EDGE
OF THE
SHADOW

The Wisdom Court Series
Book One

Yvonne Montgomery

Cover and Book design by eBook Prep
www.ebookprep.com

August, 2014
ISBN: 978-1-61417-646-6

ePublishing Works!
www.epublishingworks.com

ACKNOWLEDGMENTS

My deepest appreciation to Shane M. Ewegen for his immaculate editing skills and ongoing support.

Special thanks go to Carol Sullivan and the WaterCourse Writers Group.

I am grateful to the careful readings and suggestions of the following people: Elizabeth Cox, Kay Bergstrom, Gwen Schuster-Haynes, as well as Margot Rounds and Carol Caverly.

My gratitude to Misty K. Ewegen for help navigating computer issues as well as her literary sensibilities, and to Bob Ewegen for always having my back, and for his acute editorial assessment.

My thanks to the Boulder Chautauqua Society librarians for their help.

Thanks to Rocky Mountain Fiction Writers, always a source of information and support.

Many thanks to Nina Paules and Brian Paules of eBook Prep and ePublishing Works for their help in entering the world of e-publishing.

This book has had a strange evolution over quite a long time, and I may have forgotten to acknowledge others who helped along the way. Please forgive any oversights, for they are unintentional.

CHAPTER 1

"Mistletoe to break the lock." The woman seated at the small table sprinkled leaves into the shallow bowl next to the candle illuminating the room.

The windows at her back were closed and curtained but the flame fluttered, deepening the red of her upswept hair and gleaming along the silver threads in her robe. Her gaze darted toward the gloom in the corners as she reached into another bag.

"I call upon the spirits." Spiky thistle leaves fell to the pottery surface. Groping inside a leather pouch she pulled out dry needles. They dropped from her hand as she whispered, "Yew to raise the dead."

A gauzy sack yielded graying fronds. "Balm of Gilead, manifest the one I seek."

After a glance down at the ancient book open across her lap she murmured, "Protection born of amaranth. And borage for courage," she added under her breath, releasing the last bits into the container.

Shadows stirred along the wall as she twisted the candle from the saucer and held it to the herbal mixture, taking care to push her flowing sleeve away from the dish. Pungent smoke drifted upward as she replaced the taper.

A breath of air touched her and she and turned, half-glimpsing motion but unable to find its source. Again the flame wobbled, and behind her the curtain billowed upward. The border of the coarsely woven material brushed the wick as it fell back into place.

A tiny spark gnawed along the threads until it blazed.

Andrea Bellamy steered her overloaded Toyota past the wrought-iron fence where a plaque was attached to the gatepost. *Wisdom Court* was etched in gothic letters.

The arrow-tipped palings restrained lilacs and forsythia bushes screening the courtyard formed by three houses. Behind them great slabs of reddish sandstone thrust from the mountainside toward blue sky.

Andrea turned off the engine. Here would be the start of her new life. For the first time since her daughter's birth, she was on her own. For an entire year she would work at becoming a painter. That dream had seen her through the dark days following her husband's death, and had kept her going when her job as a forensic artist at the Tacoma Sheriff's Department became hard to stomach.

Now her challenge would be to answer the questions haunting her sleep since her acceptance at Wisdom Court. What if she didn't have real talent? Was it too late to develop her skills? Hastily she dug into the handbag on the seat beside her, pulling out the dog-eared letter she'd received from Caldicott Wyntham four months earlier.

> *...You have been chosen to receive a Wyntham Grant from the Wisdom Court Foundation.*

The grant goes to noteworthy women artists and scholars who have not yet gained the recognition of their peers. Several years ago I purchased one of your paintings, "Between Worlds" and it has sparked my imagination many times since. Your work deserves a greater audience, and it is my hope that the year in Boulder can help you gain it.

"It will." Andrea whispered the words like a mantra. "It has to." Her living expenses were assured. Art supplies would be paid for and she'd been promised a studio.

A bird trilled nearby and Andrea glanced up, looking past the rearview mirror. No need to remind herself of the laugh lines at the corners of her eyes, or the silver in her chestnut hair. Forty-three can't be too old for me to change my destiny, she told herself. I won't let it be.

The car door creaked open and she scooted off the shabby upholstery. Every muscle in her body protested as she tugged at her sweater and tried to dust off her jeans.

The breeze was crisp with pine and cool on her skin. Still ahead lay meeting the other associates living at Wisdom Court. She pushed a hand through her hair, wishing she'd done more than wash her face at the last gas station. *I'll make a great impression*, she thought. Not that anyone was around to impress. The courtyard was deserted and quiet, except for a rippling fountain at its center.

Andrea approached the middle building, a tall old farmhouse with a vine-covered front porch, dodging the water pooling like liquid footprints across worn cobblestones. She climbed the steps, took a deep breath and reached for the doorbell. Her hand was shaking. Andrea made a face and pushed the button.

After a minute she knocked firmly, and the door swung open.

She peered inside. In the foyer a staircase climbed to an open landing on the second floor. Light from large windows cast shadows of the railings onto the oaken floor.

An indescribable odor reached her nose and she sneezed. Venturing inside, she called, "Hello?" No response.

Where *was* everybody? Her ears caught a fragment of sound and she pursued it through an arched doorway. The air was thicker here, the sounds more distinct. She walked down the narrow hallway past a gallery of framed portrait photographs nearly covering the grass-green wallpaper.

Voices came from an open doorway ahead and Andrea stopped beside it. "How *could* you have had an open flame so near the curtains?" exclaimed one, and a woman sputtered in apology.

"'Would-haves and could-haves are broken paving stones on the road to what is,'" was the brusque reply. "Mary Tolliver Bell, eighteen thirty-seven to eighteen ninety-two."

Andrea choked back a laugh. She'd caught sight of three women seated across the room when a russet whirlwind raced toward her, barking fiercely. Andrea took a hasty step backward from the snarling dachshund whose tail wagged madly even as it continued its fierce warning. The women gaped at her.

Andrea offered a smile. "Hi. I'm Andrea Bellamy." She raised her voice over the barking. "The new associate."

"Oh, my sainted aunt," sputtered a tiny woman with hedgehog hair, and all three surged to their feet. The next few minutes passed in a flurry of explanations, all punctuated by the dachshund's crazed yapping.

"Strudel!" The small woman's face scrunched up at the noise. "Aura Lee, can't you make her hush?"

The Amazon in stained purple robes bent to grasp the dog's collar, her brassy hair escaping from a clip. "You know how territorial she is, Noreen. I'm sorry," she added to Andrea. "It's been an upsetting day. Usually she's not this bad."

Andrea leaned down and extended her closed hand for the dachshund to sniff. "She's just doing her job." Strudel licked her knuckles and rolled onto her back, offering her belly for petting. Andrea laughed as she straightened. "Good dog."

"You can see how ferocious she is." A slender woman regarded her with friendly gray eyes. "I'm Rose Hertzberg, the director here. It's so good to meet you." Her damp silver-blond hair hung to her shoulders, and she appeared unaware of the dark smudge on one cheek.

Rose motioned Andrea toward an overstuffed sofa. "Have a seat. The fire department left a while ago, and a stiff drink was the only response I could think of. I'll bet you could use one, too, after your trip." She headed for the built-in sideboard holding an array of bottles. "Tell me everything's ready for Andrea, Aura Lee."

"Um, almost." Aura Lee's face was wreathed in smiles. "Goddess bless!" She sat down next to Andrea and held out one hand. When Andrea offered her own, she grasped it and turned it over, focusing on the palm. She clicked her tongue. "You're a Scorpio, aren't you?"

Andrea tried to pull away, but the older woman tightened her grip. "My birthday's in July."

Aura Lee's face fell and she released her hold. "You're a Cancer? I picked up an impression of Scorpio. Something about your eyes, I think, and the color of your aura—"

"Oh, stop for now, Aura Lee. Let the poor girl catch her breath." Noreen nodded cordially from the wingback chair near the fireplace.

Andrea blinked. The woman was so small that her legs didn't reach the floor. Her short salt-and-pepper hair stood on end, as if she'd run her fingers through it repeatedly.

"Miss Wyntham was excited about your acceptance of the grant." Noreen's air of pleasure dimmed. "I'm sorry you won't get to know her."

Andrea had looked forward to telling Caldicott Wyntham in person just how much the invitation had meant to her. "Isn't she here?"

Noreen shook her head, eyes somber. "She died a couple of months ago. Didn't you read about it?"

"Look at her face," murmured Aura Lee. "She didn't know."

Rose handed Andrea a glass of scotch and sat on the other chair. "I'm so sorry. Caldicott was ill for a short time. I thought I'd notified you, but with all the details…"

Andrea was surprised at her sharp sense of loss. "I was so busy getting ready to come here. I haven't paid much attention to anything else." She took a quick drink of the scotch and swallowed it with some difficulty. "I'm sorry I won't get to meet her."

"I'm sure she would have liked you." Aura Lee's mouth worked for a moment. "I'll go fix some tea," she said gruffly. "Come on, Strudel." She strode from the room, the dog trotting behind her.

Rose looked after her. "She misses Caldicott. So does Strudel."

Noreen nodded. "Caldicott was the heart of this place, and it doesn't feel right without her." She glanced at Rose. "Can you manage here now? I left my computer running when the firemen arrived."

"Of course."

"I assume I'll see you this evening, my dear," Noreen said to Andrea. "Welcome to Wisdom Court."

Rose sighed as Noreen whisked out the door. "We had a small fire here today," she explained. "Not much damage, but everyone's upset."

"Oh, no! That explains the smell. I'd be upset, too."

Rose glanced toward the doorway. "I need to check on a couple of things before I take you up to your room. If you can wait just a minute, I'll be right back to get you settled in."

"That's fine. It'll give me a minute to realize that I'm actually here. I need to…" Andrea paused.

"To catch up to yourself?" Rose patted her shoulder as she passed by her. "Make yourself at home."

Andrea sipped the scotch as she wandered through the spacious room, sighing as the muscles in her legs loosened.

She stopped before a framed eighteenth century map of the Americas. It was easy to picture her daughter, with her brand new teaching degree, pointing at a newer version in her school classroom and answering students' questions. After her walking tour of Scotland, Grace would be teaching in Sacramento.

Her year at Wisdom Court would make it easier to build a new life without more than Grace's occasional presence. It had been just the two of them for so long. If only David had lived to see the person she'd become.

With the ease of long practice, Andrea pushed the thought to the back of her mind. For the first time she noticed the gentle sound coming from the window. On the sill she found a small dish fountain where water bubbled over a slab of slate. She smiled at the miniature porcelain crane peering into the tiny pool below it.

Andrea sank onto the sofa in front of the fireplace and found a coaster for her glass, wondering idly what the burgundy velvet curtains hanging above the mantel covered. She yawned and thought about getting up to see, but the pillows were soft. She slipped into sleep.

In her dream she drove over endless hills leading to the mountain in front of her, but never drew nearer to it. The rutted road jostled the car, and she bounced on the seat, struggling to hold onto the wheel.

"What did they do, spike your drink?" asked a deep voice near her ear. Andrea felt a hand on her arm and the shaking began again. "Come on, lady, time to rejoin the world."

Her eyes flew open. A man was looking down at her and when she started to push herself up he raised his hand in a cautioning gesture. "I didn't mean to startle you." His smile was crooked, his brown eyes assessing." Aura Lee sent me to tell you tea's ready in the kitchen."

Disoriented, Andrea stared at him, trying to summon a name, not finding one. "Have we met?"

"Nope. I'm Neal Cameron, on the Wisdom Court board." When he extended his hand, she put her own into it and he pulled her to her feet. "Come on. Aura Lee made scones."

For someone calling himself a board member, he looked pretty casual. Andrea wondered why he'd come to tea with black streaks on his faded jeans. More were on the rolled-up sleeves of his blue work shirt. She took a closer look as he tugged her down the picture gallery hallway. Neal Cameron was tall and well built and moved with easy assurance. Straight brown hair fell over his forehead and in profile his nose had a bump suggesting it had been broken. His square jaw was set. Nobly searching for the elusive scone, no doubt.

"Here she is, Aura Lee," he announced as they entered the roomy kitchen. "She was busy dreaming."

Aura Lee turned from the stove, dismay clouding her blue eyes. She'd traded the purple caftan for a loose green dress, and her hair was pinned in a neat upsweep. "I'm sorry, dear. I thought you'd need something to eat after that long drive."

"I am a little hungry." Andrea glanced at Neal. "Thanks for fetching me."

"Don't mention it." He lifted one brow. "Well now, Aura Lee, I think it's time we got down to basics."

Rose entered from the door across the room. She, too, had taken time to change clothes. In faded blue jeans and a white sweater, she looked younger than she had before. "Don't you mean down to business? Thanks for helping with the clean-up, Neal." She smiled warmly at him and kissed his cheek. He returned the salute.

"The wind's coming up," said Aura Lee.

Rose frowned toward the windows. Outside the light was fading and the aspens near the house fluttered. "Do you think I ought to cover the hot tub?"

Neal glanced up from the butter dish. "I'll check it when I leave."

The floury scent of scones made Andrea's stomach growl. Neal shot her a smile. She felt a shift in awareness so powerful that the air changed. Before her eyes, his face began to transform, other features replacing his own until her vision went black. She cried out.

"Heads up, Rose."

Andrea heard the faraway voice and the room swam darkly around her. When she felt a warm grip on her shoulders she came back to herself and looked around, blinking. Neal was holding her up, his eyes shadowed with concern. Rose was at his side and behind her Aura Lee was talking.

Neal pulled her over to a chair at the table and when Andrea felt the edge of it against the back of her knees, she sat down hard, letting her head fall forward. "Sorry." The thinness of her voice frightened her.

Rose pushed a glass into her hand. "Here, drink this." The rim of the glass knocked against her teeth and she gulped brandy, choking at the heat in her throat. Someone thumped her back and she coughed again.

Rose knelt to look into her face. "You fainted. Are you all right?"

Andrea took a deep breath. Her heart was hammering and she was light-headed, but mostly she was embarrassed. "I'm okay. I don't know what happened."

Rose set her palm against Andrea's forehead. "You're not feverish." She glanced over her shoulder at Aura Lee. "Do you think we should call Jerri's office and get her checked over?"

"I doubt she needs a doctor." Neal squatted in front of Andrea and peered at her. "What can you tell us? Are you sick? Have you been exposed to anything?"

Andrea shook her head. "I didn't get enough sleep. I drove all night."

The worry in his eyes dissolved in a glimmer of humor. "So you're dead on your feet and hungry, too?"

"Don't forget the scotch," added Rose.

"Brandy on top of it." Neal stood up. "What do you think? Some scones and a nap?" When Rose nodded, he added, "If Aura Lee's scones can't cure what ails you, Andrea, her brownies can. I've been trying to get her to make a batch for two weeks. Haven't I?" he asked the older woman.

Aura Lee ignored him. She slid onto the chair beside Andrea and clasped her hand tightly. Her face was alight with excitement. "What scared you so much?"

Andrea stared at her.

Aura Lee said patiently, "Think, now. Did you see anything…odd? Maybe strange lights, or shining orbs?" Her hand tensed on Andrea's. "Was there an unusual aroma?"

Andrea glimpsed Rose behind Aura Lee's shoulder. She was gaping at Aura Lee in disbelief. Beside her, Neal Cameron frowned.

"Did you see a messenger materialize? Is that what frightened you so?" As Andrea drew breath to ask what she meant, Aura Lee's voice faltered. "Did someone mention Cottie to you? Caldicott Wyntham?"

Andrea blinked, at a total loss.

Aura Lee waited for an instant, then whispered, "Tell me. Please. Did you intercept a message for me from the Other Side?"

CHAPTER 2

Late-day sun lit the Wisdom Court kitchen windows, and the copper pots on the overhead rack glowed like medallions. Kerry Tomlinson didn't notice. Her green eyes shot sparks as she dumped cartons of Chinese carryout into serving dishes. "It's insane," she snapped. "Aura Lee could have died in that fire. *Then* she'd have been able to communicate with all the dead people she wants."

Rose sagged on a barstool at the butcher-block island. Helping clean up the damage to Aura Lee's room had killed the afternoon. Trying to ease her disappointment that Andrea's blackout hadn't been caused by an apparition had required almost as much energy. Now Kerry was on a rant.

"Andrea drives fifty percent of forever to get here." Kerry scowled over her shoulder at Rose. "She walks into a madhouse, where the inhabitants are reeling over the effects of a *summoning* spell, for God's sake." She knocked over a carton of steaming broccoli beef onto the countertop. "Shit." Frowning, she shoveled the food onto a plate.

"She gets dizzy and Aura Lee asks the poor woman

if she's just met Caldicott's *ghost."* Tugging open the door under the sink, she pitched the empty cartons into the wastebasket.

Rose wished she'd kept her mouth shut. Kerry had the right to be upset over the spells, especially after today's fire. But at Wisdom Court women could think what they liked. Since she'd come to work on Caldicott's biography, Kerry had grown ever more impatient at Aura Lee's fixation with the paranormal.

Rose pulled a tissue from her pocket and wiped her nose. "Aura Lee's trying to deal with Caldicott's death, and that includes the hope that her ghost could be here. It comforts her to believe there might be a way for them to be in contact."

Kerry pushed the dishes under the heat lamp. "Isn't it unhealthy to encourage that crap, considering how mystical she's getting? And now to involve Andrea! The woman must think this place is an asylum."

This place *is* an asylum, Rose thought. Why had she let Caldicott convince her to take over as director? Someone with administrative experience, someone like Noreen, would have been a better choice. Closing her eyes, she took a deep, cleansing breath. The sunlight was warm on her face. She visualized a pool of water, its calm surface spreading through the room, soothing the air.

"Do *you* believe in ghosts?" Kerry asked irritably.

Rose opened her eyes.

Kerry scrubbed the counter top with such intensity her bobbed auburn hair flipped around her face. "Do you think the soul hangs around like a bad smell," she growled, "waiting for someone to let loose with cosmic air freshener?"

"Nice imagery," Rose said, trying not to laugh. At Kerry's snort, she straightened on the barstool. "I've seen and felt enough to wonder about ghosts. Do I have any proof they exist? No."

Kerry took a breath, but Rose pressed on. "The issue isn't what you or I believe, it's what Aura Lee believes. Why are you so bent out of shape over that?"

The color deepened in Kerry's rounded cheeks. "That kind of bullshit doesn't belong here. I thought Wisdom Court was supposed to be about the pursuit of knowledge and truth."

Rose felt an unfamiliar gratitude that she was no longer young. "As someone I respect said recently, *The strength of Wisdom Court lies in each member's right to tailor her own experience to suit herself.*"

Kerry relaxed into a disarming smile. "That's a cheap shot, quoting me to myself. Not to mention saying you respect me. Which, by the way, I consider a major compliment."

Rose returned her nod. As she slid off the stool her muscles reminded her of all the bending and hauling she'd done that day. "You deserve it. Most of the time." That elicited a mock glower and Rose started for the door. But something was off-center about the way Kerry moved the dishtowel over the counter top, and she hesitated.

Kerry draped the towel over the oven door handle with care. "I get embarrassed," she muttered. "I mean, when Aura Lee pulls out the tarot cards or offers to read someone's aura, I want to run for cover." Her eyes were puzzled. "I know this place isn't conventional, and I like that. But the women here are too savvy to go along with the otherworldly stuff. So why do we? Why don't we try to talk some sense into her?"

"Are you volunteering?"

Misery flashed for an instant across Kerry's face.

Rose sighed. "Aura Lee came to work for Caldicott at least twenty-five years ago. But she wasn't just hired help for long. She and Caldicott became friends, Kerry. When Aura Lee turned to mysticism during hard times, Caldicott accepted it, tarot cards, crystal-gazing and all."

Kerry's lips tightened, and Rose could feel her resistance. "I don't believe Caldicott would have lived as long as she did if it hadn't been for Aura Lee's care. But Caldicott gave a lot back and Aura Lee's having trouble getting on with her life without that friendship. Everyone has to make sense of the world as best she can. Aura Lee has her way, you have yours."

Rose added gently, "And Aura Lee isn't trying to force you to accept hers."

Kerry lifted her shoulders in a shrug and shot her a wry look. "Of course not, because my truth's the right truth."

Rose recognized the wavering humor for what it was. "Which truth is that?"

Kerry laughed, and the tension ebbed. "The truth that dinner's good to go and *you* have to set the table. Don't forget to add a place for Andrea." She headed out the door.

As Rose washed her hands the memory of an old peasant she'd met during a trip to Brazil years before strayed into her mind. He'd lost most of his teeth, only the back molars surviving, and his words were indistinct, as if he couldn't quite bite them off from an almost endless stream of sounds. *The young have a fever that demands change, but time does its damage and leaves behind a yearning for the familiar,* he'd said through the interpreter. Of course, he'd also claimed that a diet heavy on guava juice was the reason for his astonishing number of children. Who knows, she thought, maybe it was.

As Rose set bright place mats and old flatware on

the dining room table, she let her mind range over other memories from that long ago trip. She paused, caught by the odd thought that those remnants could be seen as ghosts of her own.

The Wisdom Court dining room evoked an earlier, more gracious age. The beveled mirror in the built-in sideboard reflected candles in a collection of holders at the center of the table. The flames flickered in the conversational currents next to a low majolica urn filled with flowers. Kerry's Chinese entrees were accompanied by two good table wines, white and red. The tradition of Thursday nights at Wisdom Court had started long ago, Andrea was told, with each member in residence taking turns supplying a main course, the others bringing side dishes if they so chose.

"Even after Caldicott started watching ER we stuck to Thursdays," Aura Lee reminisced. "We'd just record it and watch it after dinner."

"One of us sets up for the meal, and cleans up afterward. That's my job this week," Rose added from the head of the table. "The idea is to keep from sticking Aura Lee with dinner party work every Thursday. We get to share whatever cooking—or choosing—talents we have. It's the only mandated contact we have with each other."

Regal in a severe black dress, Noreen nodded. The porcupine hair of the morning had been tamed, bangs smooth across her forehead. "I was the headmistress of a private girls' school. I never had to cook, but I had to eat what was prepared to set a good example. I've had enough balanced, nutritious meals to choke a chestnut. My mission in life is to see that Wisdom Court keeps up with the latest developments at KFC and Pizza Hut."

Dolores Rivera laughed. The sculptor had arrived in

time to meet Andrea before dinner, dramatic in a low-cut crimson dress that deepened her bronze skin and set off long, straight black hair. "Our other associate, Elizabeth Schuster, makes up for Noreen's fast food by testing her recipes on us. But food isn't the point. I heard Thursday dinners began so Caldicott would know what everyone was doing."

Aura Lee's chopsticks halted halfway to her mouth. "She wasn't nosy. Cottie always said it's easy to turn into a hermit when you're in the middle of a project, and hiding away undercuts good work. I think she must have spent a lot of time alone in her life." As she lifted the broccoli beef to her lips a drop of sauce landed on her gray caftan. The sleeves were banded in silver the same shade as the shadow on her eyelids. She snatched up her napkin and rubbed at the spot, causing her sterling earrings to swing against her neck.

"What does Elizabeth do?"

Rose glanced across the table at Andrea, who gave an altogether different impression from the tired, stressed woman who'd arrived that afternoon. Dressed in a peasant skirt and black scooped-neck top, her brown eyes were alive with interest, flicking to each speaker as talk ebbed and flowed. "She's a chef from Louisiana, and her cookbook memoir is almost ready for publication. She went home to see her family this week. They live outside New Orleans."

Andrea nodded. "Sometimes I feel I've spent my adult life trying to find even a little time to myself. When my daughter was small, I'd have sold my soul for a chance to paint once in a while. Then there was my job…" Her gaze traveled over the faces turned to her. "How can you get anything done if you *don't* isolate yourself?"

"Here, here," Kerry murmured. Her green sweater

set off her auburn hair and pale skin. "Most people are afraid of being alone, and fill every second with phones, computers, iPods while they run, TV on for background noise." She bit into an egg roll. "Isolation allows you to think, to do your work."

"No, no, *jita,* you mean solitude." Dolores refilled her wineglass and passed the bottle to Rose. Her dark eyes were brilliant in the candlelight. "You're alone *with* yourself so you can create the focus for your work. Isolation is when you cut yourself off from everything and everyone else. The energy, it has no place to flow. It's like flowers without bees...the pollen just sits there."

Rose topped off her own glass and offered the bottle to Noreen. "I think we get too much cross-pollination, thanks to modern media. You can keep track of nearly everything happening all over the world. There's no judgment as to what you hear, just blah-blah bombardment from morning to night. Isolation doesn't sound bad compared to that."

"Except here at Wisdom Court, last of the salons." Noreen saluted them with a wave of her chopsticks. "Caldicott started the Thursday night tradition, and we continue it. I'll begin and announce that *Reader's Digest* has bought my boarding school anecdote for 'Laughter Is the Best Medicine.' It's not a book contract, but it's better than nothing." The others broke into applause, Kerry tapping her wineglass with a chopstick.

"She's working on a collection," Dolores explained to Andrea. "Folk tales, customs, old sayings and quotations."

"Noreen's gathering them all from the female point of view," Rose added.

Noreen nodded with a smile. "The term *'old wives' tale* is used unfavorably, especially among some academics, though a lot of folk wisdom fits in that category. So I started keeping a list of those tidbits.

"Scientific research has begun to validate some of these older scraps of knowledge. An easy example is chicken soup. My mother made a batch every time we got a cold. Now doctors know that chicken broth thins nasal mucous, helping rid the body of germs. Thus the term, 'Jewish penicillin,' from the cultural stereotype of the Jewish mother treating her children with the soup."

Her eyes kindled with enthusiasm. "Even now, history is written primarily by men. Details of everyday life are neglected for dramatic events— wars, political upheavals, and so on. Men are more represented in quotation books because they were the authors. The historical lives of women have to be found in household ledgers, or recipe books, or in a midwife's medicinal concoctions." Noreen caught herself with a self-deprecating smile. "I didn't mean to lecture. The need for isolation can be a response to the garrulous."

"No, no, how can you say that? Don't you think she's very informative?" Aura Lee looked to the others in appeal. Reassured by their various signs of agreement, she turned back to Noreen. "Isolation can be useful, though. People are more likely to get messages from the Other Side when they're alone. It's hard to receive them unless you're truly an Adept. If you're on overload, the spirits can't get through." With a sidelong glance at Rose she added in a rush, "I think we ought to consider holding a séance. People have to try to get the communications from Beyond or they can be lost forever."

Andrea cleared her throat. "You're expecting a message from someone?"

"The nearest psychiatrist," Kerry grumbled.

Noreen regarded Aura Lee with interest. "How do you know these things? Are there instructions for the various activities?"

"Only from charlatans and crackpots." Kerry reached for her glass. "No reputable scientists believe you can communicate with the dead."

"Oh, pooh," said Aura Lee. "Scientists don't know everything. They're so close-minded."

Kerry leaned forward to respond but Noreen was already talking. "It's similar to the technicians who listen for signals from outer space at those installations of huge satellite dishes. They complain that the traffic on airwaves obscures distant signals. With people, I suppose the constant clutter of life itself veils the inner voices as well as some of the things going on around them. Maybe, as you say, even signals from the other side."

Interest lit Dolores's face. "You know, it's funny you put it like that. I was thinking today about making art, what makes you do it. And people ask me where I get my ideas."

"The idea store," Rose teased and they all laughed.

Dolores's eyes danced. "Oh, yeah, would I love to find that place. But sometimes, when the work is going well, and the clay moves in my hands, I feel like I'm…touching something outside myself. As if," she went on, focusing on the wine she swirled in her glass, "there's something out there I can tap into once in a blue moon. Sometimes I can almost feel it with me while I work. A presence." She looked around the table at them. "Am I the only one who's noticed that?"

Kerry shook her head. "They call it 'the flow.' A lot of people have felt it. And it isn't limited to art. Scientists and poets have written about it, and athletes talk about the same kind of thing." Her glance at Aura

Lee held a challenge. "I don't think it does justice to human experience to associate it with some supernatural mumbo-jumbo."

Aura Lee inhaled sharply and set down her spoon with a click.

"Maybe it doesn't," Rose said quickly, "but I've felt things I couldn't explain. *Presence* may be too strong a word, but I've had moments when I've felt a breath of air on my neck or thought I've seen something out of the corner of my eye."

Kerry grimaced. "They're sensations. The body has hundreds of thousands of nerve endings. Why wouldn't you detect changes in air temperature or see nuances of light?"

Noreen nodded. "The question is, what causes those sensations? And there's the issue of why certain people perceive them and others don't, and whether some are sensitive to perceptions too faint to register upon most persons."

"Like mediums, for instance." Aura Lee's excitement was growing. "People who can direct their sensitivity toward the supernatural."

Kerry's green eyes darkened. "All you have to do is read a book or two about the spiritualism craze of the nineteenth century to see what a con job that is."

"What interests me are things the artistic and the spiritual have in common," said Dolores. "Those feelings of connection with *something else* remind me of church. I have rituals that help me get ready to work, and they have almost a sacred tone to them. When I think about how they're alike, it's hard not to feel I'm communing with something—or someone—outside myself."

"You're talking about a state of mind, a change in brain wave activity that allows a different kind of energy to be used." Kerry paused to choose her words.

"That's one of the most magnificent things about being human, that we're able to think and function in a variety of ways, on different levels."

"Exactly!" Galvanized by the exchange, Aura Lee leaned forward, draping her sleeve across her plate. "On that we totally agree, Kerry. Human beings are able to do so much they're not even aware of. Simple intuition sharpened into channeling," she added softly. "There are few who can be in touch with what lies beyond our earthly life." She noticed the stain on her sleeve and frowned. "Rats." Dipping her napkin into her water glass, she dabbed at it.

Color suffused Kerry's face and Rose stood up. "My intuition says it's time for dessert. Andrea, if you'll help me with the plates, I'll show you where everything is."

Andrea pushed back her chair and gathered several dishes. When she followed Rose to the kitchen, Dolores and Noreen were chatting about an exhibit at the University. Kerry and Aura Lee were silent. The door swung shut, cutting off the conversation.

Rose waved a hand toward the cabinets near the sink. "The bowls are on the second shelf and there's a tray right there with the cookie sheets." She pulled a carton of ice cream from the freezer as Andrea put the dishes in the sink. "Mocha Fudge Revenge coming up, don't hold the calories." She hunted for a scoop, and then noticed that Andrea was regarding the sink with undue attention. "What's up?"

"Oh, sorry." Andrea opened the cupboard door and found glazed stoneware bowls. "You'll have to show me the ropes for the next communal dinner. Is there another scoop?"

Rose dug into the container. "I'll do it. You can take it easy this time and wow us when it's your turn." She flipped ice cream into a bowl. "The meals are just a way to maintain contact with each other. Caldicott figured food was as good a way to create a sense of community as any other."

"It makes sense. I definitely fit into the chooser category, though." Andrea watched Rose but her mind was still back at the dinner table. "What is it that you do at Wisdom Court? I assume you sort of run the place."

Rose glanced up, and the curiosity in Andrea's face prompted her own sense of irony. "That describes my style exactly: I sort of run the place." She dug into the ice cream. "I came here a few years ago to help Caldicott. We'd met in a yoga group some time before that. As it happened, she became ill not long after I got here. The day-to-day details got to be too much for her." She picked up a morsel of ice cream on the counter and popped it into her mouth. "Now, what did you really want to ask me?"

Andrea lined up the bowls on the tray. "Am I imagining the tension between Aura Lee and Kerry? They're so on edge with each other."

Rose filled the last bowl and jammed the lid back onto the carton. "Your intuition's good." She returned the ice cream to the freezer and rinsed her hands under the faucet. "Aura Lee's fascination with the magical arts, for lack of a better term, has been around for a long time. Since Caldicott died, though, she's become convinced that she's sending her messages from beyond the grave.

"Kerry was brought here to write a history of Wisdom Court—in effect a biography of Caldicott— but she died about four months after Kerry got here. It throws her that Aura Lee wants to contact Caldicott through a séance. Maybe Kerry's afraid it might undermine Caldicott's reputation. Not that Caldicott would care."

Andrea set the last bowl on the tray. "And that's why Aura Lee got excited this morning when I got so dizzy."

"Yes." Rose hefted the tray and headed for the dining room. "Could you open the door?" As she passed by Andrea, she added, "We're all still distracted because of Caldicott's death. You'll have to bear with us."

Aura Lee was addressing Noreen with enthusiasm. "I haven't been able to contact Cottie directly, but my channel keeps telling me she wants to commune with us."

Rose set the tray on the sideboard.

"Your channel? Wants to commune?" echoed Kerry. "Do you know how crazy that sounds?"

Aura Lee stood up and swept the folds of her caftan to one side. She rounded the table with impressive dignity and stopped beside Kerry. "Disbelievers can't affect the truth. I just ask you to keep an open mind. And I'm asking a favor from all of you." She looked at each of the women in turn. "Notice what's around you. Cottie is here in the house, and she's trying to tell us something. It would be awful to miss it, and even worse to refuse to recognize it." She turned on her heel and sailed through the door to the kitchen.

The others exchanged glances. "Well," Noreen began, but Kerry surged to her feet.

"All I recognize is she's taking this spiritualism garbage too far." Kerry marched out of the dining room. A few seconds later the front door slammed.

Dolores reached for the wine bottle and emptied it into her glass.

"Anybody up for doubles on the ice cream?" Rose asked.

CHAPTER 3

Andrea woke to darkness heavy with potpourri. Her cheeks were wet, and her heartbeat thumped in her ears. Fumbling for the bedside light, she found the switch and turned it.

Shadows leaped from the corners to loom over the bed. A sliver of light glimmered from the edge of the cheval mirror across the room, the rest of the glass almost black.

At the scratch on the door Andrea's heart rose in her throat. She threw back the covers and swung her legs over the side, ready to run. The scraping sound came again. Andrea forced herself across the room. Her fingers closed round the knob and she yanked the door open.

Strudel trotted into the room, her tail wagging.

Andrea sank down beside the dog, running shaking fingers over her fur. "What are you *doing* here?" Strudel cast her a trusting glance and rolled onto her back to present her belly.

"You scared me half to death, you rotten dog." A draft at her nape gave her shivers. "Come up on the bed with me before I freeze to death." She slid her hands under the dog's back to pick her up. When she heard the creaking of the door hinges, she swung round.

A slice of light crept toward her across the Persian rug.

"Are you all right?" a voice whispered. Aura Lee stuck he head around the molding, her hair hidden by a crocheted net festooned with pink bows. "There you are, Strudel."

Slipping into the room, she glided across the rug. "I heard you call out, dear. May I?" She nodded toward the chair near the bed and took the dog from Andrea's arms. Her gown billowed as she sat, settling the dog on her lap. "Get back in bed, dear. I wanted to make sure you weren't ill, or hadn't gotten dizzy again."

Andrea walked back to the bed on shaky legs and got under the covers. "Why would you think I was ill?" She pulled the comforter up around her neck.

"When I heard you scream, I thought any number of things might be wrong." Aura Lee's face had creased in lines of concern. "By the Goddess, you must have been sleeping deeply."

"I screamed?" Andrea blinked. "I'm sorry."

Aura Lee clicked her tongue. "I should have made you a sleep posset, especially after your long drive. And there was your possible encounter this morning. The first time you meet a Visitor can be a strain," she added, "even when the spirit is friendly. Which Cottie is, of course."

The last thing Andrea wanted to think about was a ghost. "Aura Lee, I didn't really see—"

But the older woman was reminiscing. "Cottie loved the visual arts, and was always alert for new talent. That day we were driving along the coast and the sun was hot for early spring. I was thirsty.

"A half hour out of Monterey we stopped in a small

town. The restaurant served lemonade garnished with mint. It tasted so good." She pressed her lips together in memory. "They had a show...badly organized. Prints and oils, and a few photographs, were all jumbled together. Cottie saw your painting right off. 'They don't know what they've got there,' she said and she was right."

"The compliment in her letter meant so much to me," Andrea murmured. "Selling that painting was one of the hardest things I've ever had to do." It was the work of an afternoon during Grace's first year of college. When the idea drifted across her mind, she'd just painted it until her arm was a heavy weight. The effect she sought was inspired by old Victorian story pictures. In a play of contrasts, she'd depicted a youth nearly hidden in the purple shadow cast by an old house. In his dark clothes he almost merged with the green vines twisting over the wall next to him. The grassy area on his other side was lit by afternoon sunshine and was divided by stepping-stones extending toward an open gate. The play between the dark and the light hinted at secrets, lending the work clandestine air. Andrea knew it revealed her as none of her other work ever had.

"Is it here at Wisdom Court?"

Aura Lee eyed her in puzzlement. "Of course it's here, hanging in the parlor. Didn't you see it?"

Andrea glanced away. "I didn't get the whole tour, what with everything going on this morning."

"You can see it tomorrow." Aura Lee settled into the chair cushions. "You're tired, I know, and it's too soon to expect Cottie to have said much, but I'd be grateful if you could tell me if she's calm." She looked hopeful. "Being a ghost doesn't necessarily mean serenity, or she'd have crossed over, but it would make me feel much better to know she's not *uncomfortable* in her new condition."

A current of cold air brushed against Andrea's neck, and she pulled the bedding closer. What could she say?

Strudel growled deeply. Hinges creaked, and she and Aura Lee turned to see Rose in the doorway, ghostly herself in a long white robe. "What's going on?" she asked sleepily. "Is anything wrong?"

"No." Andrea rubbed her face with both hands, wondering if the other Wisdom Court inhabitants would appear, one by one. "I had a bad dream and woke Aura Lee. I'm sorry I disturbed both of you."

"Don't be silly." Rose approached the bed, observing Aura Lee's comfortable situation. "What kind of dream?"

"I don't remember." Andrea tried to recapture the remnants that had frightened her. Strudel yawned hugely, her pink tongue curling. The contrast between that image and Aura Lee's attempts to collect messages from Caldicott Wyntham hit her with sudden humor. A glance at Aura Lee's hairnet had her choking back a giggle.

"My dear, don't be upset." Concerned, Aura Lee leaned forward to pat her hand. "Hysteria can be as upsetting to the Representatives as it is to humans."

"Hysterical about what?" Rose frowned. "What representatives?"

Aura Lee clicked her tongue. "Of the Other Side, of course. They only make visitations to pass on messages that cannot be denied. They don't mean to frighten the living, as a general rule."

Rose grimaced. "Do messages have to be delivered in the middle of the night?"

"I've done some research," Aura Lee said modestly. "Most sources say that to be receptive you have to be close to sleep or even hypnotized. I think that's why so many people are afraid of visitations. They're in sort of a vulnerable state anyway."

"Obviously." Rose brushed her curling hair off her face.

"Fear makes people think ghosts mean them harm," Aura Lee continued. "Usually they aren't interested in *haunting* but in finishing something left undone. Or in revealing something hidden."

Rose pondered that. "I guess most of the ghost stories I've read would support that theory." Her bemused gaze wandered toward Andrea and her eyes sharpened with realization. "Good Lord, I'm sorry. Here we are rambling about ghosts, and you're tired to the bone. We'll talk more in the morning."

Andrea nodded.

Aura Lee stood up with Strudel in her arms and headed for the door. Rose followed behind her, pausing as she stumbled over something, and bent to retrieve it. "This must be yours." She laid a narrow sketchpad on the comforter.

Andrea had thought to record first impressions but she'd fallen asleep after only a line or two. "Thanks." She set the pad on the nightstand. When she saw what was on the first page, she snatched it up again.

"What's the matter?" Rose's gaze went from her face to the sketchpad.

Aura Lee trailed back across the room.

The sketch was of a man in a black coat. Thin-faced, he had an angular jaw and stubborn chin. Black hair grew in a widow's peak and bold brows frowned over almond-shaped eyes. His nose was straight and well formed, his lips firm and unsmiling. A dark tie set off his high, old-fashioned collar. The drawing was made in the economical style she'd developed as a forensic artist. She'd never seen the man before.

Aura Lee peeked over Rose's shoulder. "By the

Goddess, who's that? He's very handsome."

"Maybe someone I drew on the job." Unable to look at it any longer, Andrea fumbled with the cardboard cover, flipping it over the paper.

"A criminal?" Aura Lee cast a disillusioned look at the sketchpad. "What a shame. He doesn't *look* bad, does he?"

Rose frowned at Andrea. "Are you all right?"

"I'm fine." Who was the man? Where had the sketch come from?

Aura Lee leaned toward her, eyes sparkling. "You drew it tonight, didn't you? Was it in your dream? It could have been automatic writing." At Rose's scowl her eagerness dimmed. "You sit with a pen and the spirits write their message with your hand."

"Aura Lee, what the hell?" Rose held her robe more tightly to her.

Aura Lee stamped her slippered foot. "We should use automatic writing to allow Cottie to get her message to us."

"For God's sake, it's three in the morning and Andrea's already having nightmares. Give it a rest."

"Of course, you're right," Aura Lee said contritely. "Maybe I should fix her some tea. Calendula, perhaps. Or chamomile."

Rose took a deep breath. "That's very kind but let's just let her go back to sleep. It's been a stressful day. Can you drop off again?" she asked Andrea.

"Sure. Sleep sounds good."

Rose nodded and walked to the door, Aura Lee behind her. Strudel watched Andrea over Aura Lee's shoulder as they went out.

Rose paused. "Don't forget. If you need anything, just call us." The door clicked shut.

Andrea forced herself to breathe slowly and closed her eyes. She tried to imagine something soothing. A waterfall: a silvery stream coursing over a steep bank, reflecting sunlight. Behind her eyes the flowing current smoothed into a mirror surface where the image of the man on the sketchpad grew until he filled her mind, staring at her, challenging her.

CHAPTER 4

French doors opened to a room where tall windows looked out on mountain grass and scotch pines. The sloping ceiling was itself glass, narrow double panes joined together with leaded strips. The floor was dark slate.

"The east guest house has a traditional studio," Rose told Andrea. "Since Dolores is set up there, we thought this would do."

Andrea barely heard her. She approached the low cabinets along the edge of the room and opened a door, finding empty shelves inside. She explored another, seeing where she would put supplies. Damp canvases could be racked inside the vented compartment in one corner. The cupboards above had drawers and cubbyholes for paints and brushes.

Rose came up beside her. "The light will be strongest at late morning and early afternoon. If that's a problem, we'll figure something else out."

"Are you kidding? I've never had such a wonderful place to work in before." Andrea's gaze swung around the empty room but in her mind it was already filled with canvases covered in color.

"Coming through." Neal Cameron maneuvered a large box through the door and carried it to the far wall. With a grunt he lowered it to the floor. Andrea noted the bunching of shoulder muscles under his blue tee shirt, the tightening of faded jeans over his backside. She could just hear her daughter's voice: *This guy is a serious babe.*

"Whew." Sweat shone on Neal's forehead. His greenish eyes held a teasing light. "You paint with rocks, right?"

Andrea shot him a guilty look. "I had to overload all of the boxes to get everything in the car. Here, I'll help."

He shook his head. "You want to make me look bad in front of Rose? It's taken years to convince her that I'm not all brains. Don't blow my cover."

Rose's eyes twinkled. "Don't kid yourself, Neal. I always think of you strictly as brawn." She patted his shoulder and moved to the door. "I've got tons to do. Did Aura Lee tell you about the pipe in the laundry room? Could you check it before you go?"

"Yeah, sure."

Rose nodded. "Yell if you need me. You, too, Andrea. I'll be in my workroom, making fountains." She went back into the kitchen.

The mood of easy relaxation left with her. Neal's gaze made Andrea aware of how quickly she'd dressed that morning, how little attention she'd paid her face. She was irritated with herself for thinking about it. "You don't have to unload the car for me. Really, I can do it." Will power kept her from lifting her hand to smooth her hair.

"That doesn't mean I can't give you a hand." Neal headed out the door and Andrea followed, increasing her pace to keep up with his long strides.

As they emptied the car, embarrassment grew over

the number of belongings she'd packed. I should have thrown in my old recliner while I was at it, she thought grimly while lugging another heavy box.

They were nearly finished when Neal pulled another crate to the edge of the trunk. He hefted it and turned back toward the house. "More books, right?" he asked as he passed her.

"Afraid so." How could she know which books she'd need? And her totems: a fertility rattle Grace gave her, a bear claw to increase her power, a soapstone figure of a woman embracing her pregnant belly. All had sparked her imagination.

By the time they were done, Andrea was starving. Strange dreams had broken up her sleep, and thanks to the midnight gathering in her room, she'd overslept, missing breakfast.

Aura Lee appeared in the studio doorway. Her flowing gray garment reminded Andrea of a nun's habit. It was easy to imagine a white wimple framing her rounded cheeks.

"It's a gorgeous day and you two have been working hard." Aura Lee handed Neal a large wicker picnic basket. "I just mopped the floor, so the kitchen's off limits. Take Andrea up to Chautauqua to see the view."

Aura Lee was a born matchmaker. Andrea's cheeks grew hot at the idea. She cast Neal a glance, only to find him watching her with a crooked grin. "That's a great idea," she said hastily, "but I'm sure Neal has lots to do."

"Neal's hungry." He lifted one side of the basket lid and peered inside. "Sandwiches, apples. Cake. German chocolate?" he asked. Aura Lee nodded. "Excellent. Let's see, beer, potato chips, napkins." He pulled a sketchpad out of the side pocket and raised a brow.

"In case she wants to draw. There are pencils inside and I tucked a space blanket in the other pocket so you can relax."

Neal bent to kiss Aura Lee's cheek. "You're an angel." He looked at Andrea. "How about it? You have enough energy to walk a few blocks for some great scenery?" Andrea gave a fleeting thought to the studio and setting up her equipment. Reading her mind, Neal said mildly, "You can do it all later. And you have to eat, right?"

Her stomach gurgled on cue and she slapped a hand over it. "Okay, okay."

Within fifteen minutes Neal was leading her around the side of the house, brushing past a mock orange bush just about to bloom. The spicy scent tantalized her nose and with a shock she realized that only two days ago she'd driven past snowdrifts in Montana.

"There's a break in the hedge along the road and we'll be able to cut across to the trails. How hungry are you?" At her quizzical expression he added, "If you can hold out for about thirty minutes—forty tops—we'll hike up to the Amphitheater Trail. It's about a half-mile, but worth it. You game?"

"Sure."

Neal strode across the street bordering the Wisdom Court land. "This is probably what you came in on, Baseline Avenue. It runs along the Fortieth Parallel." He pointed up the hillside. "That's the road you see from your studio window. It goes to the top of Flagstaff Mountain."

Andrea looked behind them. Wisdom Court receded into the shadow cast by the peak.

They walked up a narrow lane beside a creek lined with clusters of willows and wild plums just leafing out. At the end of the trail was a cul-de-sac at the mouth of a ravine Neal identified as Gregory Canyon.

A sign posted near the canyon warned hikers to beware of bears waking from hibernation. Neal smiled at the shifting expressions on Andrea's face as she read it. "They go after the chokecherries along the creek. Which don't grow on the trail we'll use."

They stopped at the bridge across a small creek nearly hidden behind thickets where nesting birds twittered. In the distance Neal could hear a canyon wren. Behind him Andrea leaned against the railing, gasping for breath. "Altitude bothering you?"

"A bit." Her cheeks were flushed and sweat slicked her forehead. She looked fit, even eager to continue, but he knew how long it took to adjust to higher elevation. Boulder was fifty-two hundred feet above sea level and they were still climbing up the trail. "You know, we could save the Amphitheater for another day. There's a closer spot where we could spread the blanket and eat. It has one of those great views Aura Lee was talking about."

Andrea breathed deeply. Her eyes held gratitude. "Sounds perfect."

After they climbed steep steps made of logs, the trail angled, cutting through chiseled boulders on the mountainside. Small wildflowers sprouted from fissures in the stone. At intervals more logs were set to restrain falling rocks and mud. A walkway complete with a handrail spanned the talus that buried the slope.

Andrea was beginning to flag when Neal grabbed her hand. "We're almost there." He pulled her up the next switchback and boosted her to the clearing that lay above the trail like a balcony. Winded, she sank onto rough grass.

Neal pulled the space blanket from the basket and snapped it open. The sunlight flashed on the folds of metallic fabric, blinding him for a second. "Here, let's get this underneath you." He levered Andrea up by one arm and tossed the cover across the ground in front of several small boulders. "Okay, sit." He placed the basket on the opposite corner to keep the breeze from flipping it over and knelt at the other edge. "Here's some water. As soon as you can breathe, we'll eat."

Andrea didn't answer, and when he glanced at her, he understood why. Though she was struggling to catch her breath, her eyes were fixed on the panorama that extended for miles.

Before them fell the hillside they'd just climbed, and beyond it lay the Boulder Valley. Sunlight shimmered like diamonds on three small lakes to the east. From the slope where they sat the foothills of the Rocky Mountains stretched northward. Below them the city sprawled across the valley floor, lines softened among multitudes of trees.

"It's magnificent." Andrea turned toward him. Her hair drifted over half her face, and she pulled it back across her cheek. "I nearly drove off the road yesterday because I wanted to see everything as I came into town, but *this*...this," she said between breaths, eyes returning to the vista before her, "is probably the most beautiful place I've ever seen."

Neal was surprised by the pleasure he felt. *Taking credit for the scenery,* he thought wryly. He inhaled the scent of pine on the breeze, and heard a dog barking in the distance. He reached into the picnic basket. "The sandwiches are tuna salad—one of Aura Lee's specialties. She puts in apples and walnuts and who knows what else."

A couple hiking on the trail above their little bank called a greeting. Andrea waved at them. She unwrapped her sandwich and took a bite. Neal tossed her a small bag of potato chips and held out a bottle of beer.

"Aura Lee does good picnic." Andrea looked at him with curiosity. "Is this on your list of duties at Wisdom Court?" Before Neal could say anything, she frowned. "I'm sorry, that sounded awful. What I meant was, have you brought other uh—people up here?" Her cheeks reddened.

Neal smiled. "You mean, what's a nice guy like me doing in a place like this?"

"Something like that." Andrea took a swig of beer.

"A few years ago, Caldicott needed work done— one of the houses had foundation problems—and I'm an engineer. We'd met at a party, had taken a shine to each other—she was an amazing woman. She asked me to be on the board to keep an eye on the physical plant. I started hanging out because I liked her, and the others. Good company."

Andrea nodded in agreement. "Yeah, from what I've seen so far. Do you hike a lot around here?"

Neal shook the bag of chips absently. "Normally Chautauqua is crawling with hikers, especially on weekends. Sometimes I'll take one of the trails for a break, especially when I've been at Wisdom Court. I can get a nice little hike in without spending much time at it."

Andrea bit into another potato chip. "I'm glad you brought me up here."

"My pleasure." He poured chips into one hand. "Is this your first trip to Colorado?"

"Yes." Her gaze wandered back to the horizon. "We have mountains in Washington, but not like these. I can't wait to paint them, if I can get a handle on them, that is."

Neal regarded her with curiosity. "You aren't sure you can?"

Andrea took the piece of cake he offered. "The

landscapes I've done are places I know well, so I'm not only seeing them, I'm feeling them." She nodded at the view. "This is all new and big, and I haven't absorbed it, you know?"

"Sure. You get past the point of noticing details. Here, all you see *are* the details. It's like that the first time you consider any big project. You look at all of it,"—he waved broadly—"and you get overwhelmed. When you break it down into separate parts you can get a handle on it."

Neal studied the landscape below, wondering how painters chose a place to start. He shifted his gaze back to Andrea, to her frowning absorption in the rocks above them. "You do what you've always done before, I guess, and hope for the best." He reached over to flick crumbs off her chin.

She wiped the same spot with a napkin. "One of the reasons I'm at Wisdom Court is to figure out if I can become the artist I want to be."

The heat of the sun was making him drowsy. He swallowed the last of the beer. "So what were you doing before you came here?"

The breeze again blew Andrea's hair into her eyes and she pushed it back behind her ears. "I was a forensic artist for the Tacoma Sheriff's Office. You know, crime victims described suspects and I made sketches that could help track them down. Kind of like boardwalk portraits, only from verbal descriptions rather than live models."

"Sounds harder than with models. Did you use those things I've seen on TV shows? The cards with the different noses and ears and so on?"

"The Identikit." Andrea shook her head. "Sometimes, but I worked better listening to witnesses. I think showing them all those unrelated body parts can be confusing."

Neal pointed silently toward the sky. A redtail hawk, wings outstretched, was circling slowly over the meadow extending toward rows of cottages. They watched its graceful arcs for several minutes.

With a satisfied sigh he leaned back and folded his hands across his belly. "So, how'd you get invited here? Did Caldicott see some of your forensic sketches?"

Andrea chuckled. "No. She saw one of my paintings and liked it."

Neal glanced at her left hand, noting that she didn't wear a wedding ring. "Rose said you have a daughter. How old?"

A burst of laughter came from four young women on the trail below them. Andrea watched their easy progress down the pathway. "Grace is twenty-three, just starting her first year as a teacher in Sacramento. She went to school out of state, but it still seems so final." She dusted off her hands. "Don't get me started on the empty nest bit. Do you have any kids?"

"A son. He lives in Denver with his mother. We're divorced," he added. "He graduates from high school this year if all goes according to plan."

"That's nice." Andrea had slipped the sketchpad from the side pocket of the picnic basket and rummaged deeper for a pencil. "Are the two of you close?"

"Yeah. Jason's a good kid." Neal flashed on a memory of Jason's grin as he'd tossed him the keys to his car last weekend. Jennifer thought him too young to have his own car, but she might feel better if it were a graduation present. As long as she saw it as his trying to buy their son's love, it wrecked the whole idea. His eyes drifted shut against the sunlight and soon he was asleep.

* * *

A gust of wind flipped the corner of the blanket onto Neal's face and he swatted at the light touch. When he opened his eyes, it was to see how far the sun had gone behind a thick gray cloud promising showers. He stretched and sat up. A quick look around found Andrea still leaning against her rock, the sketchpad in her lap. "Andrea?"

She didn't answer. Neal pushed himself up and moved closer. "Andrea." He knelt next to her, searching her face. Her eyes were open and she appeared to be staring at something in front of her. His gaze followed hers, but the pink pasque flower in her line of vision didn't appear unusual. He shook her shoulder and she shuddered. "What's going on?"

At the sound of his voice, Andrea's gaze swerved toward him. She was pale, her eyes confused. "What happened?"

"You were staring off into space." He glanced down at the sketchpad and frowned at what was on the page. The power of the drawing took him by surprise. "Maybe you got lost in your work."

Andrea peered down at the notebook in her lap and gasped.

Neal wondered what had possessed her to draw such a threatening scene. She'd portrayed a young man at the edge of a steep bank behind him, alarm on his face. A jagged rock formation loomed above him.

"It's well done," he said carefully. "Scary, though. Almost claustrophobic."

Andrea jerked the cover over the sketch with a snap. Her face was bone white.

Neal realized she was struggling for control. "I'm no critic, of course, but you're very good. There's a lot of emotion in that sketch."

She pushed herself up and he extended a hand to steady her. Her fingers were icy cold. "You feel okay?"

"Fine. Can we go back?"

Neal was certain now that something was wrong. "Sure, if that's what you want."

He loaded the picnic basket and helped Andrea from their picnic spot to the trail. He couldn't figure out what had spoiled the mood. She'd gone from enchantment with the view to what looked like outright fear. *Maybe something I said,* he thought glumly as followed her down the path. They walked back to Wisdom Court in silence.

CHAPTER 5

Rose stared out the living room window at the aspen and cottonwood trees shuddering in the rising wind. She was cold, even with a sweater. The nights were still chilly, spring or not. She turned away from the glass, gaze going to the portrait of Caldicott Wyntham over the fireplace.

The painting was done after World War II, when Caldicott was in her thirties. Her gray-green eyes gleamed with humor under flaring brows. The curved mouth hinted at mischief, and her firm chin offset an aristocratic nose. Chestnut hair was worn in an upsweep, emphasizing her graceful neck. Captured in the brushstrokes was the charisma that had remained throughout her life. She'd had the mettle to create Wisdom Court, and the ability to direct it to prominence.

From the outset her plan was for women to live on site. After buying the old farmhouse beside Gregory Creek, she built the two wing houses to allow for expansion. Then came the alumnae group that was the foundation of both recruitment and fund-raising efforts. After the cobblestone courtyard was laid around the fountain, what Boulder called *that Wyntham woman's place* had become known as *Wisdom Court.* The play on her name was a nod of respect.

Rose sighed, thinking of the forceful old lady who had maneuvered her into running the place. Caldicott never did tell her where the money for Wisdom Court had come from. The nineteen-forties had hardly been a time of great opportunities for women. What would she think of how things were going now, and how would she view Aura Lee's resolve to make her the focus of a séance?

Clattering from the kitchen was a reminder of Aura Lee's current activities. She'd been cooking all afternoon, no doubt planning to lull her into a receptive mood. The davenport table near the window already held two of her favorite appetizers, mushroom caps stuffed with crab pate and creamy shrimp dip with butter crackers. Rose sniffed the air in appreciation. Beef bourguignon. She was going all out.

Rose turned as Aura Lee came into the room. "It smells good. Is anybody else joining us for dinner?"

The purple scarf at the neck of Aura Lee's turquoise hostess gown wafted behind her as she moved toward the sofa. "Andrea said she'd be here, and Noreen's a maybe. I made enough to feed everyone."

"Let's have a drink first. What would you like?" Rose crossed to the breakfront cabinet.

"Sherry, please." Aura Lee sent a fidgety glance toward the arched doorway that opened to the hall. "Andrea looked peaked when she got back this afternoon." At Rose's raised brow she added, "She and Neal went up one of the trails for lunch. When they got back, her aura seemed thinned out."

Rose handed her a small glass of sherry and tasted

her own Chardonnay. "Maybe she's tired. It takes a while to get settled in."

"I guess so." Aura Lee sipped her drink. When she lowered her glass, her blue eyes were resolute. "We need to talk, Rose. Now, before anybody else shows up."

Rose sat at the other end of the sofa, tucking her legs underneath her. Noticing the unhappiness in her face, Rose wondered again how she could help her come to terms with Caldicott's death. "What's on your mind?"

Aura Lee met her gaze with dignity. "You already know. I've been talking about it enough."

"A séance."

Aura Lee's brow wrinkled. "I know everyone's been dancing around the idea, or, more likely, ignoring it. But I have good reasons for wanting to hold one."

"All right, tell me."

"You know I'm very sensitive to feelings, Rose. Who else," Aura Lee added in a wobbly voice, "was able to tell what Cottie wanted even after she couldn't speak? I *sensed* what she needed toward the end." She groped in her pocket for a tissue and dabbed at the corners of her eyes.

"You were her dearest friend. I know how much you miss her." Rose paused. "Caldicott's gone and the notion of trying to bring her back bothers me. It feels disrespectful."

"Usually I'd agree with you." Aura Lee leaned forward anxiously. "But Cottie *isn't* gone. I can feel her, Rose, here at Wisdom Court. I *know* she's trying to tell me something."

Rose blinked at the fervor in her voice. "What exactly would be involved in a séance?"

Aura Lee let out a short breath. "There are rules and

rituals," she began carefully. "We would form a circle and burn certain herbs to create a place of safety and focus on receiving her message."

"Who do you mean by we?"

"Why, everyone here at Wisdom Court."

Rose groaned inwardly. She could just imagine the reactions of the others. Noreen would be curious enough to give it a try. Elizabeth might laugh and agree for the hell of it. Kerry—she'd be livid. Dolores would go along. Andrea was an unknown quantity. As for her, Rose thought ruefully, it came down to how long she could hold out against the pestering.

Something had to be done to help her through her grief. "I'll talk to them." She raised a cautionary hand in response to the joy dawning in Aura Lee's face. "No promises, except that we'll talk about it. Okay?"

Aura Lee surged to her feet. "I knew this was going to happen. The cards foretold a good outcome, and I'm sure that extends to the séance, too. I'll cast the runes tonight to make certain." She headed out of the room, scarf fluttering in her wake. "I'll check on dinner."

Rose finished her wine. Wind buffeted the windows, and she thrust herself off the sofa, suddenly anxious to pull the long curtains shut. She tugged the cords, feeling an odd sense of reprieve when they met over the window, swaying gently. Time for hors d'oeuvres, she told herself firmly, and reached for a plate.

Andrea's eyes snapped open at the sound of Grace's scream. She bolted up, snagging her legs in the comforter. In confusion she looked to the window where draped sheers filtered the dying light of early evening. She wasn't at home. She was at Wisdom Court. Grace was in Scotland. There'd been no scream.

Her gaze went to the sketchbook on the nightstand. The events of the afternoon came back, the hike with Neal, their lunch together, and the sketch she couldn't remember drawing.

The walk back to the house had been awkward, the earlier, easy mood dissolving in their silence.

She showered, grateful for the accustomed rites of grooming. Under the flowing water life was reduced to well-known steps. Finally, wrapped in the fuzzy yellow robe Grace had given her, she combed her drying hair.

She'd put it off as long as she could. Andrea picked up the sketchpad. When she lifted the cover to reveal the sketch done the night before, her hands trembled.

She could almost believe someone else had drawn this serious young man. But the smudged thumbprint on each side of the septum was her method for shadowing the nostrils. Here in the cross-hatching was her suggestion of hair texture. If she hadn't drawn it, the person who did had mimicked her style.

Andrea looked beyond technique to the person on the page. He was just a man, twenty-five to thirty at a guess. No, not just a man, she realized, examining almond-shaped eyes and lips pressed together in determination. Offsetting his good looks was an air of strength. She could see it in the jaw above his stiff collar, and could read it in the way he held himself. Here was a man who would take on the world.

She turned the page to look at the sketch she'd drawn today. It was the same man. He was half turned toward the slanted ground behind him. The jagged rock formation above him was menacing, as if it could fall on him. His hair appeared wet, and his collar, so stiff in the first sketch, was crumpled. He was scared. *Who was he, and why the hell had she drawn him?*

Andrea dropped the cover. She'd worked like a maniac the last month to tie up the loose ends involved in moving to Colorado for a year. The long drive had worn her out. Maybe her subconscious had mixed up a few features from drawings she'd done before and presented her with a man she'd never seen. "And had me sketching him in my sleep," she whispered.

Andrea put the pad back on the night table. For fifteen years she'd worked with hundreds of victims and witnesses. She had a gift for hearing descriptions and translating them into images that had often helped in identifying the bad guys. But she hadn't produced portraits out of the blue, and she'd always been awake while she sketched.

Andrea started at the knock at the door. "Yes?"

"Are you coming to dinner?" came Noreen's muffled voice. "Aura Lee just started dishing up."

Andrea glanced down at her bathrobe. She could throw on a sweat suit and wear her slippers. "I'll be right down."

"Okay."

Andrea pulled on her clothes and was tying one shoe when her elbow caught the edge of the sketchpad. It fell to the floor, the cover flipping open to reveal the top drawing. The beautiful young man stared up at her and her throat went dry. His image provided no answers, only a sense of urgency she couldn't understand.

What could make her create and forget not one, but two sketches? Was she having a breakdown? She closed her eyes at the thought. The weird moment yesterday when Neal's face seemed to melt—*that* she'd been able to pass off as a fit of dizziness. Today he'd probably decided she was a few shingles short of a roof, but she hadn't frothed at the mouth or anything. Could she be reacting to some odd form of stress?

The thought got Andrea halfway down the stairs. *What if it isn't stress*? The little she knew of her family tree didn't yield anyone who had been all-out crazy. There was speculation about her great-aunt...*what was her name? Ruta, Ruthann, Ruelynn*? "Great-Aunt Rutabaga," she said aloud.

A butter-smooth voice said, "You look like you don't know whether you're coming or going." An African-American woman smiled at her from the foyer. The paisley shawl around the shoulders of her gold tailored suit set off cocoa brown skin and tilted eyes viewing her with amusement. Her hair, black frosted with gray, had been plaited into tiny braids, all cascading over the broad gold band framing her face.

Although comfortable in her sweat suit moments before, Andrea realized she looked like a frump. She continued down the steps. "I'm decision-challenged, that's all." She extended her hand. "My name's Andrea Bellamy." Her fingers were firmly squeezed.

"Elizabeth Schuster."

Ah, the cookbook writer from outside New Orleans, Andrea thought. "Did you have a good visit with your family?"

"You might say that." Elizabeth unwound the shawl from her shoulders, draping it over the newel post. "My husband, Lovell, and I had our usual fight. After that we spent *quality* time together." Her eyes twinkled. "Then we were able to catch up with each other and talk about the kids and the restaurant." She adjusted the gold bracelet on one wrist. "Every month it's the same. Good thing my stay is only a year. I don't think Lovell would be much inclined to keep goin' after that."

Andrea considered the difficulties the Wisdom

Court grant might cause for a recipient's family. "Isn't it hard to be away from them?"

"Sure it is. But this is *my* time. You think I haven't spent years taking care of all of them and cooking for the restaurant, too? Believe me, I have. It's not gonna hurt Lovell or the girls with me out here. Besides, the twins are in college." Her eyes gleamed with shrewd humor. "When my cookbook starts selling, they'll find all kinds of ways to help me spend the money."

"Oh, yeah," Andrea said with feeling. "My daughter just graduated. Someday I might get solvent again."

"What's your thing?" At Andrea's lifted brows, Elizabeth waved a hand. "What'll you be working on here? Wait a minute—you're an artist, aren't you? I remember Rose saying something about a painting of yours."

"Yes, I paint." Andrea frowned, wondering suddenly if she would have the same trouble with painting as she was having with sketching. Wouldn't that be a kick in the teeth, she thought with bitterness. *I could create a whole portfolio without having any memory of doing it.*

"Well, you don't look happy about it." Elizabeth studied her. "Isn't it what you want to do?"

"More than anything," Andrea said. "I just have to make sure I know what I'm painting." At the bubbling laughter from the other woman, Andrea stared.

"Lord, I love this place. Things are always hopping, always something new to keep me interested. D'you know, I've never been bored here." She put her arm around Andrea's shoulders and gave her a quick hug. "I don't have any idea what you're talking about, honey, but you've got to admit, it's not boring."

Andrea smiled reluctantly. "You've got that right."

Elizabeth dropped her arm and headed down the hallway. "I smell beef bourguignon and I'm starving.

Let's go get us some dinner."

As they walked into the dining room, Kerry leapt to her feet, scurrying around the table to greet Elizabeth. "When did you get back?"

Returning her hug with enthusiasm, Elizabeth extended a hand to Dolores, who was standing behind Kerry. "The plane got in at five-thirty, but it took forever for the luggage to get unloaded. You know the drill. I'm lucky I'm here, with all those clouds piling up, because it looks like all hell is going to break loose before too long."

"It's good you're back. I'll get you a plate." Aura Lee went to the kitchen, bringing back a place setting and a wineglass.

When everyone had resettled around the table, Elizabeth surveyed the company. "It's so good to be back, but I swear you all look like you've been working yourselves to the bone. Rose, you've lost five pounds at least. Kerry, if you don't stop wearing those god-awful coveralls, I'm gonna burn 'em." She took a healthy swallow of wine. "Aura Lee, you've got a secret."

Her voice was tinged with humor, but Aura Lee went pale. "How did you know? Who told you?"

Elizabeth's eyes narrowed. "I'll never reveal my sources." She turned her laughing gaze to Noreen. "You find out everything, Noreen. What's this woman been up to?"

Before Noreen could answer, Aura Lee stood up. "Rose, this isn't the way to get everybody in favor of my plan. Why didn't you wait until later?"

"I haven't talked to anyone," Rose protested.

Noreen frowned in full schoolmistress mode. "Don't be melodramatic, Aura Lee."

Pausing at the door to the kitchen, Aura Lee turned to look at them with tragic eyes. "Rose promised a serious discussion about a séance, but I know how it will be. Kerry will snipe and Elizabeth will laugh, and who knows how the rest of you will react. This is important!"

"For God's sake," Kerry groaned. "Not the séance bit again."

Aura Lee took a step toward the table. "Enough, Kerry! I'm sick of your disrespect. We need to contact Cottie before something terrible happens."

Lightning cracked and the window lit up. The overhead chandelier blinked out, leaving only the candles at the center of the table. Thunder roared like the end of the world, and Dolores screamed. Seconds later a tree branch crashed through the window and a rush of cold air snuffed out the candles. From upstairs came a series of crashes ending in a loud crack of splitting wood.

The silence in the heavy darkness was deafening. "Okay, okay," quavered Kerry. "I vote for the séance."

CHAPTER 6

The next morning they found a large branch of the old cottonwood had pierced the attic roof and lay across the tongue-in-groove floor. A broken rafter sagged over furniture shrouded in sheets, squashing boxes under its weight.

Daylight speared through the jagged hole onto fluttering leaves. Further back the sun struggled through dirty gable windows, dust motes turning the air to gauze. Rose flashed to thoughts of the garret where Jo March wrote her stories, and the austere chamber where Sara Crewe yearned for her father.

Behind her Kerry murmured in distress. "Oh, no, look at those boxes." She scrambled across the floor to a steamer trunk, the top creased by a tree branch. "We have to get this out of here. No telling how much harm's been done, or to what. I knew we should've come up last night to check things out."

"By flashlight? We had enough to do covering the dining room windows." Rose turned at a noise behind her. Noreen had climbed up the steps, holding the rail in a death grip.

"Elizabeth's off to Denver for the TV interview, so

that's taken care of…" Noreen's voice trailed off. Her gaze traveled from a crushed hatbox to file folders spilling yellowed papers onto the floor. By the time she peered up at the hole in the roof, her hands were clutched tightly at her waist. "Lightning," she lamented. "Can you believe it could strike so near the house, with the mountains right up against us?"

Rose's pant leg caught on a broken branch. She tugged it free and reached Noreen's side, putting her arm around the older woman's shoulders. "Everything will be okay."

"But look at it," Noreen fretted. "Will the roof have to be replaced? Do you know anything about such repairs?"

"A little. We'll take care of it." Rose turned her back to the attic stairs and steered her through the debris. "Neal's on his way over. Could you help Aura Lee fix some tea and maybe some pastries to keep us going?"

Noreen nodded. The anxiety in her eyes was fading and color had come back into her face. "You're right, tea would be good. *Thank God for tea! What would the world do without tea?* Sydney Smith, seventeen seventy-one to eighteen forty-five," she added gamely. "I'll go down and help Aura Lee." Gripping the railing, she descended the steps.

"Well, at least she's quoting, even if it was a man." Kerry brushed leaves off her pants.

"I wish she didn't always feel so responsible," Rose murmured. "It takes away from her own work."

"Always the headmistress, I guess." Kerry surveyed the chaos around them. "Where can we take all this stuff? Imagine having construction people up here."

Rose reminded herself that Kerry had a vested interest in preserving information about Wisdom Court. Any threat to that would naturally upset her.

Kerry slumped against a shrouded dresser. "I didn't mean to snap at you. I've been pecking away one box at a time, but it never occurred to me that leaving the rest up here would be a problem. Who knew a damned tree would break the roof?"

Rose pulled a branch to one side and reached for another. "Further proof you're not omniscient."

Kerry looked around the attic with a frown. "If only I'd taken more boxes to my place to sort through them there."

Rose tugged at a crumpled dustcover under a fallen chair and used it to dry an area of the floor further from the roof damage. "Let's shift what we can away from the tree."

They started piling papers and scrapbooks into empty boxes Kerry found in the recesses over the eaves. Dolores arrived and soon the stairs echoed with the thump of her Doc Martens as she carried boxes down to the library. Kerry took more while Rose tried to clear the floor, sweeping up leaves and stacking broken branches in one corner. A batch of sodden photographs required jury-rigged drying lines in Andrea's studio.

Heavy footsteps heralded Neal's arrival. "The damage in the dining room is minimal. We'll have new glass here by this afternoon." He looked around the attic and whistled at the destruction. "Must've been a hell of a boom when it hit. Any problem getting the power back on?"

"The power people were here first thing this morning."

Neal set down his battered toolbox and ran a practiced eye over the ceiling. "I can't tell if the other rafter was affected. It doesn't look cracked from here. We're lucky the whole roof didn't cave in." He pulled a spiral notebook from his back pocket, and took the pen behind his ear to make a note. "We'll need to cover up that hole. Where's the ladder?"

"Back shed." Rose had been making her own list. She'd have to hire a hauling company to carry off the wreckage. The insurance company might require bids for repairs. Would they need permits? Inspections?

Soon the tall stepladder rose through the attic entrance, followed by Neal. He eased it around the railing and propped it against the wall. "How much of this stuff are you taking downstairs?"

Rose glanced around the space. "The rest of the boxes and those two trunks for sure. I'm hoping we can push the furniture into the corners. Will that allow enough room to work in?"

"Maybe."

Dolores trudged up the steps, Kerry close behind her. "Noreen said to tell you tea and fixings will be ready in about fifteen minutes."

"Thanks. Kerry," Rose asked, "do you want the trunks taken to your place? The other option is to put them in the library."

"Definitely the library," Kerry said. "I'm still tripping over my own stuff."

Neal unfolded the legs of the ladder and placed them across a smaller branch. "What's with Noreen? I saw her when I came in and she looked kind of drag-tailed. She feeling okay?"

"I sent her downstairs," Rose said. "I don't want her to trip over these branches. And I can't quite see her carrying boxes down those stairs, can you?"

Dolores made a sound. "Not me. I'm a lot younger and I'm sucking air like a fiend."

Neal had the stepladder directly under the hole in the roof. "She'd carry boxes if she needed to." He climbed nearly to the top and began checking around the edges of the break. He wiggled the end of one board gently. "Noreen's one tough lady after herding teenage girls for all those years." He put a little more pressure on the plank and moved it back and forth slowly, leaning on it to check its strength. Without warning it snapped off above the jagged end and fell toward the clutter below. The weight of the board threw Neal off balance and he lurched to one side, taking the ladder with him. Both fell heavily onto the floor, across the larger tree limb.

"Madre de Dios!" Dolores shrieked.

Kerry dropped the box she'd picked up and scrambled toward Neal. Dolores followed, Rose right behind her. The leafy boughs obscured Neal's head and torso. One of his legs extended through the gap between the ladder steps. Rose felt ice down her spine. *What if he broke his leg, or his back? What about his neck?*

"Stay there!" Neal's order brought them all up short. He shifted his body and under the rustle of leaves they heard the dry whisper of wood moving against wood. Freeing his foot from the ladder, he eased his legs off the branch, onto the planks.

"Are you hurt?" Dolores spoke carefully in a low voice, in case anything louder could cause the floor to crumble.

"Couple of bruises." Neal brushed at the twigs and leaves in his hair and on his shirt.

Rose saw the red streak across his forehead. "You're bleeding!" She started toward him but Neal held up a hand.

"Don't come over here. I'm not sure the floor will hold us both now." He scooted himself back against the largest branch, wincing as he extended his arm.

"What is it?" Rose demanded.

"Shoulder." Neal pushed the rubbish off the planks nearest him. He slowly pressed against the boards immediately around and under him, testing their solidity. When he moved one leg, a faint cracking came from beneath him. "That doesn't sound good." His fingers continued delicately along the surface of the floor. Blood dripped over one brow and trickled into his eye. He rubbed at it with the back of his hand, smearing it down the side of his face.

From downstairs came the familiar slam of the front door. Dolores eased back toward the stairs and then swiftly moved down them. "Bring back some clean cloths," Rose called after her. She turned to Kerry, waiting tensely beside her. Rose said in a low voice, "I think you'd better call an ambulance. He could have a concussion."

"I don't have a concussion." Neal frowned in concentration, his hands moving over the wood.

"Then I'll call Jerri. You're bleeding, Neal. She'll want to check you out."

"Wait a sec." His frown deepened as his fingers felt across the grain. "There's a hell of a crack here." A creaking noise was followed by a clatter. "Well, that would explain it."

"Explain what?" Rose tiptoed closer. "Is the floor going to crash in or what?"

"Probably not," Neal said dryly. "If it were, we'd know by now. What I thought was a split from the fall was a cut piece, a cover for a deliberate opening."

"Let me see." Kerry thrust through the damp leaves and branches until she was close enough to peer over Neal's shoulder. "It's a hiding place!" Kerry allowed Rose enough space to kneel beside them.

The recess was between two joists and in it was a bundle wrapped in coarse fabric. Rose recognized it as a feed sack, making out the faint outlines of flowers on the grubby material.

Neal lifted out the packet and set it on the floor. He

pulled back the cloth, nose wrinkling at its musty odor, revealing a candy box decorated with the picture of a girl wearing a bonnet. The flush on her cheeks was faded and her smile had yellowed but the gilt scallops edging her image gleamed in the muted light.

Neal raised the lid. Inside was a book with the word "Diary" etched on it. Two dried roses bound with a frayed ribbon lay on top of it. Under the volume was a folded scarf, black net edged with blue ribbon. A smaller box with worn corners lay beside the scarf.

Kerry reached past Neal's shoulder toward the flowers. Her fingertips brushed the dry petals and the blossoms crumbled into dust. "Oh, no." Two drops of blood fell onto her sleeve. She jerked toward Neal. "Oh, God, I forgot about your head."

He pressed the heel of his hand against his eyebrow. "I'm fine. You know how head wounds bleed. Sorry about your shirt."

Kerry glanced down at the ancient sweatshirt. "Don't worry about it." She looked toward the door at the sound of voices from the stairs.

Dolores trotted up the steps, a bottle of rubbing alcohol and several washcloths in hand.

As Aura Lee came into view, she was brandishing a vial of iodine in one hand, a box of Band-Aids in the other. "I told you, Rose, we should cleanse the attic before you started working in it, but you didn't pay any attention. None of you ever listens to what I say."

She stepped on the hem of her green caftan as she reached the top step and impatiently swept the fabric out of the way. "With that lightning bolt, who knows what kinds of energy were released. It wouldn't have taken any time at all to run a sage smudge around the corners for protection, but no one listened. Now see what's happened!"

"I'm the one to blame for the fall." Neal's smile was

crooked. "I got careless."

Aura Lee's gaze went from the hole in the ceiling to the blood on his forehead. "There's a disturbance at Wisdom Court."

Kerry pushed herself up from the floor, clutching the candy box like treasure. "A weather disturbance."

Aura Lee was ready for an argument but Neal cut her off. "Aren't you going to staunch my wound?" He lifted a brow. "Ouch. Dammit, that's going to cramp my style."

Rose got to her feet and rubbed at the muscles in the small of her back. "What style is that?"

"You poor boy." Aura Lee made her way past the branches and dropped down beside him. "Did you break anything?" Under green shadow, her eyes shone with sympathy.

"Only my winning streak." His smile was rueful. "You know you're losing it when you don't make sure your ladder's stable." Aura Lee snatched a washcloth from Dolores's hand and applied it vigorously to Neal's forehead. "Ow! What is that, steel wool?"

Aura Lee pressed the cloth onto the cut now bleeding freely over his eyebrow. "It would serve you right. All of you waltzing up here as if nothing serious had happened."

"I'd call a hole in the roof serious." Kerry stepped over the branches, the candy box grasped tightly. "I'm going to take this downstairs for a quick look. I'll be back."

Aura Lee turned toward Rose, curiosity flaring in her eyes. "What's she got?"

Rose told her about the box they'd found in the hidden recess and sighed at her dawning excitement.

"Do you know what this means?" The words nearly burst from Aura Lee's lips. Neal was forgotten. She didn't notice when he took the cloth from her hand to press it to his head. "Perhaps you've found a Revealing Document." She frowned at Dolores's giggle. "It could be the secret history of a restless shade here at Wisdom Court."

Rose caught the quizzical glance from Neal and tried to smile. "You make it sound as though we've got a regular haunted house. Since when do we have 'restless shades?'"

A shadow darkened Aura Lee's eyes. "I told you about Cottie, Rose. I think I can feel others as well. Maybe this diary is involved somehow with the disturbances."

"We'll see. Kerry will let us know if it has anything to do with Caldicott."

Aura Lee's forehead wrinkled with worry. "Do you know last night was three months to the day since Cottie's death? And there was a full moon." When no one responded, she appealed to Rose. "Can't you see? That lightning strike was no coincidence. We should hold the séance here in the attic, soon."

"We'll talk about it tonight, all of us." When Aura Lee opened her mouth to respond, Rose added, "I promise. We'll make a decision tonight."

From downstairs came an outraged shriek, then a bellow. "Aura Lee!"

CHAPTER 7

Andrea dropped her handbag onto the foyer table and rubbed the back of her neck in irritation. She hadn't minded giving Elizabeth a ride to the bus depot for her trip to Denver, but Saturday traffic in Boulder was like bumper cars in a construction zone.

What was next on the agenda? All she wanted to do was paint, to lose herself in colors, but that probably wasn't going to happen until the roof was dealt with. She hadn't even had the chance to check the studio windows for damage.

The air was split with a screech from the kitchen. "Aura Lee!"

Andrea ran down the hall, dimly aware of muffled barking. As she reached the doorway between the parlor and the kitchen, Noreen snapped, "Watch out!" She was across the room beside the sink, where water dripped from the counter onto the floor.

Feet skidding, Andrea clutched at the doorframe to steady herself. In front of her a sheet of water extended across the ceramic tile to the other wall.

"Did a pipe burst?"

"What's going on?" Dolores said at her shoulder.

Rose was right behind her.

Before Andrea could answer, Aura Lee bumped into Rose. "By the Goddess!"

"Careful," Noreen growled as Aura Lee started gingerly toward the sink. "I almost fell getting here to turn off the water."

"What water?" Neal brushed past Andrea into the room. "Where from? The faucet or the valve?"

"The faucet. Whoever left it on also left strawberry hulls and a plate of scones in the sink. They clogged the drain." Noreen scowled at Aura Lee. "You said you'd get the rest of the tea ready while I checked for mail. What were you thinking?"

"Don't blame this on me." Aura Lee frowned back at her. "When Dolores ran in here to get first-aid for Neal, I turned off the water and went upstairs with her. And the strawberries were on the counter, along with the scones."

Noreen swung toward Neal in concern. "First-aid for what?"

"I'm fine," Neal assured her. "I just fell off the ladder, no big deal."

Aura Lee tiptoed across the wet floor to the counter. Rose followed her, stopping for paper towels from the storage closet.

A gloppy mess of berries, leaves, and pastry filled the strainer Aura Lee plucked out of the sink. "I didn't put any leaves in the sink. I saved them in the colander for the compost bin, just like always."

Kerry came through the dining room doorway. "What's up?" She pushed past Dolores, gaze moving over the indoor lake. Her face was smudged, her sweatshirt cobwebby. "Wow, a flood. Did we piss off God or what?"

"Kerry!" Dolores clapped one palm over her mouth. Her brown eyes danced as she lowered her hand.

"Don't be sacrilegious. It's bad luck."

Kerry shrugged. "So how would that change anything around here? Day before yesterday it was a fire, last night the roof caved in, and today we need blueprints for an ark. We're on a roll."

"I gotta say, as a group you people defy the odds." Neal turned toward Rose, giving Andrea a good view of his face. The Band-Aid across his eyebrow didn't hide the scrape on his forehead, and the scratches on his cheek were beginning to develop bruises of their own. Blood had dripped on his shirt.

"Are you sure you're all right?"

Neal raised a brow at the note in Andrea's voice. "Ow." He smoothed the Band-Aid over his eye. "I screwed up and didn't follow my own safety rules." He glanced at the wet floor. "Lot of that going around these days."

Rose sighed. "Things have been out of balance lately."

Noreen nodded gravely. "Positively Elizabethan, my dear. The very solar system is off kilter and won't spin normally until things are brought right." At their amazed silence she added, "Well, I did teach English before becoming a headmistress."

"There's more to it than that," Aura Lee said in a thin voice. "If I didn't leave the faucet on, and you were getting the mail, how do you explain the water all over the floor?"

Rose dropped a sopping wad of paper towels in the sink. "You're sure you turned it off? You were concerned about Neal. It would've been easy to forget, and think you had."

Aura Lee set down the strainer. "I'm positive I turned off the water. It's hard to believe that Cottie would try something as clumsy as this, but Goddess only knows what entered the house with that thunderbolt. We could have all kinds of spirits in here trying to get through to us." She lifted her chin stubbornly. "We must have a séance. We didn't talk about it last night, but we're all here now. Except for Elizabeth, and she won't mind. I *know* this awful feeling I have could be put to rest if Cottie had her say."

"It would mean that all of us participate," Rose warned the others.

Kerry shook her head in defeat. "I give up. Let's do the damned thing and then we can get serious about figuring out what the hell is going on around here."

Aura Lee ignored her. "Caldicott met a medium not long before she died. She was interested in holding a séance," she added pointedly, "but we didn't have time. I'll call the woman for an appointment. The ambience in the attic would be perfect for receiving messages."

"Why did she want to have a séance?" Neal asked. "I never heard her even mention such a thing."

"She'd felt some things here, she said." Aura Lee looked at him uncertainly. "She didn't talk much about it."

"Caldicott had a very open mind," Noreen pointed out. "I don't have a problem with an attempt."

Rose pulled a mop and cleaning rags from the broom closet near the basement stairs. "Let's clean up this mess, and then I, for one, could do with some lunch."

"I have an idea," said Dolores. "My show is next month and I'd like your reactions to what I've finished so far. I was going to ask you all to the studio in a few days, but we could do it today. Order pizza, have some wine—sort of a late lunch, early dinner. What d'you think?"

There was a murmur of agreement. "That invitation

includes you, Neal." Dolores held out a cloth to him. "I'd love to get a male's perspective on my latest sculptures."

Neal handed the rag back to her. "Can I get a rain check? I need to get that hole in the roof covered before it storms again. Sorry I can't stay to help."

"I bet." Dolores grinned at him. "Let me know when you want to see the work."

Noreen was directing Aura Lee and Kerry in getting the stools out of the way. "I'll get the area under here," she told Kerry, "if you'll take the section in front of the sink. Dolores, by the refrigerator?"

The landline rang, and Rose picked up the receiver.

"Can we talk for a minute?" Neal cupped Andrea's elbow and steered her toward the hallway.

"Sure."

Neal smiled at her and tucked a strand of her hair behind her ear. At her reflex step back, his hand dropped to his side. "I wanted to ask how you're doing. You were upset yesterday, and I thought maybe I'd said something to bother you."

"No, not at all." Andrea had a mental image of his expression if she told him about sketching pictures while she was asleep. "I'm fine. I can't imagine what made me act that way, maybe the altitude or something."

"I was afraid I might've pushed you to climb too far. I guess this isn't the best time to ask if you'd like to go hiking again." His smile returned. "We could have dinner together some night instead."

Andrea felt color rise in her cheeks. He wanted to go out with her after yesterday? His collar was open and she kept her gaze on the shirt button at the base of his neck. Just above it she could see his pulse beating. Hers was pounding.

Neal broke the lengthening silence. "Just a thought,

Andrea. No big deal."

Her glance flew to his face. "Sorry, it's just that it's been—"

Kerry hurried past them toward the basement in search of more supplies. "Neal," she called over her shoulder, "Rose wants to talk to you before you go. In her office."

The warmth had faded from Neal's eyes. "Don't look so worried. Dating board members isn't required at Wisdom Court."

Andrea reached for his arm. "Neal, let me—"

He patted her hand and turned away. "No problem, Andrea." He walked toward Rose's office.

Behind her Dolores called, "Hey, catch!" Again her reflexes were too slow. A clean rag hit her in the face.

"Well, shit," Andrea muttered.

The floor was dealt with, and they grabbed snacks to tide them over as they scattered to get ready for the art show. Kerry's thoughts flew to the candy box they'd found in the attic. She'd emptied it before the kitchen disaster, and had opened the diary to the first page. Running her finger over the copperplate "J" and "A" and "C" as well as the bold strokes of the year, 1908, had given her an odd, melancholy feeling. The journal had no apparent connection to Caldicott Wyntham, but it was a voice from the past.

Kerry rushed to the library and settled into a chair at the long table where she'd left the box. She lifted out the book and when she opened it the spine cracked. With care she turned past the frontispiece:

> *Mister Stanley Thornton, my employer, gave this Diary to me as a Remembrance of my birthday. It will be the account of my new life in Boulder. In these pages I shall set down my progress as I make my way in the world. I*

pray for the souls of my mother and father, and trust in the protection of our Heavenly Father. Jessamine A. Cunningham. May 14, 1908.

She didn't have time to read any more now. Kerry closed the journal and put it beside the black net scarf, smoothing down the blue ribbon along the edge. The smaller box was dark green and inside it a necklace lay on yellowed satin. Smiling in delight, she pulled out the ornament, running the tarnished chain over her fingers. The silver pendant had lines etched from its center point, and a triangle of metal lay flat on the disk. When she touched it, the triangle shifted and she lifted it up with her fingernail. It was a miniature sundial, the triangle the gnomon meant to cast a shadow that told the hour. Tiny chips were arranged on the radiating lines. Diamonds? At the end of each line was an engraved numeral.

A rustling came from the doorway. "Kerry. I thought you'd gone back to your place." Rose had changed into a long khaki skirt topped with a creamy white turtleneck. Her silver-blonde curls were gathered in a clip at the nape of her neck, and gold hoops swung from her earlobes.

"You look really nice," Kerry said.

"Thanks. I decided to treat Dolores's presentation as the opening it is." Her gaze went to the jewelry in Kerry's hand. "What do you have there?"

"The pendant in that box we found." Kerry glanced down at her damp coveralls and noticed the leaf bits on one shoulder. "I hadn't even thought about clothes. Is everybody dressing up, do you think? Should I put on something else?"

Rose smiled as she turned back toward the door. "Up to you, dearie. I'm sure you'll look fine, no matter what you wear. You know Dolores won't care.

I'll see you there." She continued down the hall as she spoke, her final words floating back on the air.

"Balls," Kerry muttered. She set the sundial carefully into its case and returned it and the diary to the candy box. Clean, dry clothes would at least show some respect for Dolores's efforts.

An hour later, Dolores opened the door to her half of the east associate house. Kerry, freshly showered and dressed in tailored slacks and blue silk sweater, spared a grateful thought for Rose. Dolores was radiant in a red and gold Mexican dress, and her long black hair swung in a braid down her back. She took the bag of potato chips from Kerry's hand and motioned her inside. "The pizza just got here. I'm starving, aren't you? Let me get a bowl for these and we can try the dip Elizabeth brought. It looks yummy."

Everyone had gathered in the large space that served as both a lounge and a dining room. The decor was southwestern, with earthen colors and casual furniture. A Navajo blanket had been draped over the leather sofa, and a vase of blue hyacinths was set among votive candles on the stone coffee table. Several low-backed chairs were arranged in favor of conversation.

"Hey, Miz Kerry, you're looking good." Elizabeth wore the long black tee-shirt dress she'd chosen for her television interview earlier that day. It was decorated only with the gold chain at her neck.

"Thanks. You, too. Hi, Noreen." Across the dining table, Noreen was sliding a slice of pizza onto her plate. She nodded at Kerry and bent her attention to the serving dishes. Kerry glanced around the room. "Where's Aura Lee?"

Elizabeth scooped up dip with a celery stick. "On

her way, I guess." She focused on a dish. "Mmm, garlic bread. Marinara sauce, too."

"Nice spread." Andrea took a healthy portion of salad greens. "More than just pizza and wine."

Rose pushed a dish of spiced pecans aside to make room for a platter of crudités. "We can always do better than that."

"Thanks, Rose, those are perfect for the dip. Try it, Andrea." Elizabeth nodded at a square bowl. "Let me know if there's too much rosemary."

Dolores carried a tray of glasses to the table and set them near several wine bottles. "I've got Coronas in the fridge if anybody wants beer." She bent to pick up Andrea's napkin from the floor and handed it to her. "*Dios*, I can't believe how nervous I am. You guys are the most sympathetic audience I'll ever have. By the time the show opens, I'll be a wreck."

"Has anybody else seen your work?" Andrea tucked the napkin into her blazer pocket.

"No, not this batch. It wasn't ready yet." She shrugged. "The hardest part is sharing what I've done. When it's still just mine, I don't have to worry about the critics."

Andrea nodded. "But you don't get any praise, either. Or money."

"Oh, yeah, money." Dolores grinned. "I vaguely remember money."

"You like the dip?" Elizabeth asked. When they nodded, she relaxed. "My editor wants more pages, and I don't want to have to add anything else about Katrina. I was scramblin' the whole time I was home to get extra recipes I could stick in." At Andrea's questioning look, she added, "I pitched this project as a combination cookbook and memoir about starting over after the hurricane. But that part was hard, both the writing and the remembering. I figure my auntie's dipping sauce and my cherry-wine pudding—and the stories behind 'em—will fill it out a little."

They'd nearly finished eating when Dolores brought in a plate of cookies and a stack of napkins. "Grab one of these and bring your drinks. The coffee will be ready soon."

She led them to the studio where folding screens were set just inside the door. "I'm so excited." The words bubbled from her like Champagne. "The show is called, *'Wrapture,'* spelled with a 'w.' I want you to be honest with me, *amigas."*

They followed her around the screens and stopped in their tracks. "Oh, my God," Elizabeth said in a wondering voice. "They're all waiting."

Kerry peeked over her shoulder and encountered eyes gazing back at her. The objects inside *were* waiting, she thought in surprise. And damned if she didn't feel the same quiver of unease that always plagued her at having to meet strangers.

CHAPTER 8

The studio was large, with windows overlooking the space between the two Wisdom Court duplexes. Here Dolores's display shone like a small jewel in a great box. Overhead track lights deepened the reds and gold of an Oriental rug, and illuminated the iridescent screen at one end of it. A crimson love seat and two striped chairs held life-sized sculptures. Other figures stood in conversation groupings, a motionless cocktail party. Andrea had the odd sense that she and the other women were the exhibit, the terra cotta mannequins *their* audience.

Dolores grabbed a pile of small papers. "I almost forgot." She gathered pencils as well. "Would you write down your reactions to the pieces? Just a word or two," she added as she handed out the items. "The titles aren't final yet, so what you write might help me come up with some zingers."

Andrea met the sated gaze of a stout matron next to a piecrust table holding a dish of chocolates. Her gown was fashioned from flattened candy bar wrappers, the cowl collar framing her face. Chocolate smears around her mouth gave her a blissful air. The tag identified her as *Cocoa Rococo*.

"Mmm, chocolate." Andrea circled the sculpture. "Look at those eyes! You can see the greed. If we turn our backs, she'll eat all the rest."

"Not if I get to them first, honey." Elizabeth seized a bonbon from the dish and popped it into her mouth. Kerry reached over her shoulder and took one, too.

"Hey, you're eating the artwork." Dolores grinned at their horrified faces. "There's bags of the stuff in the kitchen. I'm thinking I'll have to refill that plate plenty."

Andrea touched the lady's smudged cheek. The smooth clay was cold against her fingertips. "I've never tried sculpting," she said to Dolores. "I figured it would be harder to work in three dimensions."

"Yeah, but it's so much fun. Come here, I'll give you a taste." Dolores set down her glass and folded back the screen behind the statue. She led Andrea toward a table littered with tools and lifted the cloth covering a rounded shape.

Dolores patted the ball of clay with affection. "I haven't decided yet if I'll stick with terra cotta. I enjoy working with it, but sometimes cracking is a problem." She pulled a handful from the mass and patted it into a smaller ball. "Hold out your hand."

Andrea slipped her paper and pencil into her pocket and obeyed. The clay made a satisfying *thwack* as it hit her palm.

Dolores grinned at the way Andrea regarded the stuff. "You have to let it settle in your hands, *jita.*"

Andrea kneaded the ball, squishing it between her fingers. Memories of mud pies and walking barefooted through sand came into her mind. "It's warm." She looked at Dolores in surprise. "It feels almost alive."

Dolores nodded. "Yeah, it does. I think that's why I

keep coming back to it as a medium. It makes me feel like a god forming my own little universe." She glanced around with a mock shiver. "Don't let a priest hear me say that."

"Come look at this one," Noreen called.

Andrea put the clay back on the table and wiped off her hands with a tissue. Noreen stood beside a life-sized cloth doll seated in an armchair. She was a slender nude crafted of muslin with nylon hosiery stretched over it to suggest skin tone. Her brown hair curled around gold earrings and thick black lashes set off blank eyes. The absence of irises and pupils made for an unsettling stare that kept lookout from all angles. *Self-Wrapped* was the title.

Orphan Annie eyes, thought Andrea uncomfortably. The doll sat with legs crossed, leaning forward on the verge of telling a secret. A flat unstuffed replica of the doll, including the gold earrings and empty eyes, formed a stole that draped around her shoulders, arms crossing over her breasts.

Andrea imagined having the piece in her home. She would feel watched all the time. A shiver worked its way down her spine. She pulled the paper and pencil from her pocket, wondering how to word her reaction.

Kerry met her glance over the chair. "Reminds me of a few people I've met. The eyes are open, but nobody's home."

"And they didn't set the alarm, either." Noreen shrugged when the others laughed. "Well, don't you think part of the impact comes from the dolls' identical expressions?"

Elizabeth turned away from the piece, the gold chain around her neck shifting in the light. "I get a different feeling. She looks like she wants something she don't have, and wouldn't be shy of trying to get."

Dolores brought over more wine. "She's one that

came out of the ozone, you know? Surprised the hell out of me."

Andrea shot her a glance. Had she experienced something akin to what had happened to her with the sketches? As Dolores filled her wineglass, Andrea searched her face. She smiled at her and moved on.

Rose paused beside a clay figure near an overstuffed chair. "Not only is someone at home, she's been around for quite a while." The woman leaned on a cane. Attired in a plain purple dress, her feet were planted for support in laced Etta Jennicks. Her back bent in a dowager hump and her slumped shoulders increased gravity's hold on the flattened breasts hanging nearly to her waist. Her thinning hair was pulled back into a bun, and though her face was lined and wrinkled, it bore signs of hidden youth. Lively curiosity gleamed in her eyes.

Rose smiled into the wizened countenance, then looked to the small card taped to the screen behind it: *Woman Wrapped in Time.* "I really like this one."

"Thanks." Dolores patted the statue's cheek. "I was thinking of *mi abuela* while I worked on her." A crooked smile lit her face. "That's why I couldn't leave her naked. Grandma would haunt me."

Kerry had stopped in front of the figure at the end of the row. "What in God's name have you done here?"

Curious, Andrea moved closer to see what Kerry was looking at. It was an enormous woman whose pendulous breasts almost merged into the folds of fat spilling down her torso. "Look at that skin," Rose murmured behind her. "And that face."

The others gathered in silence. The terra cotta had a bronze glaze and the burnished surface cried out to be touched. It was her face that fascinated, for looking from it were eyes that changed expression in the shifting light of the candles on the table beside her.

Dolores had imbued the almond eyes with both tenderness and pain, and the balance between recurred in the lined brow and brave mouth. This woman had suffered and still viewed the world with acceptance. *Woman Wrapped in Her Past* was the title.

"She's beautiful." Noreen's voice was huskier than usual. "Beautiful."

Kerry turned away from the sculpture. "Oh, come on."

Dolores considered Kerry with interest. "You can find beauty in surprising places."

"A figure like this," Kerry said gruffly, "belongs in a sideshow."

Rose inhaled deeply.

Andrea glanced at her. Why was Kerry so upset? She was a little overweight, but her reaction was way out of proportion.

Dolores sipped her wine as she stretched out a hand to stroke the rounded shoulder of the obese figure. "I'm sick of the way our society defines beauty in women."

"Why would you care?" Kerry challenged. "Why would somebody like you notice the imperfections of ordinary people?"

"Somebody like *me*?" Dolores's face broke from shock to ferocity in an instant.

"You're gorgeous." Kerry spat the word. "What do you know about how ugly people feel?"

"How do *you*?" Dolores's eyes narrowed. "I can't believe you'd ever think of yourself as ugly."

"You realize how subversive this is, don't you?" Rose stroked down the polished arm of the figure. "Fat people are the last group society considers it okay to ridicule. You're bucking the trend, Dolores." Her voice was calm and her perceptive gaze appraised the two women. The heat went out of Dolores's eyes and she took a swallow of wine.

Noreen recited, "*Hidden under mounds of flesh, the kernel of virtue is as concealed as is generosity in the soul of a miser.*" In the astonished silence following she drained her glass.

Elizabeth leaned toward Kerry. "Do you ever wonder if she makes these things up?"

Noreen straightened to her full height, regal despite her spiky hair. "Arlen Marie Seluscombe, seventeen sixty-seven to eighteen forty-two. And if I did invent quotes, not a one of you would know it."

Aura Lee appeared in the doorway. Black sequins on the yoke of her flamingo pink caftan glittered in the light. "We wouldn't know what?" she inquired. "Among the batch of us, we must understand nearly everything worth knowing."

"I doubt that," Rose retorted. The laughing protests of the others smoothed the edge from the atmosphere.

Elizabeth had wandered over to examine Aura Lee's outfit. "You look gorgeous, girlfriend. If this was for Jacob's benefit, I imagine the man melted into a puddle."

Aura Lee's blush was almost the same shade as her glowing hair, tonight arranged in curls held by jeweled combs. "He did say he liked my outfit, and usually he doesn't pay much attention. Pink always flatters the complexion." Under color-coordinated pink shadow her eyes sparkled.

"Who's Jacob?" Andrea whispered to Dolores.

"Her boyfriend," Dolores murmured. "Apparently they've been seeing each other for years. Would you like some wine?" she asked Aura Lee.

"Thank you, yes. We ate at that new vegetarian place on Arapaho and it doesn't have a liquor license yet. I must say," Aura Lee said at the full glass Dolores handed to her, "I've gotten used to having at least a little wine in the evening."

"What about Jacob?" Elizabeth was hunting for a place to sit down. She finally leaned one hip against a windowsill.

"He prefers beer. He says he's going to start a micro brewery and make designer beers, but his chart is all wrong for that kind of business."

"No, I mean, why didn't you bring him by to see Dolores's work?" Elizabeth gestured toward the sculptures. "I think it'd be fun to hear a man's take on these pieces." She glanced at several nude figures and winked.

Aura Lee shook her head. "His feminine side is underdeveloped. He'd probably be uncomfortable." Her gaze took in the sculptures nearest to her. She moved toward the chocolate lady and bent to examine it.

Kerry had wandered beyond the mountainous sculpture and was studying the figure of a woman whose face lifted toward the ceiling. On her cheeks were tears created out of clear, oval beads falling from half-closed eyes and extending down her neck and over her body. *Woman Wrapped in Sorrow* read the card.

Rose patted the obese statue with affection and headed toward Kerry. The gold hoops at her ears swung against her cheeks. Andrea watched her, thinking how she'd defused the situation between Kerry and Dolores with nothing more than her own tranquility.

Andrea looked for a place to set her glass. She'd had enough wine. The earlier throbbing over her eyebrow had become a full-blown headache. At the sound of a rising voice, she turned toward the end of the room.

Noreen had rubbed her short hair into a porcupine bristle. "It's always the same. Victorian women took arsenic to attain that pale look fashionable at the time. And they tortured their bodies with corsets to achieve the wasp-waisted figure." She caught Dolores's grim nod. "There's no difference between that and the pointed shoes in the 'sixties. *Nineteen*-sixties, that is. Do you know how many women have corns and hammer toes because of those things? We all just wore them."

Rose nodded. "Yes, but did you ever try to find something else halfway fashionable at the time? There wasn't anything, unless you wanted to wear men's work boots or nurses' shoes."

Noreen nodded judiciously. "That's true. Come the revolution, we'll take the shoe and fashion designers out into the streets and make them wear their own designs."

Elizabeth's eyes lit with humor. "That'll show 'em. Women focused so much on their bodies 'cause they weren't used to having power over anything else."

"If you're saying that the power women have gained in other arenas have stopped their focusing on their bodies, I have to disagree," Noreen returned. "All you have to do is survey article titles in women's magazines to forget that idea."

"*How to Lose Forty Pounds in Forty Days,*" Dolores responded promptly.

"*How to Look Like a Love Slave for Your Husband,*" matched Kerry. Her tentative smile deepened as Dolores returned it.

"*Ten Sexual Strategies to Make His Eyes Cross,*" Rose offered.

Noreen's eyes twinkled at their laughter. "Face it, women have been programmed to deal with unhappiness by changing their looks or their decor. That feeds into the notion that perfection is possible, whether you're talking about your body or your work or your household standards. And that's the source of real depression. Perfectionism is the Devil whispering in your ear, *You can be flawless."*

The overhead lights flickered.

"Oh, God," Elizabeth sighed. "Nobody's happy with the way things are and they can't think of any way to make them better. I'm afraid for the future of my girls. What about you, Andrea? What's your take on the modern woman? Is your life perfect?"

Andrea heard her from a distance. The air was beating a rhythm against her ears. "I don't know anything that's perfect." Her paper and pencil dropped from her hand.

Elizabeth bent to pick them up, glancing at the paper as she rose. "What's this? Dolores said to write down your reactions."

Andrea shook her head, at once regretting the sharp motion. The ache in her temples was growing stronger.

Elizabeth gave her the paper. "Looks like a sundial."

Aura Lee peered at the paper in Andrea's hand. "Is it a necklace? It has a chain," she explained when Andrea stared at her. She wiggled her fingers at Dolores as she approached with more wine. "Did you see what Andrea drew?"

Dolores glanced at the sketch. "A sundial? Nice." She set the bottle on the broad windowsill. "I've never seen one used as a pendant." The lights fluctuated again, and Dolores cast a worried look toward the ceiling.

"What did you say?" Kerry pushed past Aura Lee and caught sight of the drawing Andrea held.

"Andrea drew it instead of coming up with word reactions. Not what I had in mind, by the way. I thought I might get some more title ideas from what you all wrote. I have trouble with them."

Kerry inspected the sundial and looked at Andrea with fierce eyes.

Andrea frowned. "What's the matter?"

Kerry reached blindly for the wine and filled her glass. As the others resumed their conversations, she drew closer to Andrea. "When did you look inside the box?"

"What box?"

Kerry's mouth tightened. "I would've shown it to you along with the others. You didn't have to grandstand."

Andrea rubbed at the pain in her temples. "I didn't look in any boxes except the ones I've been unpacking. If you've got a problem, can we talk later?"

"We'll talk now." Kerry's cheeks were flushed and her eyes flashed. "You were in the house. You went to the library and rooted around for what we found. We don't do that kind of thing here. We respect each other's privacy."

Andrea stared at her in disbelief. "Are you crazy? I haven't been searching through anything." Another pain stabbed at her temples. "Skip it, Kerry. I feel horrible and I'm going back to my room." She turned to walk away but Kerry stepped in front of her.

The other women had drifted toward them. Rose looked in concern from one to the other. "What's going on?"

The overhead lights blinked out, leaving the few candles set around the room the only source of light. Kerry didn't notice, gesturing toward Andrea furiously. "It's about the box we found in the attic. You saw it, the jewelry box with a sundial pendant in it. Just like that one." She pointed at the sketch. "She probably dug through it right after I left to change clothes. We can't work together if we can't trust each other."

"What's with the lights?" Elizabeth demanded.

"I'll find the fuse box." Rose headed toward the back of the studio.

Andrea felt the gorge rising in her throat and knew that if she didn't leave she would vomit on the floor. She felt air currents swirl around her as she dodged around the terra cotta figures, and the candles were snuffed out. "By the Goddess!" screeched Aura Lee.

Andrea reached the studio entrance and darted across the shadowed living room to the door, fumbling with the knob until she finally was able to turn it. She stumbled out into the still night.

CHAPTER 9

Andrea opened her eyes, wondering what had awakened her. Sunlight shone through the sheers across the window and birds were singing. The air was scented with baking bread. As she yawned the memory of her encounter with Kerry the night before caught her in mid-stretch. "Hell," she whispered. So she'd sketched a sundial. Having a meltdown over it was unreasonable. No, it was weird.

With a groan, she pulled the covers over her head. *Weird* was not knowing what was going on inside her own head. What the hell had made her draw the sundial in the first place?

She'd have to deal with Kerry and the others. What did they think of her after last night? Instead of defending herself against Kerry, she'd run away. The only good news was she hadn't thrown up on them.

Andrea flipped the sheet back and swung her legs over the side of the bed. Something landed on the floor with a soft thud. It was the sketchpad. Bending down for it, she suddenly was enveloped in a sense of *déjà vu*. That first night she'd retrieved the pad off the floor and had found in it the drawing of the young man in danger.

Dropping to her knees, she picked up the tumbled drawing pad. Smoothing page by page she contemplated the images. First the likeness of the unknown man, then a quick sketch of a flower seen along the Chautauqua trail with Neal. The sheet after that had the image of the man done during the picnic. Andrea leafed through the other pages, finding only blank paper. She slumped in relief.

Her bare knees rubbed against grit. She pushed herself up and felt granular roughness against her hands. Touching her tongue to the tiny white crystals on her palm, she tasted salt.

Andrea looked more closely at the Oriental rug and saw a thin line of salt extending the full length of the bed. She followed the trail around the end board and found more on the other side. She climbed onto the bed and peeked over the edge. Her bed was encircled with it.

Andrea slid off the bed and examined the room. Nothing else appeared to be out of place and the rest of the rug was clean—not a dust bunny to be found. Why would somebody put salt around her bed? Andrea considered the women at Wisdom Court, and stopped. She didn't even know them yet and already she was trying to decide who might be playing tricks on her.

Suddenly, she wanted nothing more than to get away from the place. Groping for clothes, she stepped into jeans, pulled a shirt over her head. All she'd done since her arrival was ask questions without answers. She dragged the comb through her hair and slammed it down on the dresser. She was tired of being afraid.

After the briefest possible time in the bathroom she threw open her door and dashed into the hallway. Halfway down the stairs she encountered Aura Lee, but before the older woman could say a word, Andrea announced, "I'm going for a walk."

"Why, so am I." Aura Lee beamed at her. Today she wore an amber sari and several strings of beads. "I'm just heading to the store to pick up a few things. We could go together."

"Um, that would be—"

Aura Lee patted Andrea's shoulder. "You have something else in mind, don't you?" She smiled at Andrea's surprise. "I have psychic tendencies. You run along now."

The warmth in her eyes prompted Andrea to say, "If there aren't too many things, I could get them for you."

"Aren't you sweet. Are you sure?" Aura Lee frowned at her. "You're not here to run errands, you know. You have your own work to do."

"Just this once. I won't tell if you won't."

Aura Lee nodded in solemn agreement, but her eyes twinkled. "Thanks, dear. Just a gallon of milk and a dozen eggs. If you walk down Ninth Street, you'll pass Clifford's where we have an account. They're open on Sundays. If you go somewhere else, I'll pay you for whatever you spend."

"Okay." Andrea continued down the stairs. Her hand was on the doorknob when Aura Lee called after her.

"Oh, and could you get some salt? We're almost out."

Andrea slammed the door shut behind her.

The noise of the door brought Kerry to her front window, coffee mug in hand. Tilting up a couple of slats to see better, she saw Andrea stride across the courtyard. When she'd disappeared behind the hedge, Kerry turned back toward her study. *Wonder what she's running from now.*

The candy box from the attic was on her desk, along with three of Caldicott Wyntham's leather-bound journals stacked at the edge. After her run-in with Andrea, Kerry had gone to the main house with Rose and Aura Lee to take the box from the library. She'd told Rose she wanted to explore the diary.

She wasn't about to leave it where anybody else could ransack it. Kerry lifted the lid and opened the velvet case. She pulled out the sundial, letting the chain hang over her hand.

Underneath the grime clouding the compass she could see the needle dancing. She folded the gnomon upright and stared at the tiny shadow cast by the lamp. On the reverse side was an inscription, but she couldn't make out the whole thing. Her fingers curled around the edge of the disk. It was such an elegant little instrument. If lightning hadn't struck the old tree, it would have remained concealed as long as the house lasted.

Kerry lifted the cover of the diary and reread the dedication. Jessamine Cunningham had probably been one of the poor souls who'd set out to find a new life in the West. Instead she'd lost both parents and had gone to work for the man who'd given her the diary. Kerry spared a thought for Mr. Thornton, kind enough to give his employee such a gift for her birthday.

Jessamine's writing commenced in neat copperplate, but as the spring days lengthened into summer and her duties as Mr. Thornton's hired girl multiplied, the entries became hurried scrawls. She wrote of long laundry days and the endless battle against dust and dirt in the house. Weeds threatened the kitchen garden, as did grasshoppers and cutworms. The hearty meals she and the housekeeper, Mrs. Selkirk, prepared became more elaborate when Mr. Thornton's sister and nephew arrived in Boulder for a visit. The more formal paragraphs of the opening pages gave way to scribbles reflecting the girl's loneliness and fear for her future.

June 3, 1908.

When Papa and Mama lost the farm in Missouri two years ago, I thought that was the worst. Now I would go back to those days in a second. At least we had each other. I feel so lonesome that sometimes I wish I'd died too. Mr. Thornton is kindly, but I'm still hired help and not his kin. He's got his older sister and her son Edward, who is not very nice. When they was here they treated each other like strangers, though Mr. T. went fishing with Mr. Edward.

June 15, 1908

It is beautiful in Boulder. The air is clean and crisp like apples, and sometimes all the colors look sharp in the thin air. The mountains reach up so high they probably touch Heaven.

Today a batch of climbers from the Chautauqua climbed up the meadow. From here the women, in white shirts and skirts, looked like giant butterflies over the waving grass. Mr. T. said they was going to the Royal Arch, where the rocks make a bridge that frames the valley. I wish I could see it.

I said that to Mrs. Selkirk and she looked at me like I was witless and set me to polishing the silver. She is a good woman, I reckon, but I don't think she likes me. When I make a mistake, she acts like I did it on purpose. I try and stay out of her way.

Kerry's sympathy was with the girl, trying to meet

the exacting standards of the straight-laced housekeeper, shut off from people her own age. Though her parents had been killed in a wagon accident, she'd found a job and worked to better herself. Her descriptions of the books she read during her scarce free time were earnest and sometimes insightful.

The girl had guts, Kerry thought admiringly. I wonder if I'd have done as well in her circumstances. She turned a page of the diary and continued reading.

Andrea followed the sidewalks down the hill, anxious to put distance between herself and Wisdom Court. The different designs of the houses caught her eye, and she began to enjoy looking around. A stone residence constructed in the clean lines of the Prairie style was next door to a Craftsman bungalow where a black Labrador slept on the porch. A blonde woman smiled at her from behind the screen door.

For several blocks most of the homes were two-and three-story Classical and Colonial revivals but a few blocks later she found a tiny castle built from rock with a crenellated tower above the main door. The surrounding fence was covered with honeysuckle vines and the sweet, haunting scent made her feel she'd traveled back in time. If a princess with a veiled headpiece had waved at her from the tower, she'd not have batted an eye.

The neighborhood was an old one, judging by the height of the trees. Maples shook out their new leaves in the breeze and aged pines and spruces brushed at the air, releasing their sharp scent. The mountains looming behind them surely held up the bright blue sky.

Clifford's was built of river rocks that might have been left over from the castle. The little store was across the street from an old cemetery. Andrea gazed toward the headstones among the trees, tempted to explore before buying the milk and eggs. To say nothing of the salt, she thought. But she was thirsty and she went into the shop. A radio propped against the cash register was blaring big band music, and the air was thick with the scent of overripe oranges.

Andrea found the milk and eggs. The salt was on a shelf near the coffee maker, and she set down the other items to reach for the largest foam cup she could find. The tattooed young woman at the checkout stand smiled at Andrea around the gum she chewed in time with the music. Her spiky black hair and vermilion bangs quivered as she rang up the purchases. "Nine eighty-three."

"I'm staying at Wisdom Court," Andrea told her. "Aura Lee said they have an account here?"

"Sure thing." The girl slid a form from under the counter and slipped it into a slot on the register. The machine whirred and spat out the receipt. "Just sign at the bottom."

"So you're a Wisdom Court woman." The old man in the lawn chair behind the counter squinted at her under shrubby brows. Sparse white hair tufted from the center of his head like milkweed fluff. His eyes darkened with trouble as he watched her.

Uncomfortable now, Andrea made a business of signing the invoice, finally daring another glance at the old man.

"I remember when Miz Wyntham bought that old house," he said abruptly.

The checkout girl murmured, "Grandpa," but he ignored her. "People talked about her and her women's school, or whatever she called it. Like college students wasn't bad enough."

"Is that so." Andrea pushed the bill and the pen

across the counter. She sipped her coffee as the girl bagged her groceries.

"Yes, that's so." The old man's mouth moved silently, rehearsing what he would say next. He blinked several times. "She wasn't friendly. Put herself above everybody else, like she was better than us."

Andrea groaned inwardly. "I never met her." She took the plastic sack and picked up her cup.

"Tried to talk to her." The old man watched her, lips still moving. As she turned to leave, he muttered, "Tried to tell her about the house. Something's wrong about the house. They say it's haunted. You might meet 'er yet."

Andrea stopped. "What do you mean?"

"Grandpa! Stop that. I'm sorry," the young woman said with a worried glance over her shoulder. "He gets confused...he doesn't mean anything by it."

Andrea nodded without expression.

"Was always somethin' off about it," the old man insisted in a reedy voice. "Wasn't just me that noticed."

"What kind of things were 'off?'" Andrea asked. Could he possibly be referring to the kind of thing that was happening to her? When he didn't respond, she added, "Do you tell people that story just to frighten them?"

Resentment kindled in his narrowed eyes. "You're another one of 'em, ain't you? Pay no mind to the signs—"

"Grandpa, that's enough!" The girl jerked her head toward the door. "I'm real sorry. You better go."

Andrea pushed the door open and left. Outside she drew in a deep breath and let it out, glad to be out of the funk of the store. What could Caldicott have done to him that he should talk about her like that, even after her death? A woman like her, someone who charted her own course, could have been enough for him to make mischief. But what had he meant about the house?

Andrea waited for a break in the traffic and crossed Ninth Street, stopping at the iron fence bordering the cemetery. Beyond it lay a forest of headstones— granite, sandstone, marble. Some still stood upright, but many were tilted with the weight of years. Sipping her coffee, she slowly walked along the fence line, noting the different designs of the tombstones.

Andrea reached the gate and had started inside when she heard a horn. She glanced around and saw Dolores waving at her from her little pickup truck. "Can I give you a lift?" she called.

The milk weighed a ton and she wasn't looking forward to carrying it uphill. "Yeah!" The driver in the car behind Dolores leaned on his horn as Andrea hurried to the truck. The door swung open and she hopped inside. At another horn blast from the car, Dolores gunned the engine. "*Dios*, he's in a hurry." Her brown eyes were snapping with good humor.

Andrea set the bag on the seat and fumbled with the seat belt. "Thanks for stopping."

"No problem." Dolores glanced at the bag. "You get any chocolate?"

"Nope, just milk and eggs for Aura Lee. And salt."

"Too bad. I could do with a Snickers. Or maybe a Mounds bar. Mmmm, yeah, coconut." She downshifted as they approached the next intersection. "I'm going back for one."

"No."

Dolores turned toward her, gold hoop earrings swinging against her cheeks. "How come?" She'd raised her foot off the accelerator and the pickup was slowing. Again the horn blared from behind them.

Dolores shot an irritated look over her shoulder and pushed the pedal down. "What's up?"

"I had a run in with the old guy in the store. Maybe you could get your candy bar someplace else." Andrea thought about telling her what he'd said, but decided to let it go.

Dolores sneered. "So long, jerk."

"Huh?"

She glanced over at Andrea. "Mr. Horn Guy behind us just turned off. Good riddance. I've still got a bunch of chocolate at home. Like I need it." She shot another look at Andrea. "I'm sorry about last night." She shook her head. "Kerry hasn't been here all that long, and she's mostly working, you know? One thing I've noticed is that she obsesses about anything to do with Caldicott. Of course, she's writing about her life, but that doesn't explain what was going on last night."

Andrea stared out the passenger window. "I guess I figured you'd all think that I'd done whatever she was so mad about." She turned back to Dolores. "I didn't."

"Why would you expect us to think that?"

Andrea shrugged. "I didn't defend myself or shove her accusations down her throat or anything. I was so upset that all I really wanted was to disappear. That isn't the best way to impress people of your honesty."

"Look," Dolores said, "I know it's hard at first at Wisdom Court. Everyone else has been around for a while and you feel like you'll never crack the code. We've all been there and we've all had to make our own places. It's one of the best things about Wisdom Court, believe it or not. It's what keeps the chemistry changing and dynamic."

"I've had plenty of dynamics, thank you very much. I could do with a little peace and quiet so I can get started on my painting."

Dolores turned onto Baseline and geared down to

climb the hill. "It'll happen. One of the things you need to remember is that everybody's on edge right now. Nobody's used to life without Caldicott, and we're all hurting. Especially Aura Lee."

Andrea frowned. "I'll talk to Kerry. I didn't see whatever was in that box she was talking about. I don't even remember drawing that sundial, for that matter. I didn't have anything in mind at all." She slanted a look at Dolores, wondering if she dared bring up the notion of sketching things without knowing it. Hadn't Dolores said she sometimes felt as though what she sculpted was a surprise to her?

"So what's it to Kerry if you draw a sundial?" Dolores shrugged. "It was a nice little sketch and she went ballistic. I'm just sorry it happened. By the way," she added, "since you escaped before I could ask, did you like my stuff?"

"Oh, yeah. I think you've said so many things on so many levels that I'm just blown away."

A pleased smile curved Dolores's lips. She flicked on the turn signal and they swung into the drive toward Wisdom Court. "Thanks. Everybody was enthusiastic enough for me to go ahead and mount the show. If you all hated it, I would've had to think it over." The pickup rattled down the lane. "I just wish Caldicott could have been here for it. That woman knew what she liked, but she also knew plenty about art. I miss her."

Andrea thought about what the old man at the store had said. The women who lived with her, who had really known her, were the ones she should pay attention to. "I'm so sorry I didn't meet her. She changed my life."

Dolores nodded. "Yeah. Mine, too."

The sound of Dolores's pickup pulling into the parking area jerked Kerry back to the present. She looked up from Jessamine Cunningham's diary, her gaze sliding to the face of the mantle clock. "Holy shit," she muttered. Over an hour had passed. What she'd planned to do was cross-index Caldicott's first three journals. Now it was nearly time for lunch.

Kerry stood up and stretched her arms over her head. A faint headache throbbed between her eyes. It was probably from trying to decipher Jessamine's worsening scrawl. It had been worth the effort, she thought with pleasure. The entries had gone from the early lists of chores and mundane details to her feelings and observations of the people she encountered. Her thumbnail sketch of the pharmacist's wife who had snubbed her on the sidewalk in front of her husband's drugstore had made her laugh out loud.

Kerry glanced again at the clock, then slipped the diary into the desk drawer and locked it. "I'll be back later," she murmured. She almost felt that Jessamine could hear her.

CHAPTER 10

Andrea set the grocery bag on the kitchen counter and began emptying it. The air smelled of lemon and a spice she couldn't identify. She sniffed again. Thyme, maybe, but she always confused that with basil. She'd put the eggs and milk in the refrigerator and was searching for a place for the salt when Aura Lee swept into the room carrying a laundry basket.

"Thanks so much for getting those things, dear." She hefted the basket onto the counter. "You saved me a trip."

"No problem." Andrea nodded at the salt. "Where does this go?" Besides my bedroom carpet, she wanted to add.

"The pantry's right here." Aura Lee reached for a handle on what Andrea thought was merely a tool rack and opened it, revealing shelves of canned goods and baking supplies. "I'll take it."

Andrea held onto the box. "Aura Lee, I found a line of salt around my bed this morning. Do you know how it got there?"

Aura Lee beamed at her. "Of course, but it wasn't this kind." She took the box of Morton's from

Andrea's limp grasp and set it on a shelf. "It wouldn't work as well. I use only the purest sea salt, I promise you."

"But why? What possible reason could you have for—"

"How did you sleep last night? You didn't have any nightmares did you?" When Andrea shook her head, Aura Lee nodded, pleased. "I didn't think so. You looked much more rested when you went running out of here this morning, much more energetic than you have been."

"Okay," Andrea said. "I don't understand what you're talking about."

Aura Lee clicked her tongue. "My dear, it's perfectly simple. If you circle a bed with sea salt, the sleeper will be protected against harm, be it in dreams or in reality. You were so upset the other night with that nightmare and the sketch you drew. I just wanted to help you get some sleep."

She *had* slept well. "Well, thanks. I appreciate the thought."

Aura Lee snapped a green towel from the clothesbasket and swiftly folded it. "Happy to help, dear. Will you be here for dinner tonight?"

"I guess so. I'm going to paint now." Feeling awkward, Andrea paused in the doorway. She felt as if she ought to say or do something else in response to Aura Lee's kindness. "Do you need any help with dinner?"

Aura Lee glanced up from the dishcloth she was folding. "It's all under control. You run along and paint, dear."

Andrea's gaze traveled around the studio. Photographs from the attic hung like wet laundry from the rope strung across one end of the room. Several boxes were stacked in a corner. No matter. For the next year, this was the most important place in the world.

As she picked up a canvas, thoughts of organizing her supplies dropped out of her mind. She needed to pick up a brush, to feel the power waiting inside her since the invitation to Wisdom Court. She was charged with energy. If she could capture just a fragment of those feelings…

She unfolded an easel, set the canvas in place. In moments she began to apply the wash of liquid white that would lend to the look of the sky as she'd driven into Boulder. The clouds had billowed like celestial sails across sapphire seas. Could she capture it? The stab of doubt stopped her mid-motion. She forced herself to rummage for brushes, unwilling to let uncertainty take hold.

The familiar preparations, mixing pigments and setting up her palette, were like warm-up stretches for a ballerina. With the first daub of paint on canvas the dance began. Everything narrowed down to colors and shapes and their fascinating interaction.

A crash from overhead brought Andrea back. The light through the studio windows was the silvery gray of late afternoon. She went to the sink for water and gulped it down, not caring that half dripped down her chin. She hunted for the paint thinner under the sink and set to cleaning the brushes still clutched in one hand. Droplets of color were scattered across her pullover; she muttered to herself for having forgotten a smock.

Rolling her shoulders to loosen them she waited for the water to run hot from the faucet. She was so tired. Scrubbing at the paint on her hands, she then splashed her face with water, and dried it with a clean rag.

Her stomach growled and she realized she was starving. Aura Lee would probably give her a snack.

And coffee, hot and sweet, enough to put a little zip back into her.

Andrea rubbed cream into her hands and was heading for the door when she glanced back at the painting. She stopped and her breath slid out of her. The ethereal sky she'd set out to portray was nothing like what was on the canvas. Ferocious dark clouds menaced a sharp sandstone embankment scarred by a ledge cut into rock. Naked branches of a dead tree clawed at the clouds overhead like a cadaver hand. Where had this come from?

The power of the work was undeniable. Caught between fear and an odd pride, Andrea went closer and leaned in to study the brushstrokes. Near the stark tree was the outline of a man, his head tilted up to the sky. No face, but the widow's peak formed by his hair was distinct.

Andrea made a wordless sound. Was it the man of the sketches? She forced herself to scrutinize every detail of the figure. What he looked toward she couldn't tell. She had no memory of painting any part of it.

Bile rose in her throat. If she let herself, she'd splinter into bits. By the time she got to the back door of the house, she was running. She heard a voice behind her yelling her name but didn't stop.

Instinctively she retraced the way she'd gone with Neal, striding along the street and crossing the parking area. The altitude finally slowed her down. She was gulping for air by the time she reached Gregory Creek. Bracing herself against the bridge rail, she gasped for oxygen, frightened by the thunder of her heartbeat and the black edging her eyesight.

Andrea blinked and felt a tear spill onto her cheek. She dashed it away with the back of her hand. Breathing deeply, she focused on control. She was alone with whatever was happening inside her.

From a distance she heard the crunching sound of footsteps on gravel.

"Excuse us."

Andrea jerked around, nearly bumping into the man and woman waiting for her to leave the bridge. "Sorry."

The thickset man consulted the Rolex at the cuff of his crisp white shirt, but the woman beside him ventured a smile, kindness warming her pale eyes. "Are you all right?" She paid no attention to the man's impatient gesture as he stepped off the bridge, but instead waited for Andrea's response.

"I'm okay." Andrea cleared her throat. "Thank you." She motioned toward the steep hillside. "I'm not used to the altitude."

The woman nodded in understanding. "It affects everyone at first. Where are you headed?"

"The trail to the Amphitheater."

"You'd better go slow. It takes a while to acclimate." She passed Andrea and strode to catch up with the man. The two of them scrambled up the trail veering off from the stream.

Andrea felt steadier for the woman's interest. People were frequently compassionate. Hadn't all of the women at Wisdom Court—except for Kerry—been considerate since she'd arrived? How long would that last if they knew she was delusional? She laughed grimly at the thought and the sound scared her.

She set off on the path and within minutes was at the wood sign marking the Amphitheater Trail. The ruggedness of the course gave her pause, but she was in no mood to go back.

Her leg muscles protested at the high stone steps set into the hill but she ignored the pain. She miscalculated a step and tripped, nearly falling to her knees. Grabbing at the nearest support, a shrub growing out of the hillside, she regained her balance. Frightened, she gazed down the steep rock fall to the sluggish rivulet in the fissure below.

This was the same place she'd been on Friday, but the sun was behind clouds and today the mountain offered no welcome. Her fingers brushed against the small red flowers that reminded her of poppies.

She talked herself up the trail, staying near the slope, away from the edge. Her feet slipped repeatedly and she vowed to buy hiking boots at the first opportunity. She would enjoy hiking. In time her lungs would increase in capacity and she wouldn't feel so much like throwing up. She would learn to know these mountains so she could paint them as they deserved to be painted. The image of the canvas back in her studio intruded, and she pushed it out of her mind. All she had to do was put one foot in front of the other. All she had to do was breathe.

From the peak roof Neal saw Andrea run across the backyard and up the hillside. He called to her but she didn't pause. He frowned. Had she not heard him or was she ignoring him? For the umpteenth time he wondered what had gone wrong when they'd hiked together. She'd been cool to him ever since, and downright closed-off yesterday when he asked her to dinner.

Behind him Denny Corbin said, "Hey, what'd you do, offend the lady?" He was on the ladder braced in the attic, his head and shoulders above the edge of the hole. He'd been ripping away damaged shingles with a pry bar in order to staple down the sheet plastic they'd brought that morning as a temporary cover. His curly blond hair waved in the breeze and he shoved it out of his eyes. "She's a looker. You forget yourself with that sweet thing?" he demanded, grin mocking.

It hit too close to the mark. "Get back to work, you slacker." Over the last two years Denny had become Neal's right hand man, but his idea of wit was to rib him on his social life. Twenty-five and single, Denny seemed amused by his employer's stops and starts in the world of dating.

Neal returned the one-finger salute Denny sent him. He caught another glimpse of Andrea's blue shirt past the bushes along Baseline and frowned again.

Sometime later thunder rumbled to the west and Neal surfaced from the problems of splintered rafters and a cracked floor joist. The sky was darkening, particularly over the mountains. "Shit," he muttered. He needed a few more minutes to finish tacking down the plastic. He didn't take time to measure the furring strip for the final section, just broke it over one knee and stapled it along the folded edge. "Here, Denny, put this in your tool box." He handed over the staple gun. When he saw lightning over Gregory Canyon, he remembered Andrea. "Did that woman come back? The one we saw leave earlier?"

Denny was winding the extension cord from hand to elbow. "I didn't see her, man." He jerked his chin toward the clouds piling up over the Front Range. "Looks like something's headed our way. Think we oughta bag it for a while?"

"Have you got that side fastened down?" When he nodded, Neal said, "Okay, you go ahead."

Denny eased across the expanse to the ladder at the side of the house and started down. The wind came up, whipping his hair around his head. He hesitated, looking back at Neal. "You coming?"

"In a minute." Neal scanned the area where he'd seen Andrea, alert to a glimpse of blue shirt or chestnut hair, but didn't see any sign of her. She'd probably come back already. He climbed down the ladder. No reason to worry. Odds were she was in the house.

The intermittent wind made taking down the ladder difficult. Neal and Denny lashed it to the pickup, then made sure the plywood panels stacked nearby were bound and under cover.

With each passing minute, the worry gnawing at Neal's gut grew stronger. "You finish up," he called to Denny. "I need to check something in the house."

Denny waved at him and Neal headed inside. The rooms were quiet and empty. He called Andrea's name, then Aura Lee's, but no one answered. The tension along the back of his neck intensified. She went for a walk, he told himself. She has enough sense to get out of the rain. The thought brought him no comfort. Filling his mind was how totally lost in her own thoughts she'd been the day they'd hiked together.

He slammed out the back door. "Denny," he called and got an answering shout. "I'm heading up to Chautauqua. I'll be back soon."

"Are you crazy?" Denny protested. "Man, that storm's gonna hit any minute."

Neal ignored him and strode across the yard.

Crossing Baseline, he dodged a car accelerating off the curve of Flagstaff Mountain Road. The wind had picked up speed and he could feel electricity building in the air. He told himself that all this worry was for nothing. She'd have come back hours ago. Maybe she was out on some errand. He picked up speed.

Neal was almost running by the time he reached the bridge over the creek. And then it struck him just how impossible his rescue mission was. He didn't know which direction she'd gone. He'd been assuming she'd go back where they'd hiked together. It was just as likely she'd started up Gregory Canyon, or headed south on the Bluebird-Baird Trail.

A gust of wind pushed him against the railing. He heard voices behind him. A man and woman were coming down the rocky byway from the Bluebird-Baird Trail. She was in front, picking her way over the rugged terrain. "Hurry up, Jess," the man bellowed. "We've got to get out of here before the storm hits."

She made it over the loose rock, flashing a relieved smile as she approached the bridge. "It's getting wild up there," she shouted to Neal over the wind. "I'd wait it out if I were you."

"Jess, we don't have time to stop." The sleeve of his white shirt was torn and graying hair blew into his eyes. He glared at Neal and roughly grabbed the woman's arm. "If you're stupid enough to go up there in weather like this, you deserve what you'll get."

"Don't worry about me." Neal started past them, then played a hunch and turned back. "Did you see a woman come this way? Reddish-brown hair, wore a blue shirt?"

The man tugged at her arm, but she'd already stopped. "We saw her here on the bridge. She said she was going up to the Amphitheater."

"Thanks. Thanks very much." Neal raced toward the trailhead, and rain began to fall.

Thunder crashed overhead. Neal bounded up the big blocks of stone, on the alert for any sign of Andrea. The wind rushed down the cleft created by the trail and more rain rode on it. The path was hard to see and he had to slow down to avoid falling when every instinct pushed him to hurry.

The rain slid off the stone slabs winding upward. The rubber soles of his boots slipped repeatedly. By the time he neared the jagged rocks of the Amphitheater, he was slowing down in spite of himself. He followed the bend in the path entering the area. Lightning flashed, and he saw her. She stood motionless, circled by the misshapen stones of the formation.

"Andrea!" He scrambled toward her. She didn't move and he grabbed her by the arm, swinging her around to face him. He yelled over the wind, "Are you trying to get yourself killed?"

"Neal?" Shaking with cold, she stared at him in confusion. "What are you doing here?"

"Come on." He pulled her upward toward cover. Time and erosion had created clefts in the rocks above them. Not deep enough to be called caves, they offered limited shelter.

He dragged Andrea behind him, thrusting her into a shallow fissure in the rocks. Her back scraped against the craggy interior as Neal pushed in beside her. The deluge had begun in earnest. He shifted his body, blocking the rain from hitting her. Between the thunder and the downpour, they could have been in the middle of a waterfall.

Andrea found she could breathe more easily. She was grateful for Neal's warmth, but she knew his back was exposed to the storm. "You're getting wet."

He lowered his mouth to her ear. "What did you say?"

"You're getting wet," she said more loudly. "Your back."

"I'll live." He pulled away from her a little and, in the flash of lightning, she could see his face. He was dripping rain, and his eyes were dark with worry. "What the hell were you thinking of, standing out in the middle of a thunderstorm?" His hands tightened on her shoulders. "You might've been electrocuted."

The rough rock was cold against the length of her spine. Andrea shivered. "I don't remember what happened. I saw somebody…something." She shook her head. "Then you were there yelling and you dragged me in here. That's all."

"Jesus, lady, you are something." He radiated heat from his hands, from his body pressed against her. "You can't go into mountains, even this close to home, and not watch out for yourself. You could've been hurt. You could have been killed."

Andrea began to tremble in a reaction that had nothing to do with cold. "I didn't mean to—"

His grip on her shoulders strengthened and he said something under his breath that she couldn't hear. Before she could ask him what it was, he bent his head and took her mouth. His lips moved against hers and she felt his tongue against her own. For a shocked moment she held herself still. Then she leaned into him. She kissed him back, greedy at the rush of pleasure. Her arms were at her sides and she struggled to get them free. He lifted his head. "Let me go."

Her voice was little more than a whisper but he loosened his grip on her and stepped back. Andrea closed the small gap. She ran her hands up his arms and grasped his shoulders, drawing him back to her. His lips skimmed over her face, finding her mouth once more. Everything else had left her mind. She knew only how vital it was to be close to him.

Lightning crackled, thunder crashing almost at once. They pulled apart in alarm. She looked up into his face as another bolt lit the sky. His brown hair was dark with rain. His gray-green eyes were feverish, his mouth taut. She pulled his head back down to hers.

Want became need. Andrea clutched his shoulders and kissed him with desperation she hadn't known before. Reality narrowed to the tension in his arms around her, and the power of his body moving against her own. She pulled back for air and in that instant lightning flared again.

At what she saw, time tilted on its axis. His hair was black, drenched, slicked back from a widow's peak. Rain slid down now-olive skin, and in the flash of light his eyes were black, were almond-shaped, were aglow with passion. He was not Neal.

When the recess went dark again he pulled her closer to his body. She screamed. Fighting insanely, she shoved him with all her strength. He stumbled back and she pushed out of the crevice.

The wind slammed against her, driving rain into her face, whipping her hair around her head.

"Andrea, *Andrea!*" The hoarse shout came from behind her, and in horror she wondered whose voice she heard. Tripping, nearly falling, she slipped over the tumbled rocks as lightning sizzled around them. "Andrea, wait!"

She found the trail and flung herself down it, frantic to get away. At the sound of stones sliding against each other she turned and saw him lunge toward her.

CHAPTER 11

Andrea ran.

The wind forced rain into her eyes, making it nearly impossible to see the trail in the dimming light. She lost her footing on the slippery rocks, falling against rough granite, ripping the sleeve of her shirt and scraping the skin beneath. Pain spurred her on.

Lightning jolted shadows into motion and thunder shook the ground. Gravel all but pitched her onto the talus below. She ran into a tree, clinging to it until the sound of footsteps drove her forward.

As she reached the creek Andrea faltered, shivering convulsively, gasping for air. She started across the wooden footbridge, clutching the rail to keep herself upright. The adrenaline fueling her flight was ebbing fast. When she heard a noise behind her, she stumbled against the handrail.

"Either you're neurotic," Neal said with difficulty, breathing heavily, "or flat out crazy."

Andrea flashed on the image of his features shifting before her eyes. In spite of exhaustion she took a trembling step away from him.

"If you run now I swear to God I'll drag you down

in the middle of the road." He stepped swiftly toward her across the bridge.

She had no doubt he would. He came up behind her, so close she felt the heat of his body. When he grabbed her arm she shrank from him.

"Dammit." His hand tightened as he swung her around toward him.

His face was in shadow.

At her sound of distress he stepped closer and she pulled back instinctively. He shook her by her arm. "Jesus, what's *with* you?" The words were forced out between deep breaths. "Up there you kissed me back. Why the hell did you run?"

He paused for her answer but by now the terror-fed strength carrying her down the mountain was at an end. Her teeth were chattering.

"Wait a minute," Neal growled. "Did you think I was going to force you—do you think I'm the kind of bastard who would *attack* you?" He let go of her but when she swayed he grabbed her arm again to brace her. "Let's get out of here."

Neal kept hold of Andrea's wrist, pulling her along beside him as they headed toward Baseline Road. She had caught her breath but her mind was in chaos.

She'd *seen* that transformation. Neal's features had changed from his own to the almond-shaped eyes, the widow's peak and the black hair of the man in the sketches. Andrea's heart pounded at the memory. She'd been crushed in Neal's arms, had been kissing him for all she was worth and then she'd been held by whom? By what?

Andrea stumbled on a rock and Neal jerked her upright before she fell, but she hardly felt the impatient motion.

As they passed under a street lamp already alight in the early dusk caused by the storm, she forced herself to look at him. He was Neal, his face hard, anger coming off him in waves.

He pulled her through the break in the hedge and strode across the grassy verge with her in tow. The glass fixture above the back door spotlighted the steps, creating an island in the deepening twilight. Neal dropped her arm to propel her up them with a hand against her back. He reached around her to open the door, but the knob barely turned. "Do you have your keys?" he demanded.

Andrea shook her head and then jumped when he banged his fist against the door. At the click of the bolt turning, he started back down the steps.

She turned. "Neal?"

He looked back at her, and the bitterness in his eyes scalded her. Then he was gone.

Behind her the door swung open, spilling light onto the flagstone. Aura Lee's fiery red head appeared for an instant at the edge. "By the Goddess!" She tugged Andrea inside. Her orange sari swirled about her legs as she turned, pulling the door behind her.

"You're just in time." She bustled ahead into the kitchen.

Andrea was enveloped in warm air perfumed with cloves and cinnamon. She limped to the nearest chair and sank onto it.

"Wait till I tell you." Aura Lee turned around, eyes widening as she took in Andrea's appearance. "Sweet, suffering seraphim. What happened to you?"

Andrea let her eyes close. Where to begin? She felt a cool hand against her cheek and when she opened her eyes, Rose was beside her.

"You need something to drink?" she asked with concern. When Andrea shook her head, Rose pulled out a chair and sat in it. "Do you want to tell me about it?" Her voice was kind.

Andrea desired nothing more than to recount everything to Rose. Composed and waiting, her silver blonde hair pulled back at her neck, she was the embodiment of sanity. The mental image of her compassion transforming into disbelief kept Andrea from spilling out the details of what had happened with Neal. "I went up to Chautauqua," she said low-voiced. "It rained and I slipped on some rocks."

The front doorbell chimed as Aura Lee came back with a first aid kit. "That must be Belinda," she exclaimed, eyes alight. She tossed the box onto the table and hurried toward the entrance hall.

Andrea looked after her. "What's going on?"

Before Rose could tell her, Kerry appeared in the doorway. Her auburn hair was disordered, her mouth sulky. "What's up?" she asked Rose. She didn't look at Andrea. "I've got other stuff to do, you know."

Rose was tending to Andrea's arm. As she tore open an antiseptic pad to clean the scrape, the sharp medicinal scent cut into the air. "I imagine our medium has arrived."

Rose rubbed the cold pad against the scrape and Andrea's breath hissed out at its sting.

"Medium?" Kerry shoved her hands into her jean pockets. Color rose in her cheeks. "For a séance?"

Rose smoothed a large Band-Aid over Andrea's wound. "Someone Aura Lee knows had time tonight." She repacked the first aid items and took the kit over to the counter. "You're invited, of course."

"Yeah, like I could get out of it." Kerry sat in the chair vacated by Rose, frowning absently at Andrea. "You've got mud on your face." Her glance at Rose was challenging. "So, have you met this medium before? Madame Something, I'm sure."

Rose tore a paper towel from the dispenser and held it under the faucet. "You know, Kerry, no one's forcing you to attend the séance." She wrung out the paper towel and brought it to Andrea. Her eyes were twinkling. "You could spend the evening alone, wondering madly about what's going on over here."

Andrea wiped the towel over her face. The warm moisture felt wonderful.

Kerry stood up, brows gathered in a frown. "You're evil, Rose. I can't help being curious. I just hope that Madame Whatsit puts on a good enough show to make it interesting."

Aura Lee rushed into the room trailing excitement and the scent of patchouli. "Come on, come on, we're ready now. Dolores and Noreen are with Belinda in the living room. Where's Elizabeth? She's supposed to be here! Kerry, would you bring the tray up?"

Rose straightened the beads nearly hanging down Aura Lee's back. "Elizabeth went to get the biscotti at her house, remember? She'll be back any minute. Take Andrea with you and I'll help Kerry with the tea things. It might be easier to have it down here before we go up."

Aura Lee hesitated. Under the orange shadow smudging each lid, her eyes were apprehensive.

Sleepy from the comfort of the warm room, Andrea wondered if Aura Lee bought eye shadow to match every outfit.

"It's silly to be so worried, isn't it?" Aura Lee tried to smile, but her lips trembled. "I've felt Cottie's presence every day this week, but what if she doesn't try to get through to us?"

Rose gave her a quick hug. "If she doesn't tonight, there'll be other times. All we can do is try. Take a deep breath and try to relax. That's it." Rose glanced at Kerry, concern in her eyes. "Let's gather what we need and get started."

Belinda Smythe had already gone ahead to make

ready for the séance. The narrow stairs squeaked in protest as the rest of them climbed to the attic, their shadows marching up the stairwell over rosebud wallpaper.

"I feel like I'm in the middle of a Gothic novel," Kerry muttered. "I need a long nightgown and a candle, though. And for the rest of you to disappear."

Andrea tightened her hold on the railing. Caught up in the preparations, she hadn't mustered the energy or force of will to avoid the occasion. Her legs felt weighted with iron. Muscles she'd never met ached with each step.

"What about a Mr. Rochester?" Noreen asked Kerry gravely from behind her. "You'd want him to be here, wouldn't you?"

"Nah," Elizabeth said near the top of the stairs. "She'd want somebody more emotionally intelligent."

Rose chuckled and the cups on the tray rattled. "A sensitive hero."

Noreen snorted. "Where's the romance in that? The whole point is to watch while the worthy young governess tames the savage rich man."

"Yeah, savage." Dolores was carrying Strudel under one arm. She flashed a smile toward Kerry over her shoulder. "Someone to match your passions, *chica.*"

"For sure." Elizabeth chuckled. "Miz Kerry here would just have to sweeten up Mr. R. and turn him into a pussy cat. You could do it, too, honey."

"Charlotte Bronte's spinning, you guys," Kerry followed Dolores up through the trapdoor. "Wow, this looks different."

Aura Lee had accomplished miracles in a short time. The furniture was pushed against the walls, shrouded in dust covers. The overhead fixture, a glass pendant, cast a feeble glow.

The black plastic sheeting covering the hole in the

roof dully reflected the light. The floor had been cleared of branches and debris, in their place an ancient rug with fading garlands framing fleurs-de-lis. Fat pillows were arranged around a red pottery bowl filled with herbs, a burning white candle at its center. Four flickering candles were equidistant around the bowl's circumference.

On one of the pillows sat Belinda Smythe. She was monochromatic, her graying blonde hair and tanned skin blending into her sand-colored pullover and matching leggings. Seated in the lotus position, her thin hands rested on her knees, the first two fingers and thumb of each hand touching. Her gaze followed each of the women as they approached the circle.

"Is there a smoke alarm up here?" Kerry asked. She caught sight of the seated woman and frowned.

Aura Lee stationed herself near an old dresser where she took the biscotti from Elizabeth and set it near the cups Rose had brought. She gestured toward the seated woman. "Belinda has had a lot of experience in making contact with spirits. We're very lucky to have her as our Spirit Guide this evening. Thanks again for coming, Belinda."

"You're welcome, Aura Lee." Her voice was deep and melodious. Kerry and Andrea exchanged surprised glances. "I'd like all of you to join the circle." She caught sight of Strudel and blinked. "Do you think it wise to expose the dog to the séance?"

"Oh, she seemed so lonely—" Aura Lee dithered.

"She'll be frightened on her own." Kerry's voice was flat.

Dolores bit back a smile and bent to lower the little dog to a pillow. She sat down beside Strudel, tucking her long flowered skirt around her.

Belinda Smythe lifted her shoulders. "Whatever you think best." She gazed around the room. "I've cleansed the space with sage and have placed candles to represent the four quarters. Red for fire, blue for water, green for earth, silver for air," she explained, looking at each of them in turn. "White is in the center to represent the Goddess."

Kerry rolled her eyes and released a long-suffering sigh.

Aura Lee frowned but her voice was calm. "Some of us are a little uncomfortable with the idea of speaking with the dead."

Belinda nodded. "I've come to believe that some skepticism can be useful in these efforts. The spice in the recipe, if you will." She gestured toward Kerry. "Be seated and we'll begin."

Reluctantly Kerry approached a pillow and sank onto it. "I'll try to control my doubts."

"It doesn't matter. If you're all ready now, we'll get started."

Aura Lee motioned toward the cups and the silver urn. "I thought we might have tea before we started, just to relax us and put us in the right frame of mind."

Belinda blinked and her shoulders shifted uneasily. "Ordinarily that would be a good way to begin, but I'm feeling some…strange influences here. It would be wise to start the séance right away."

"Oh, how exciting." Aura Lee eagerly seated herself in the circle.

Rose's gaze met Andrea's across the bowl of herbs. Her gray eyes were questioning.

Noreen had arranged herself on a cushion, her short legs folded in a perfect lotus position. Elizabeth tugged at the skirt of her red dress, shifting as she sought a more comfortable pose. Belinda inhaled deeply, her chest rising and then falling as she exhaled.

Aura Lee began to breathe in the same rhythm. In

spite of her orange caftan, and her precarious perch on the pillow, she had a certain dignity.

Andrea willed Belinda to help Aura Lee achieve the closure she longed for. If she could just be reassured that her friend was all right, she'd be so much happier.

"Oh, I forgot to turn off the light." Aura Lee pushed herself off the floor, reaching up to pull the chain on the overhead fixture. Shadows slid from the candle-lit corners toward the center of the room.

Belinda again took several breaths and slowly bent forward, lighting a long match from the center candle. She held the flame to the herbs in the bowl and as they caught fire, she surveyed the circle. In the wavering light her face was wiped clean of time and emotion.

She held out her hands, one to Aura Lee, and the other to Elizabeth. "Everyone join hands," she instructed, eyes closed, and they complied. "Now, let yourselves be carried on our breath. Inhale...exhale. Again. And again. As the waves of breath rise and fall, we send our welcoming thoughts toward the Other Side."

The room was silent but for their breathing. The candle flames danced in the movement of the air, the pungent smoke of rosemary and dittany wafting from the bowl.

Belinda's voice cut through the silence. "Guardians of the Watchtowers of the East, Creatures of air and intellect, we request that you bind this circle, thus protecting and guarding us." She inhaled deeply and the others followed suit.

"Guardians of the Watchtowers of the South, Creatures of fire and courage, we request that you bind this circle, thus protecting and guarding us."

Andrea felt Elizabeth's fingers tighten on her hand. She glanced at her from the corners of her eyes.

Elizabeth mouthed something to her, but Andrea couldn't make out what she said, and shook her head.

Belinda Smythe cleared her throat pointedly and Andrea jerked her attention back to the smoking herbs.

"Guardians of the Watchtowers of the West, Creatures of water and emotions, we request that you bind this circle, thus protecting and guarding us."

Smoke from the candles was blending with that from the smoldering herbs, filling the room. Noreen coughed, then murmured, "Sorry."

"Guardians of the Watchtowers of the North, Creatures of earth and strength, we request that you bind this circle, thus protecting and guarding us." They all breathed rhythmically. Andrea was lightheaded; the scent of herbs was heavy on the air.

Belinda spoke gravely. "We ask that a doorway to the Spirit World be opened to us this night. We mean no harm to anyone. We seek contact with the entity known in life as Caldicott Wyntham, to determine her wellbeing." Belinda's voice gentled. "Caldicott, we call to you. I am here with people who loved you in life and I summon you to show you can hear us. Aura Lee is here. She asks you to give us a sign."

They waited, hands linked. The attic air warmed and thickened. Their even breathing continued, interrupted by an occasional cough as the smoke intensified. Outside the wind began to rise and the plastic sheet covering the hole in the roof fluttered.

At the sound, Aura Lee looked up, face alight with eagerness. "Something's happening," she whispered.

Kerry's muffled groan was drowned out by Noreen's sneeze as the herbal smoke shifted toward her. Andrea focused on the wavering candles, caught up in their flares of orange and yellow. Sweat beaded her forehead. She wanted to wipe it away, but let her hands remain in the grasp of those on either side. The heat and heavy fragrances weighed down her eyelids. She was finding it hard to take full breaths.

A low whimpering began. Andrea opened her eyes and saw Strudel staring fixedly at the corner beyond the dresser, her tail wagging. Her whines grew louder.

"Strudel." Dolores leaned toward the little dog. *"Pobrecita,"* she crooned, "what is it?"

Strudel's ruff had risen, and her tail had stopped wagging as she looked toward the corner.

"What do you think she sees?" Noreen asked softly.

"Don't know, don't want to know," muttered Elizabeth. Her hand tightened on Andrea's. "Something's sure bothering her."

The dog's whine hardened into barking, and then she pointed her snout at the ceiling and bayed.

The high-pitched howl sent shivers down Andrea's spine. Involuntarily, she slid off the pillow and reached for Strudel.

"Holy shit," muttered Kerry. "What's gotten into her?" Strudel's cries grew louder.

Belinda Smythe waved her hands. "Everyone resume your seats," she begged. The quaver underlying her words was upsetting. "Let us resume."

Strudel leapt into Dolores's arms and barked madly at the corner. Her frenzied snarling stopped abruptly. She made a horrible whining sound, then broke out of Dolores's hold and ran for the stairs.

One corner of the plastic sheeting whipped free and a strong gust of cold air rushed into the room, putting out the candles. The burning herbs whirled out of the bowl like fireflies given their freedom.

"Quick!" yelled Rose. "The embers could cause a fire. We've got to snuff them out. Hurry!"

Andrea pushed herself to her feet. Off balance, she staggered in the dark through the flying embers toward the center of the circle. Rain and wind slapped at her face.

"Caldicott Wyntham! Come forward." Belinda's voice boomed over the shriek of the wind and the frantic slapping of hands and pillows against the floor and walls. "We are waiting for you, Caldicott."

"Shut up, you idiot!" Kerry's voice rang out, nearly as loud as Strudel's continued barking.

Someone lurched against Andrea. "Dammit, everyone just hold still for a minute!" Andrea moved her hands cautiously over her head, trying to find the light chain. Pellets of rain hit her arms. When the metal cord brushed her fingers, she grabbed it and pulled.

Light barely shone from the fixture, growing brighter, soon stabbing at her eyes. Rose squinted at her from across the room. Only Belinda had remained on her pillow. Dolores was against one wall, Strudel at her feet. Noreen and Kerry were on their hands and knees near the herb bowl and Aura Lee was pushing herself up off the floor. Her expression was an odd mixture of consternation and triumph.

Elizabeth bent and held out one hand to Strudel, then ran her fingers over the little dog's head and neck. "Ssshhh, baby. Ssshhh. It's all right." She picked her up, and Strudel's frantic barking dwindled into whimpers once more. The dachshund's gaze remained riveted on the corner across from them.

Elizabeth looked helplessly at Dolores. "Something's really getting to this dog."

"Animals can be indicators of the presence of spirits," Belinda said from her pillow. "We can watch her and perhaps determine the nature of what she sees."

Kerry was dusting bits of herbs off her pants. "No, she's scared enough as it is."

Aura Lee shot a wary glance at Belinda.

"Let's get her downstairs." Rose and Dolores helped Elizabeth, still cradling Strudel, negotiate the maze of pillows to get to the attic stairs.

Aura Lee had joined Noreen in patting the rug to make sure no remnants of the herbs were still hot. Andrea wiped at her wet face. "The rain on the rug will help dampen any sparks."

"Wait!" Belinda pleaded. "We *must* restore the circle. Someone is in here, someone has crossed over to communicate with us."

Kerry shook her head. "We're not going to torture Strudel to continue this farce." A gust of wind rushed through the hole, whipping her hair around her face.

"You don't understand what could happen." Belinda's voice held a note of urgency. "If we don't close the circle—"

Kerry pushed the hair from her eyes. "And I don't care. Come on, we're going to have rain in here any minute. The séance is over. Andrea, help me find a hammer and some nails. We've got to fasten down that plastic."

Andrea nodded and crossed quickly to the stairs. She trotted down the steps and tried not to worry at the fearful expression she'd seen on Belinda Smythe's face.

CHAPTER 12

Moonlight shone soft on wet cobblestones and rainwater running from the drainpipe rang like a tinny bell. Kerry jogged up the steps and through the outer entrance to the associate house, fumbling for the key in her pocket. Entering, she shut the door behind her and leaned against it, grateful to be alone.

Dropping her key on the foyer table, Kerry saw that her hand was shaking. "Dammit," she whispered. They'd done it, they'd tried to contact Caldicott Wyntham's spirit, and no matter how cynical she thought herself to be, the experience had been unsettling.

Aura Lee's yearning face filled her mind's eye. No message had come from Caldicott, but it was impossible to believe she'd stop looking for it.

Kerry kicked off her shoes. Aura Lee was ripe for the power of suggestion, and the instability of the weather had goosed that along. For her the plastic's blowing loose when it had was a sign that Caldicott had been there with them, and nothing would change her mind about that. But what freaked out Kerry was how Strudel had gazed at something, and had howled at *something.* What had the dog sensed to prompt those uncanny sounds?

Shivering, she rechecked the door. Locked—as if a lock would keep ghosts out. No, she wouldn't go down that road. She went into her study, relaxing at the familiar scent of books. The desk lamp cast a glow over Caldicott's journals. Protected in the deep file drawer were the candy box and diary they'd found in the attic.

The desk chair creaked as Kerry slid into it. She glanced at her watch. Sleep wouldn't come soon. Lifting the brass lamp, she slid the key from under its base. The lock clicked, and the drawer slipped open, prompting a rush of anticipation. Pulling out the yellow index card she used as a bookmark, she opened the journal to the page where she'd left off.

February 11, 1909

Mama used to say what withers people's souls is what happens to them in life or what they learn from it. Something bad must have happened to Mrs. Selkirk. Last evening Mr. Thornton passed along a copy of Charles Dickens's Bleak House to me and said I might find it interesting.

Mrs. Selkirk couldn't have gone stiffer if she'd drunk starch for breakfast. Today she told me to clean the spots on the parlor carpet. She gave me such a look when she said I had to mix up the cleaning fluid. Then she smirked when she told me what went in it. Shaving white soap wasn't so bad, but the aqua ammonia made me sneeze and the smell of the ether made me sick after a while.

I must have rubbed more than an hour at those spots where Mr. T. tracked in axle

> *grease from the tool shed. It's too cold to*
> *open the windows and didn't she love that! Do*
> *unto others, Mama and Papa said, but they*
> *didn't know Mrs. Selkirk.*

It was only one example of the housekeeper's spiteful attitude toward the girl. Jessamine wrote in her careful script of her struggle to respect Mrs. Selkirk, even though the woman clearly disliked her. Her son, Edward Selkirk, lived in the housekeeper's set of rooms and worked as a hired hand to pay for his keep. His insolence toward Jessamine was hidden well enough to make it difficult for her to complain. More than once she'd thought his mother encouraged him to treat her so.

Kerry looked up from the page with a frown. How old was Mr. Thornton at this point? Jessamine always wrote as if he was ancient, but she was only seventeen when the diary began. Women had been at a premium in those days, especially young ones. And what about Mrs. Selkirk? Did she have her eye on Mr. Thornton?

> *July 13, 1909*
>
> *I rode to the train station today with Mr. T.*
> *and his sister-in-law, Mrs. Wolcott. She lives*
> *in Omaha, and didn't stay but two weeks,*
> *thank the Lord. She came for the one-year*
> *memorial service for Mr. T's late wife. I*
> *swear she looked at me sideways, and acted*
> *like I was dirt under her feet. Mr. T. and his*
> *sister were very cool to each other at the end.*
> *I heard them raise their voices last night.*
>
> *When the train pulled out of the station, Mr.*
> *T. stuck his thumbs in his vest and winked at*
> *me! "What say we make this a little holiday?"*
> *His eyes twinkled like he was laughing inside.*
> *Next thing I knew, we were back at the house*

and he was unhitching the horse. He told me to pack a picnic lunch. "We'll walk up to the Chautauqua and see what's doing."

Mrs. Selkirk was upset when I told her his plan. I was so wound up I didn't even know what I put in the basket, just snatched up what I could. When we opened it, we found biscuits and butter and a mess of peas in the same kind of bowl as the chicken I left in the icebox! It didn't matter to Mr. T. He was dressed in his Sunday best, smelling of bay rum, but he looked at those peas and commenced to shelling and eating them right out of the pod!

Before that, we listened to a man from Chicago, Dr. Philip Tweedham. His speech was about spirituality in daily life. It was better than a sermon, very uplifting.

Jessamine's writing became so small that Kerry groped for the magnifying glass in the desk drawer. The next entry told of a milestone, and Jessamine was wary of discovery.

July 15, 1909

Today I met Kelvin Haslett, who accompanies Dr. Tweedham on his speaking tour. He is from Philadelphia and his parents are both dead. He has the most speaking eyes. He looked at me when we were introduced, and I felt so strange. Like I could fall right into his eyes, which are deep and brown as coffee. He is refined looking and polite.

Kerry smiled. Jessamine sounded smitten. A yawn overtook her and she rubbed at her eyes, and then glanced at her watch. It was after midnight. She usually stayed up later, but the séance had drained the energy out of her. She thought of Elizabeth carrying Strudel down the stairs and of the disappointed droop to Aura Lee's mouth as she'd said good night. Life was messy enough without trying to contact the people who'd left it.

Kerry slid the diary into its drawer and locked it, and replaced the key under the lamp base. She yawned again and turned out the light. What had it been like to live in the old house ninety-some years ago? Boulder must have looked very different.

She tripped on one of the book boxes and muttered a curse. Thoughts of the past scattered like confetti, and she yawned again as she climbed the stairs to the bedroom.

Andrea lay in bed, tired to the bone, yet her mind was picking over moments in the day. Flailing in the attic darkness for the string from the light. The feel of Neal's arms around her. Strudel's desolate howling. The moment when she looked at Neal and he wasn't Neal. She closed her eyes and breathed deeply to calm herself.

Soon she slept, shifting under the light covers as images flickered behind her eyes.

She was climbing up a grassy hillside scattered with wildflowers. Behind her was a landscape that took her breath away. The meadow flowed like a green skirt down the mountainside toward the town. Cattle grazed and redwing blackbirds trilled to a background chorus of sparrows. Ahead of her the Flatirons reached toward the robin's-egg blue sky. Soon she was walking among dense pines standing guard at the base of a trail zigzagging toward looming sandstone boulders.

She moved easily over the rocky talus, skimming up turns in the path with no effort. The high collar of her bodice grazed her jaw and the edge of her long skirt brushed the tops of the boots crossing from stone to stone up the trail. When she ventured into the open area hemmed in by jagged walls, she glimpsed movement and turned toward it. His familiar shape separated from the shade cast by sandstone formations.

Without speaking he came toward her, almost a shadow himself in the black suit he wore. The shimmer in his almond-shaped eyes brought color to her cheeks. He stopped in front of her and took her hand. When he pressed his mouth against her wrist, it took effort to draw breath.

Happiness flooded through her and tears spilled onto her cheeks. When he saw them, he brought her hand to the side of his face. *What is it?* he asked silently.

Wonder at the love in his face rose in her. Mute, she could only look into his eyes.

His lips curved. *I love you more.* Cupping her face in his hands, he bent to press his lips against hers. She closed her eyes to savor the sensation.

Her arms drew him closer. He enfolded her against him. *Come with me, love.* He tugged at her hand and she followed him up the trail.

The sky darkened and the wind began to rise. Her skin prickled as uneasiness replaced the enchantment she'd felt in his embrace. *This isn't right,* she thought, looking around in puzzlement. The path was gone, replaced with rocks of every size. He'd gone ahead of her and she could barely see him.

Something's wrong, she called silently. But he kept moving away from her. *Wait for me!*

She struggled over one pitted boulder, only to find a bigger one on the other side. The wind wailed, pushing to force her back down the mountain. Dark

clouds threatened and she had to strain to see through
the dust. She caught sight of him as he crested a hill.
His black hair was blowing in the wind. Then he was
gone. She was alone.

From the studio doorway Rose and Aura Lee
watched as Andrea slashed at an oversized canvas
with her brush. In the short time they'd been there,
she'd made war on it.

The paintbrush as a sword, Rose thought. A chill
crawled down her spine. "How long has she been
doing this?"

Aura Lee shook her head, arms hugging each other
as if she were cold. "Strudel woke me up maybe
twenty minutes ago." Her voice trembled. "I guess she
heard something. Oh, Rose," she whispered. "What
can be happening to her?"

Andrea slapped the brush into one of the pigments
on her palette. She turned the brush gracefully and
thrust it at the canvas in a stabbing motion. Her eyes
were wide open, but Rose couldn't tell where her gaze
fell.

Rose turned away and held her hands to her face.
What in the *hell* was going on at Wisdom Court? First
at the séance, now this morning. She rubbed at her
eyes and lowered her hands. "Has she said anything?"

Aura Lee shook her head. "I think she's asleep."

Surprised, Rose turned back. Aura Lee's eyes,
naked without shadow on each lid, were red with
fatigue. "Asleep? You mean now? Her eyes are
open."

"I know, but look at her. She's like a robot, or a
puppet." Aura Lee shuddered. "She looks empty."

"Oh, don't say that." Rose looked back at Andrea.
"How could she be doing this while she's asleep?"

"I don't know." Aura Lee's voice wobbled. "Why

hasn't she heard what we're saying?"

"There's one way to find out." Rose stepped into the studio, intent on challenging Andrea.

Aura Lee grabbed her arm. "No, no. You mustn't. Everything I've ever read says you shouldn't wake up a sleepwalker."

"She's not sleepwalking. She's sleep-painting." At a sharp little cry from Andrea, Rose gasped.

Andrea's arm moved unceasingly. Tears trailed down her cheeks.

Rose started toward her. "I'll try not to frighten her," she assured Aura Lee. "We can't just leave her like this. We have to make sure she's all right."

Aura Lee nodded, but doubtfully. They walked across the tile floor to Andrea, who continued her work. As they approached her, they glimpsed the canvas. When Rose was close enough to see the whole painting, she stopped. Aura Lee, eyes trained on the images there, walked into her but Rose didn't feel the impact.

On the top half of the canvas a wild mountainside towered toward stormy skies. Rose could almost feel the turbulence of the air and the power of earth so forged by water and wind. On a trail along the landscape were rough outlines of a figure looking up the steep hill, one arm up as if to protect himself.

Andrea ground the brush into rusty paint on the palette, then slapped color onto the picture where more rocks took shape. Observing her vacant face, Rose realized Aura Lee was probably right about her being asleep. Her eyes were open and tears spilled onto her cheeks, but she was expressionless.

She struggled over the rocks, calling silently for him, receiving no response. Where are you? Why have you left me behind? She fell to her knees in despair. He would never return.

"*No!*" Andrea jerked awake at the sound of her own voice. Her heart thundered in her chest. A dream, she told herself, struggling for calm. It was a dream. She lifted her hand to her head, and realized that she held something. She stared in bewilderment at the tightly grasped paintbrush.

"Andrea, you're all right," Rose said. "You're in your studio. You've been painting."

Andrea looked past her pointing finger at the large canvas. The tumultuous landscape seemed to explode from the canvas. Shocked, she inhaled sharply and took a step back from the easel. "I painted *that*?"

Rose nodded. She watched her anxiously.

Andrea turned back to the painting, swallowing against nausea. Her gaze moved over it as she registered the power in the brushstrokes.

When Rose's hand touched her arm, Andrea turned abruptly toward her. The concern in the older woman's eyes was mirrored on Aura Lee's face.

Andrea shook her head. Her hair tumbled about her cheeks. "I don't believe this." She stepped toward the door.

"But—" began Aura Lee.

Andrea didn't stop. "I don't know what's going on. I can't deal with it."

CHAPTER 13

Wisdom Court was quiet in the mid-morning sun as Andrea walked across the cobblestones toward the associate house where Dolores lived. Inside the small portfolio case was her sketchpad and the drawing of the sundial Kerry had so resented. She marched up the stairs and into the lobby, and before she could talk herself out of it, she rang the bell labeled *Rivera*.

Dolores didn't answer the first chime. Andrea imagined her at a critical point in her work and almost turned away but anxiety made her press the button again.

When the door opened, her gaze flew over stained work clothing and Dolores's clay-streaked hands. "I'm sorry to interrupt, but I need to talk to you."

Taking stock of Andrea, the artist's brown eyes warmed with concern. "You look terrible, *jita*." She waved her into the apartment, motioning toward the living room. As Andrea sat on the leather sofa, Dolores asked, "Can I get you some coffee or something?"

"No, thanks. I just want ask you something."

Dolores perched on a chair. "What is it?"

"The day I arrived, at dinner that night you talked about a feeling you get sometimes when you're working. A sense of connection with something outside yourself."

Dolores nodded cautiously. "Yeah. What about it?"

"I got the impression that you meant more than what Kerry called the 'flow'. You compared it to church."

Dolores relaxed. "When the work goes really well, that can happen. All of a sudden you're more, like you've plugged into something way bigger. Why?"

Andrea hesitated and then took the plunge. "Have you ever sculpted something you hadn't thought of?"

"You mean something that hits me all at once? Something out of the blue? Sure."

"No, I mean you're working on a project and what you mean it to be doesn't happen. You create a figure you didn't think of. Or you find yourself in your studio and you've made something that wasn't even in your mind."

Wariness crept over Dolores's features as she listened. "You mentioned this the other day. It's happened to you."

Oh, shit. She doesn't know what I'm talking about. Andrea felt a trickle of sweat at the back of her neck.

Dolores leaned forward in the chair. "I've had strange experiences while I was working, *jita*. It can get intense. That's why we're considered out-there, you know?" Her smile included Andrea.

Andrea didn't smile back. At that moment she'd have traded everything making her an artist to stand on solid, unimaginative ground. "That's what I'm afraid of."

Dolores frowned. "Afraid?"

"Of being out-there. Of insanity." Andrea closed her eyes at the shock in Dolores's face. "Weird things have been happening since I got here."

"Hold it a minute." Dolores jumped from the chair and hurried out of the room. She came back with a glass that she handed to Andrea. "Kick this back."

Andrea took a gulp and tequila warmed her all the way into her chest.

Dolores sat down. "Better?"

Andrea nodded.

"Tell me what's going on."

Andrea shivered reflexively. "I've been sketching a man I've never seen while I'm asleep or in a daze, or God knows what. And that sundial I drew the other night, the one that upset Kerry so much? No memory of doing that. And this morning Rose and Aura Lee found me painting in my sleep."

Dolores reached for the wooden box on the coffee table. From it she took out a cigarette and a matchbook, and lit up.

"Don't tell anybody I smoke, okay? In Boulder you're better off robbing banks than letting people see you smoke."

"I promise." Andrea leaned back into the sofa cushions. Dolores blew smoke out on a sigh. "You're a forensic artist, right? Couldn't you have sketched that face from a description and just not remembered it?"

Andrea closed her eyes, summoning the details of the first sketch. Her eyes shot open and she grabbed the portfolio. "For God's sake. I brought the damned things to show you." She spread the case across the coffee table. "Here's the first one."

Dolores examined the drawing of the young man with almond-shaped eyes and dark hair in a widow's peak.

"I've made hundreds of sketches over the years, and I have a visual memory, but this guy—I know I'd feel something if I'd drawn him before."

Dolores lifted the first sketch to look at the second. "Same man, all right." She looked under it and found the sundial drawing. "What does this have to do with the others?"

"I don't know. I don't remember drawing it, either."

Dolores put them back into the portfolio and settled into the chair, wrapping her arms around her legs. With her chin resting on her knees, she frowned in concentration. Cigarette smoke cast a gossamer shadow across one cheek. "You said something about a painting?"

"It's mostly a landscape, but the roughed-in outline of a figure is there. I feel it's the same man, and I think he's in danger."

Dolores ground out her cigarette. "I've heard of people drawing pictures of the dead—psychic painting or something. What you're doing sounds different. I mean, nobody's giving you details or anything. What's spooky is not *knowing* you're drawing."

"That's what bothers me the most." Andrea rubbed her forehead. "I can't control it because I'm not aware of it. I hoped you'd say the same kind of thing has happened to you."

"Afraid not." Dolores frowned. "Sometimes I feel like a sculpture takes over and I don't know how it'll turn out till it's done. Once in a while I almost feel like the piece has already been made somewhere else and I'm just doing the follow-up." She shrugged uncomfortably. "But I've always *been* there for the process."

They sat in silence. The afternoon sun split the shadows pooling in the room. Dolores sighed. "What about apparitions?"

"What?"

"Spirits of the dead. Have you ever felt them?"

"No."

"Members of my family have." Dolores picked at dried clay under one nail. "Sometimes spirits linger behind. Maybe you're one of the people who can sense them."

"You mean these sketches might be of someone who's haunting me?" Andrea's voice rose. "Or possessing me?"

Dolores stood up, her face pale. "Not possession. That's something totally different."

The distinction escaped Andrea. The idea of a spirit forcing her to draw pictures was almost worse than thinking she was crazy.

Dolores paced to the door and back, hugging her elbows, shoulders hunched. "I think you ought to talk to the others. This is too creepy to keep to yourself. We've all had different experiences. One of them might know something."

Andrea grimaced. "I can just hear Kerry."

Dolores nodded. "Kerry's skeptical, but she's one of the smartest women here. What made you come to me? I sure haven't helped much."

"Because you're an artist. I hoped you'd recognize what I was talking about."

Dolores leaned toward her, compassion in her eyes. "I don't know what's happening to you. You have to figure it out or it'll *make* you crazy. Tell the others all of it, especially Rose," she urged. "She doesn't judge people. And she already saw you painting, right? Let me call her now, okay?" Dolores reached for the extension on the end table. At Andrea's nod, she pressed two numbers.

Rose entered her office and shut the door behind her, leaning against it to keep the rest of the world on the other side. What a day. Finding Andrea painting in her sleep had only been the beginning. Construction details and Aura Lee's burbling over paranormal activities had kept her from stringing two thoughts together. Now that she could, there was only one question in her mind: did she understand anything that happened over the last twelve hours?

During the séance last night she'd had a feeling, as if someone else had joined them in the room. Was that authentic? Had she given in to the atmosphere engineered by Belinda Smythe?

And there was Andrea. Seeing her painting while she was asleep had scared the hell out of her. All reference points had been blasted to kingdom come.

After a few moments, the calm of the room began to work its spell. Rose took a deep, cleansing breath and let her gaze wander over the shelves. Half the room was given to books and files, the other half to her small dish fountains and the stones and containers that went into their making. Sunlight from the south window glittered from the amethyst geode in an onyx bowl, shimmering through the water trickling over purple crystals.

Rose smiled at the play of light and water and crossed the carpeted floor to her desk. As she pulled out her chair, she saw what was on the blotter.

Last night before the séance she'd finished her latest fountain. Now the indigo bowl was empty. Around its edge were the rocks she'd used: chunks of crystalline tinged with yellow; green chlorite and milky quartz. The florist's jewels serving as base for the rocks were divided into four mounds, one at each compass point around the bowl. The small pump was upside down, and the cord was neatly coiled beside it.

Rose sank into her chair and stared at the collection. She didn't usually lock her door, so anyone could have come in and rearranged the pieces of her fountain. Who would want to? Why?

At the soft knock on the door Rose called, "Just a minute." Without thinking she pulled a towel off the shelf and threw it over the remains. "Come in."

When Aura Lee entered, Rose frowned at the trouble in her face. "What is it now?"

Aura Lee settled onto the ottoman, her flowered caftan billowing around her. Her green eye shadow lent her a ghoulish air. "About last night...we may have exposed ourselves to danger."

"What do you mean?"

"We didn't close the circle. Belinda tried, but no one paid attention." Aura Lee twisted her fingers together. "We created the circle for the spirits to come to us in safety, but after you do that, you have to close it again. We all scattered when the wind blew the plastic off that hole in the roof. Then I started thinking after the business with Andrea's painting this morning. We left the door open to the other world, Rose. The spirits we called could still be in this house. They could cause problems. Maybe even Andrea's...oddness."

Rose suppressed a shiver. Spirits on the loose were the least of their worries. She leaned her head on her hand and tried to think. *Protection.* The word surfaced slowly in her mind and she pondered it.

"Rose?" Aura Lee cast her a worried look. "Are you all right?"

Rose straightened her spine and took a deep breath. She could use this. "You've brought up an excellent point. We need to explore how we can protect ourselves against...whatever you call them."

"Manifestations." Aura Lee's expression was thoughtful. "You're right, we need protection. There are steps to be taken: binding spells, fortifying measures against evil. Not that I consider *Cottie* evil," she inserted hastily. "But Belinda did issue a pretty general invitation before she got to the specific summons. There's no telling who showed up." She surged to her feet. "I'll get to work on this right away."

She was halfway to the door when Rose recalled the spell Aura Lee had devised earlier in the week. "No fires, okay?"

Aura Lee opened her mouth, and then shut it again. She nodded but her gaze slid away from Rose's face. She slipped out the door.

Rose sighed. No doubt the very best protection spells involved fire. She'd have to keep an eye out. When the telephone beside her buzzed, she picked up the receiver. "This is Rose." She listened, creases deepening between her eyes, as Dolores told her about Andrea.

"She's agreed to talk with you and I think you need to hear what she's saying." The careful emphasis in Dolores's voice was far more compelling than her words.

"I'll be there in a couple of minutes." Rose replaced the receiver and scowled. She ripped a piece of paper from the pad and scrawled where she would be on it.

As she left, Rose taped the note on the door. Dolores sounded worried. "Please," Rose whispered. "Let things settle down. Please." She tried the knob to make sure it was locked.

CHAPTER 14

Kerry finished reading an on-line article about one of America's well-known mediums. She'd made notes as she read, but when she glanced at the notebook where exclamation points were scattered among scrawled obscenities, she closed the website. How could Aura Lee stomach such baseless, unscientific garbage?

According to the website author, more than thirty-six spirits had appeared to her over a fifteen-year career, and she had guided all to their rightful places on The Other Side. That was hard enough to swallow, but some of the grateful posts from readers were painful to see.

She pushed herself out of her chair and stretched, pausing to rub the sore muscle in her right shoulder. Probably from hammering the plastic sheeting over that hole in the roof, she thought. No matter. It had been satisfying to bang on something after that séance.

From the articles she'd found so far, Belinda Smythe wasn't so bad. She hadn't led them in hymns or spells, and she at least appeared sincere. Kerry was surprised to find in herself a shred of concern over Belinda's unmet pleas that they close the door opened for spirits to come through. "I am definitely losing it."

She unlocked the desk drawer and pulled out Jessamine's diary. After the otherworldly stuff, reading an historical document would be a relief.

July 17, 1909

Dear Diary,

Mr. T. came to the wash shed while I was scrubbing clothes. He told me to finish and get ready to go to Chautauqua for one of the sessions. He signs up for the lecture series every year because his wife liked them, but he doesn't go much himself. He said today's topic, Creating Domestic Serenity, wasn't for him. Since I'm learning to keep house, he said I would benefit from it. I thanked him and asked if Mrs. Selkirk would mind if I went. "I'll mind if you don't," he said. That made me smile.

The speaker talked about how women need to make harmony in the home, but I don't think he really likes women. His eyes were mean. Mama always said to listen for the truth behind what people say. Prof. Elginetter's talk was about being master in the home. Harmony to him is that women should obey men. Papa said a man who wants a woman to be less just to make him feel like more isn't much of a man. That's a description of the Professor! Judging by the faces in the audience, I wasn't the only person to feel that way.

After the lecture, I talked to some of the women there. They were very civil and asked after Mr. T. I left for home and passed Mr. Sturtevant's photography tent, and the wind snatched up my scarf. Who came out the tent door but Mr. Haslett! He ran for my scarf and brought it back. I thought he might not remember me. But he did, addressing me by name and lifting his hat. He said he'd been arranging with Mr. Sturtevant for a photographic portrait of himself taken out of doors.

Then a gust of air blew his hat off and he had to chase it. He was laughing and his hair was wild. His eyes are dark as blackthorn sloe. He is taller than I am and when he smiles, his whole face glows. He is a most well favored man. He asked if I would like his company on the walk home and though I felt a little brazen, I said yes!

Mr. Haslett asked me about myself, and when I told him about losing Mama and Papa, his fine eyes shone with sympathy. When I explained my job at Mr. T's, he was not put off, but said it was honest work. I wish the walk had lasted longer, but he said he was expected elsewhere. When we said goodbye, he took my hand and held it with both of his own. I was afraid that he would notice my pulse beat faster. I have never felt—

Kerry blinked, aware of a sound, and sat up straight. The hair she'd been coiling around her index finger reversed itself. Had the doorbell rung? "Just a minute," she called, and pushed out of her chair. She hustled barefooted through the living room, stopping to fumble for the keys on the foyer table.

She opened the door to an empty hallway. Hearing a

slam, she trotted to the main door. As she swung it open, she saw a Federal Express truck outside the gates, the driver writing on a clipboard before climbing behind the wheel. She didn't see any packages. If he'd brought her Amazon order, he'd left it at the other house. Delivery people got them mixed up all the time.

Aura Lee came around the side of the main house and strode across the courtyard toward the other associate house, her green caftan fluttering like dragonfly wings.

Kerry pushed the door shut. She'd check on the books, another interruption. Not that she'd actually been working. Jessamine's diary was too much fun to be called work. Reading her tiny writing, though, was like trying to decipher the Dead Sea scrolls. She returned to the study, stubbing her toe on a sofa leg. Where the hell were her slippers?

She finally found them under her desk, and as she slid into them, her stomach growled. She'd forgotten breakfast. Heading for the kitchen, she heard the loud squeak of a hinge and she peered through the wooden slats in time to see Noreen scurry through the main door of the other associate house.

She let the slat settle back into place and frowned at the wall. What was going on over there?

Thoughtful now, Kerry sought clothes in her bedroom. She had the perfect excuse for dropping in. Hadn't the FedEx man just made a delivery? Wasn't she expecting an order? She pulled on jeans and found a polo shirt in the dresser. *I'll see what they're up to and then I'll come back and get serious about the boxes from the attic. And breakfast.*

Outside Dolores's living room window, water danced in the courtyard fountain, catching the sun.

Andrea was aware of the attention of the Wisdom Court women seated behind her, could feel their stares.

Rose broke the silence. "Andrea, do you mind going over it one more time? Obviously, I should've called a meeting."

"It's okay." It was uncanny how they'd all gravitated to Dolores's place after the phone call asking Rose over to hear Andrea's story. Within fifteen minutes of her arrival, Aura Lee, having read the note Rose left, was knocking at the door with a message from a former Wisdom Court associate in Italy. At irregular intervals thereafter the others had trailed in, all of them except Kerry ostensibly looking for Rose.

The portfolio was open on the coffee table and the papers rustled as the women looked through the sketches. Andrea fought against growing frustration. Each time she explained about the drawings the story sounded flatter. How could she get across the dread in her now when she looked at her own work? How could she make them understand how she felt? She'd been at Wisdom Court for all of three days. They didn't know her yet. Outside the window a crow landed at the edge of the fountain.

"So, what happened then?"

Andrea glanced over her shoulder. Kerry had two sketches in her hand. "I drew the sundial you liked so much." She turned back to look out the window. "That was the last sketch so far. No memory of it, of course. Then there's the painting. Aura Lee and Rose can describe that. I've done a fair amount of work since I got here. I just don't remember any of it."

"So that's it?"

It was the tone of Kerry's question that got to Andrea. "If you don't count seeing Neal transform into the mystery man. That was good for a laugh."

"What?"

Andrea turned around to face them. Aura Lee, seated beside Elizabeth on the leather sofa, was nearly vibrating with excitement. Noreen had leaned against the arm of the couch to look at the drawings.

Elizabeth's dark eyes were filled with compassion, and Rose watched her calmly. It was only in Kerry that Andrea saw skepticism. With relief, she realized they weren't all automatically rejecting her account.

Andrea let out a breath. "I'm so new here you don't understand how oddly I've been acting. Almost passing out when I first got here," she specified, "and running out of Dolores's show. I assume you think I'm a head case. Though only Kerry's as much as said that to my face."

"Well, jeez," Kerry said in self-defense, "what do you expect when what you describe is so irrational?"

Andrea pressed her temples with her fingertips, trying to erase the throb behind them. "For what it's worth, most of the people I know consider me a model of stability."

Rose smiled at her encouragingly. "Andrea, we don't think you're crazy."

"But it's a legitimate question."

Andrea stiffened at the somber note in Kerry's voice.

"You mentioned altitude sickness, and the stress of moving here. You miss your daughter. You're trying to adjust to a new life on your own. You don't recall the sketches you've drawn. I think that's what shrinks call 'dissociative behavior.'"

Elizabeth shook her head in irritation. "Kerry, you're just lookin' at the surface here." She glanced at Andrea. "I, for one, think there are other reasonable explanations."

"No, she's right." Andrea rubbed her upper arms, suddenly cold. "Everything she said is possible. That's why I didn't tell you about it. Even I've been afraid I'm losing my mind. Don't blame Kerry for being logical."

Kerry nodded. "It's an obvious option."

"The obvious is better than obvious avoidance of it," Noreen uttered.

Kerry rolled her eyes. "Whose is it?"

"H.W. Fowler and F.G. Fowler, *Modern English Usage.*"

"I don't pretend to be an expert in psychology," said Rose, "but I have a hard time equating what I've learned about you and any severe mental disorder."

Noreen nodded. "On an emotional level, I agree. However, neither of our opinions is scientific. While we're exploring Andrea's claims, we have to keep in mind the possibility of her debilitation."

It was her scholarly objectivity that made Andrea laugh. When the others stared at her, she giggled even harder. "Something about the phrasing," she said when she'd caught her breath. "On the one hand, you're willing to consider what I've told you isn't the result of insanity. On the other, I can see you all waiting for me to start babbling." Their blank faces quenched her humor. "Hey, I haven't had a genuine laugh since I got here."

"Oh, what nonsense." Aura Lee glared at the others in disapproval. "You can't do this halfway. Either you're willing to withhold judgment or you're not." Her face softened as she looked back at Andrea. "What I do know is that everyone here will fight to help you. That's the way it is at Wisdom Court."

Kerry had already moved beyond the emotion of the moment. "Go back to the bit about Neal changing into somebody else. What did you mean?"

"I mean that one minute I saw Neal, and the next minute he looked like the man in the sketches." Just saying it made Andrea tremble inside. "It's one of the scariest things I've ever seen, especially—" She stopped.

"Especially what?"

"I was upset yesterday when I went up to Chautauqua, and I didn't notice the storm coming. When I got to the Amphitheater, I thought I saw something—I don't know what it was, but I froze. Then Neal barreled in, and he gave me holy hell for being out in the open with lightning overhead. He dragged me to the rocks and we took shelter." She remembered the warmth of his body against hers after the chilling wind.

Elizabeth studied her. "And then?"

"He was furious—scared, too, probably—and the thunder was deafening. We were yelling at each other, and—"

"And he kissed you?" Noreen raised her brows at Andrea's surprise. "Any man worth his salt would."

Andrea's cheeks felt on fire. "Yes, he kissed me. I could see him in the lightning. When it flashed again, he wasn't Neal anymore. He had the face of the man in the sketches." Her voice was shaking now. "I *saw* him, his hair and his eyes. His head was shaped differently. His hair was darker, longer. He didn't have Neal's eyes!" The others regarded her in dismay. "Then it was dark again and he grabbed me. I ran."

Elizabeth sagged against the sofa back.

"This was right before the séance?" Rose asked.

Andrea nodded. "Neal followed me down the mountain. When he caught up with me, he was so angry." Andrea scrubbed at the tears on her cheeks. "I couldn't tell him what happened. Now he thinks I was afraid of *him*. I acted like he was going to rape me.

He'll never speak to me again."

"Why didn't you say anything when you got to the house?" Rose dug for a tissue in her pocket and handed it to her.

Andrea wiped her eyes and blew her nose. "What was the point? Aura Lee was opening the door talking about the séance."

A heavy silence held the room.

Dolores leaned out of the chair and reached for the wooden box on the coffee table. "I need another cigarette."

CHAPTER 15

No one fainted at Dolores's coming out of the nicotine closet, much to her surprise. Rose smiled at her reaction. If I didn't know it would taste like absolute crap, she thought wistfully, I'd have a cigarette, too.

The lid clicked against the box as Dolores retrieved the pack. She was already lighting up as she reached the front door.

Elizabeth shook her head and her tiny braids tumbled over the collar of her saffron jumpsuit. "Miz Dolores can smoke the kitchen curtains for all I care, as long as I get a drink." She stood up and eased her way between coffee table and sofa. "How about it, ladies? We've got a real good excuse here. Doesn't matter what time it is," she added as Aura Lee consulted her watch. "This is purely medicinal."

"I wouldn't mind a glass of sherry, but we have work to do." Noreen observed Andrea's quick turn to stare out the window at the fountain. "Something very odd is happening here. Our cozy discussion about Andrea's psychological state doesn't solve the problem."

"You have to define a problem before you can solve it." Kerry looked at Rose for support. "Aren't there a couple of former WC associates in psychology and psychiatry in the metro area? Wouldn't be hard to get her in to see someone."

Rose stretched her arms over her head in a vain attempt to reduce the tension in her muscles. "What makes you think she needs a mental health evaluation?"

Kerry let out a short breath. "You've heard what she said. A psych exam is a slam-dunk."

"*To act only upon assumption is to dive into uncharted waters: one chooses risk over measurement,*" pronounced Noreen. "Millicent Sanders Teegarden. Eighteen seventy-nine." She ignored the face Kerry made at her. "You've listened to her story and decided the psychological solution is the only one possible," Noreen pointed out. "Even you, Andrea. Rose and I are suggesting that there might be something else at work here."

The delight in Aura Lee's face could have lit a moonless night. "You've felt it, too, haven't you, Rose? Cottie is trying to contact us from beyond the grave."

"What I'm thinking is a little more every day," Rose said. "Self-hypnosis, for instance, or an illness involving hallucinations. Maybe an acute case of low blood sugar. I've heard of a bunch of symptoms from that. Andrea, when we saw you painting this morning, Aura Lee and I thought you were sleepwalking. Well, sleep-painting."

Andrea came away from the window. For the first time that morning she had a hopeful look on her face.

Noreen nodded in agreement. "The other day I came across the description of a phenomenon called Bonnet's Syndrome. It's a kind of illusion experienced at times by people with diabetic retinopathy or macular degeneration and as a result of cataracts or corneal damage. You don't suffer from any of those things, do you, Andrea?"

"No." She sounded dazed.

Elizabeth carried in a tray of glasses, one filled with sherry for Noreen. Dolores was right behind her, trailing the scent of smoke, with a bottle of Irish Cream grasped in one hand. She'd had her cigarette in the hall beside the open front door in order not to miss anything. Handing the bottle to Elizabeth, she put away the lighter and cigarettes. "What do you mean, self-hypnosis?" Behind her, Elizabeth filled glasses.

"I've experienced it in yoga practice. Focusing on a sound, on a fixed visual point, even listening to music can lead a person into a trance state, although you're usually still conscious during such things. Just extremely relaxed." Rose paused, her mind tumbling with possibilities. "Then there's the whole issue of dreams."

"Ooh, dreams," Aura Lee murmured happily.

Moving her feet to allow Dolores to sit on the rug, Kerry took the glass offered by Elizabeth. She regarded Noreen and Rose with growing interest. "You're talking research. That's my favorite thing."

Elizabeth gave a drink to Andrea. "Okay, those are good for a start. And don't forget allergies. Sometimes people have the most amazing reactions to certain substances." She caught the arrested expression on Dolores's face. "What?"

"Substance abuse." Dolores's gaze darted to Andrea, who was lifting the glass to her lips. "Do you use drugs?"

Andrea tilted the glass toward her in a silent salute. "Alcohol upon occasion. I smoked some pot when I was in college, but I didn't like the way it made me feel."

"Did you ever drop acid?" Kerry asked. "I've heard about former dopers having flashbacks from drinking orange juice."

"Sorry. I was too scared to try it."

"But that brings up another issue." Dolores's voice lifted in excitement. "What if somebody drugged Andrea? Not us," she added. "But what if someone wanted to make Andrea believe that she's losing her mind?"

"Gaslighting her?" Kerry had begun to wind a piece of hair around one finger. "I love it as a plot device, but she just got into town and says she doesn't know anybody besides us."

When Elizabeth waggled her finger at her, Kerry grinned. "Ha, ha. I don't have time to drive anyone crazy."

"There's a straight line I'm not gonna touch. How about it, girl? You have any old lovers trying to get even for being dumped? A secret twin wanting to cheat you out of your birthright?" Elizabeth twisted an imaginary moustache.

Andrea sipped her drink thoughtfully.

Rose noticed the hole in one leg of Andrea's jeans, catching sight of a scab on her knee. Her chestnut hair was limp and the shadows under her eyes and lines around her mouth revealed her fatigue. But her eyes were coming back to life.

"I'm an only child and my parents are dead. And I don't recall the last time I had a lover."

"No wonder old Neal looks so good," Kerry cracked.

Elizabeth's eyes widened. "Honey, Andrea could be a nymphomaniac and 'old Neal' would still look fine. The man is a hunk."

Kerry chuckled along with the others. "And you a

married woman!"

"Married, not dead." Elizabeth smiled comfortably. "Mmm-mmm. That man is good enough to eat and he don't need cookin', either."

Dolores giggled, one hand over her mouth, at Aura Lee's scandalized expression.

Rose noted the color rising in Andrea's cheeks. "Okay, I think we can agree nobody's drugging you. Any more thoughts?"

Aura Lee nodded. "A few. Even skipping over the supernatural we could be talking telepathic imaging or strong ESP. Boulder is just the place for this kind of thing. Oh, yes," she added at Kerry's scowl. "Almost anything can happen here. Maybe it's because the inner layers of the earth are out in the open along the Front Range, or maybe because of the effect of the mountains on the weather. You hear a lot of strange stories if you listen. On the supernatural side, of course, we've got automatic writing—I mean painting—and haunting, maybe poltergeist activity. Even possession."

Dolores stared at her, laughter stilled.

"Possession?" Kerry hooted. "Upchucking pea soup and extreme neck stretches, right?"

Aura Lee stiffened in indignation. "No, personal control taken over by some other entity. And I'll thank you to keep a civil tongue in your head, young lady. We're brainstorming and the rules don't allow making fun of anybody's ideas."

"Sorry," Kerry said, chastened. "I didn't mean to diss you."

Aura Lee nodded. "Apology accepted."

"You mentioned drugs." Noreen tapped at her lips with one finger. "Another possibility might be drug interactions." She turned to Andrea. "Are you taking any prescriptions or over the counter remedies?"

Andrea shook her head. "Nothing on a regular basis. Vitamins and Midol almost every month. That's all."

"Kerry, don't jump down my throat," ventured Dolores, "but we have to at least consider the mystical along with the other options. I've known people who've had experiences." Her emphasis of the final word was slight.

Noreen's eyes sharpened. "What kind of experiences?"

"Have any of you ever seen a ghost?"

"Certainly," Aura Lee said seriously. "More than once."

"Oh, please." Kerry twisted the cap back onto the Bailey's bottle with force. "Don't go there."

Dolores's lips tightened. "My grandmother saw her father—my great-grandfather—after he died."

Kerry nodded. "People are overcome with grief and they want one more chance to see their loved-ones. Ghost sightings aren't unusual between deaths and funeral services."

"No, it wasn't like that." Dolores took a quick sip of her drink. "My great-grandfather worked in a mine in Mexico. The village was far away, so he stayed at the work site during the week. When my grandmother was ten she was helping get the younger children ready for bed one night. She tucked in her sister and went out to the cistern to get water. She saw a man standing nearby. His face was in shadow and she was afraid.

"She started to run inside, but he raised his hand and she saw the bracelet on his wrist. She had braided leather thongs together, setting in beads from an old necklace to make her father that bracelet. 'Papa!' she called, and the man smiled and nodded. She started toward him, but he motioned her to stop and she saw he was covered in blood. She ran to help him but he was gone. The next day her mother got word her husband was dead. The support beams in the mine collapsed, killing seven men. They never recovered the bodies."

"She was only ten." Kerry's voice was kind. "Wouldn't it be natural for her to imagine a final goodbye from her father?"

Dolores's smile was sad. "Sure. But to her dying day, *mi abuela* swore she'd seen her father after he was dead. I can't prove it, but I honor her by believing what she said was true."

Aura Lee rose off the sofa and bent to enfold Dolores in a hug.

Noreen cleared her throat. "This kind of thing is difficult to assess because, by its nature, it's subjective. I think the paranormal investigators who measure temperatures and electrical outputs are on the right track. Most of the accounts I've read have been descriptions of physical reactions accompanying sensory stimuli."

Aura Lee, having resumed her seat, nodded with enthusiasm. "That's why I've been certain Cottie is still nearby. It's not because the room goes cold or I feel a chill down my spine." A sweet smile lit her face. "I have the same sense of well-being I always felt when I walked into a room and she was there. How can you quantify something like that? So," she added, voice hardening, "you put up with the sniping of people who think you're foolish or irrational."

Kerry's eyes widened at Aura Lee's potshot. "If that's aimed at me, I guess I deserve it. But I lived with more than enough wishful thinking and irrationality when I was growing up. I learned a person's life is determined by how she defines reality. Taking things on faith without question can be dangerous."

"Where did you grow up, girl?" Elizabeth asked.

"One of California's flakiest communes." Kerry's lips twisted. "Fortunately for me, the elders were too lazy to home school us kids, so we went through the public school system. It was enough. Now," she said briskly, "about Andrea. I assume you had the requisite physical exam before you came."

Andrea nodded. "Passed with flying colors. Physically and mentally." She finished the drink and set the glass on the table. "My life is stable. My daughter and I have lived in the same house for twenty years and I've worked at the same job for the last fifteen years."

"As a forensic artist. What does that involve?" asked Kerry.

"I turn the details told to me by crime victims into fairly accurate drawings of the people who harmed them." Andrea shrugged. "Or so they said at the Tacoma Sheriff's Office. Not much to build on in the present circumstances."

"We have to start somewhere." Rose met her gaze. "As you said, you're new here and we don't know you. If we're going to have a chance to help you, we need more information."

"I know."

The conversation ebbed and the sound of twittering birds graced the lull. Then came the rumble of a diesel engine, ending the moment of calm.

Dolores got up to investigate. "It's the guy who works for Neal—what's his name?"

"Denny." Rose saw Andrea's start at the mention of Neal.

So did Noreen. "Is Neal coming today?"

Rose shook her head. "Denny's in charge today. Neal's boy is sick with the flu and he thought he might have to take him to the doctor."

"Too bad." Noreen stared at Andrea until she shifted uncomfortably. "The more I think about what Andrea's told us, the more I believe we need to look beyond the obvious and the easy."

"Like she's touched in the head?" Elizabeth rolled her glass absently between her palms. "My Auntie Olivia always said the dead are around us. She had a friend who talked to them, tried to help them to the other side. Now, a lot of people thought that woman was batshit crazy. Others paid her good money to talk to those dead people for them. All I know is that nobody ever proved it either way. So how do you plan to get to the bottom of this thing?"

"Another séance!" Aura Lee looked from face to face in eagerness. "If Cottie could be contacted, she could look into it for us."

"Oh, God." Kerry pushed herself up off the floor. "I'm willing to do what I can in the way of research. I'll look things up, and check on the Internet to see if other people have had similar experiences, but that's it. If you're serious about table-tipping again with Belinda Smythe, count me out."

"Now, Kerry, the mark of a true scholar is an open mind," Noreen said in reproof. "If we're going to help Andrea, that's what we all have to start out with."

"There's a difference between an open mind and a total lack of sense," Kerry pointed out.

Dolores laughed weakly. "Are we going to be ghost busters?"

"Not at all. We'll examine the data we have. We need to learn the identity of the man in the sketches." Noreen ticked off each task on the fingers of one hand. "We have to know if Andrea is sketching and painting an actual place. In each of the pictures, the landscape is roughly the same." She looked at each of them in turn. "What if it's a real place? What if she's the trigger for what's happened thus far? What if other associates have encountered similar things here?"

"You're getting a lot of mileage out of what-ifs" Kerry muttered.

"Maybe. But a hypothesis that Andrea's pictures have come from outside her is as valid as assuming they're evidence of mental illness. Either way, one must strive to prove one's hypothesis."

"Well, yes," Kerry allowed. "I guess we could start from either end of the problem and still get to the truth."

"The truth is out there." Elizabeth grinned at Kerry's dirty look. "Why don't you make it a competition? First to prove that Andrea is or isn't nuts gets a prize."

"And your point is?" Rose inquired.

"That everyone's all gung-ho to start researching and figuring out this and that. What do *you* think of all this, Andrea? Just wade right in like everyone else has."

Andrea saw through Elizabeth's flippancy to her concern. "It's okay, I'm grateful to all of you for taking what I've said seriously. The worst thing about the last few days was feeling so alone." She swallowed. "Now I don't."

"Didn't I tell you?" Aura Lee beamed at the circle of women. "It's like the Three Musketeers around here, except there are seven of us. All for one and one for all."

Andrea blew her nose. "I may be a wacko but I'm your wacko?"

"Exactly." Rose stood up. "You'll just have to put up with our help."

"Until we're all completely crazy." Kerry shook her head in resignation. "All for one."

CHAPTER 16

The afternoon sun beamed through the bedroom transoms, turning the second-story hallway into a luminous passageway. Andrea liked the idea, having passed her own way through panic to acceptance. She wasn't alone anymore. The Wisdom Court women were on her side.

Her shoes whispered on the flowered carpet runner. Aura Lee and Rose had left on errands, and she was alone. The hush in the house, edged as it was with an undercurrent of outdoor noises, was more like a mood than a suspension of sound.

She heard footfalls and glanced behind her, thinking the noise came from downstairs. When the pace of the steps quickened, she searched the hallway for their source.

Catching a tiny movement at the corner of her eye she swung round. The china knob on the door to the attic turned. Her breath caught.

The door creaked open and Neal shouldered through it carrying a large box.

Andrea exhaled in relief.

Turning at the faint sound, Neal saw her.

Embarrassment over their last encounter washed color into her cheeks.

His mouth tightened. He pulled the door shut, bracing the weight of the box against the doorframe. As he walked toward her, she saw that his gray T-shirt was smudged with thick dust and his faded jeans were grimy.

When he passed by her without speaking, remorse swept through her. She'd let him think she was scared of him. "Neal?"

He stopped, then turned back to face her.

Andrea was surprised at how tired he looked. Lines of fatigue bracketed his mouth, and his eyes were without expression. Illogical as it was, she wanted to see the friendliness that had formerly warmed them.

"What happened up at the Amphitheater wasn't your fault, Neal." She realized how impossible it was to tell him what she'd experienced. *I thought I saw you mutate into someone else, but I still really like you.*

Neal bent to set down the box. "I haven't been able to figure out *what* happened," he said, voice rough. "Let alone whose fault it was."

Her heart skipped at the way he moved, at the pull of his shirt across his shoulders. What was it about him that made him so much more alive than other people? "I didn't mean to act that way. I was upset by something and the storm scared me."

His expression remained guarded. When he took a step toward her, she moved back and her shoulder nudged open the door behind her. He stopped and held out one hand in a cautious gesture. "I freaked out when you ran away from me." His hand dropped to his side. "You were afraid, but there's no way I would hurt you."

"I know," Andrea said miserably. "I wish I could

explain."

Neal took another step toward her and she smelled his scent, a combination of sweat and soap. Irish Spring, she thought, and a series of images flashed through her mind: of her husband David lying on the couch, hooking her by the wrist and pulling her down beside him. Of his walking out of the shower, towel draped at his hips, gray eyes dark with thoughts slowed under the spray of hot water. Of his warmth against her back in the middle of the night. Grief clutched at her with strength unknown to her for five years or more. Andrea fought back pain for all she'd lost so long ago.

"What is it?" Neal searched her face, eyes intense. "What's wrong?"

Dismayed at the sudden rush of emotion, Andrea shook her head, wishing she could empty her mind. "Old memories, things that can't be changed." She let out a breath, pushed her feelings back under guard. "Don't worry about it."

The concern in Neal's eyes flattened to bitterness. "Quit playing games. You open up and before I can react you shut down again. You keep giving me mixed signals and I don't like it."

"I don't like it either!" Andrea was furious at herself for the awkwardness she couldn't escape, angry with him for seeing it. "It's too tangled to explain."

He moved closer and rested his hands on her shoulders. Desire flowed through her like an electrical current.

"Tangled for you, maybe," he said with grim amusement. "Every time I get near you, it's pretty damned simple for me." His hands moved down her arms and when he reached her wrists, he pulled her against him.

Andrea's eyes shut as she absorbed the feel of him.

His chest was broad and sheltering, his arms strong, warm. She'd known this sense of homecoming once.

The clock downstairs chimed the quarter hour, the notes distant. Neal lifted his head and Andrea looked up at him. His brows drew together in a frown but before he could ask any more questions she brushed his lips with hers. His arms tightened, and he deepened the kiss.

His fingers smoothed through her hair and then held her as he traced the outline of her mouth with his tongue, setting off nerve endings she'd forgotten were there. When his tongue surged into her mouth, she pressed herself to him, savoring the heat of his arms around her, attuned to the hammering of his heart against her breasts.

Neal looked behind her. "Is that your room?"

At her nod he eased her back, swinging the door behind them as they made their way to her bed. When she felt the edge of the mattress against her legs, Andrea sank backward, Neal following her. His hands smoothed the cloth over her breasts, down her torso and over her thighs. Her muscles melted in response. She sought his mouth again, exultant at the reawakening of her body, so long asleep.

Shifting her weight, she opened her thighs and brought him closer. Short breaths, small groans, muttered words. The world turned crimson behind her eyelids.

He pushed aside her shirt, her jeans, the fabrics rubbing against her skin, bra straps sliding down her arms, silky panties easing down her legs. His hands were strong against her breasts, his mouth hot and wet around her nipples. She gloried in sensation.

The change came on so gradually she didn't know when anxiety overcame anticipation. A tendril of aversion snaked down her spine, triggering tension along the way. His arms held her too tightly. His breath came in uneven gasps. The heat of his body was overpowering, but a chill spread through her.

Abruptly Andrea pushed against his shoulders.

He groaned, as if in pain. He leaned his head against her neck, and the patch of skin where he touched her burned. His mouth moved up her neck and found her lips once more.

Andrea fought against the kiss, but he clutched her still more tightly. His lower body moved against her, hard and demanding. *This is wrong.* Futilely she tried to free herself, palms slipping on the crisp surface of his shirt. The scent of starch teased her nose. Her mind spun with images, of lightning stabbing the dark, of thunder rumbling destruction, of Neal's features melting into those of the man she had sketched.

A small, terrified sound escaped from her.

He crushed her to him and she thought her ribs would break. She couldn't catch a full breath. Heat came off him in waves but her teeth were chattering with cold. A low humming sound filled her ears.

She'd almost lost consciousness when his grip loosened and he sagged against her. Andrea gulped in a breath, then another.

He mumbled something into her shoulder.

Andrea felt him turn toward her. She kept her eyes tightly shut. What if it wasn't his face? Here in daylight, what if he was the other man? She forced her eyes open, and looked at him.

Neal stared at her from glazed eyes. His face was flushed, hectic red extending down his neck and bare chest. "Bay rum. Grandpa wore it. Haven't smelled it in thirty years." His head fell onto her shoulder and he slumped against her.

"Neal?" Andrea shoved with all her strength at his

shoulders and tried to wriggle out from under him. She was pinned. "Neal, get up!" She shifted as violently as she could but there was no moving him. His breathing was shallow.

She fought against panic. "Neal, wake up!"

"Andrea, are you okay?" The door hinges squeaked. After a moment of sharp silence, the hinges sounded again. Rose's voice retreated. "I beg your pardon."

"Rose! Don't leave. Help me."

Rose was beside the bed a few seconds later, her horrified face appearing above Neal's shoulders. "What's wrong?"

"I don't know." Andrea tried again to squirm out from under him. "Help get him off me. Hurry. He's in trouble."

Rose put her weight into pushing against Neal, and Andrea managed to free herself. He pitched over onto his back and Rose fell onto the mattress beside him. Andrea scrambled to her knees next to him, hands patting over his face. "He's burning up with fever."

"Let me see." Rose leaned against his shoulder and rested her palm against his forehead. Neal groaned, recoiling in pain. He opened his eyes and frowned up at her.

"Don't feel so good," he rasped. He looked past Rose to Andrea, eyelids at half-mast. He fumbled for her hand and clutched it. "Rain check?"

Andrea couldn't repress a smile. Instinctively her fingers tightened around his.

Rose clicked her tongue. "How about we get you an aspirin or two?" She flipped the bedspread over Neal's legs. "Andrea, hand me his shirt. You might want to get dressed, too."

Andrea glanced down at herself. Before she could dive for her clothes, she felt a tug on her hand. Neal glanced at Rose as she headed for the bathroom. Then his bleary gaze returned to Andrea. "What happened?"

"I don't know." She'd felt the same sense of intrusion as she had on the mountain. Would he have changed into the other man? Andrea pulled against his grasp.

He held on. "Unh-huh. No more running." He took a shallow breath and closed his eyes. "Promise?"

Andrea stared at his heated face, at his lips tight with pain. She nodded and realized he couldn't see her. "Promise." She stroked his cheek.

Neal sighed and slipped into sleep.

A bar of sunlight from the shuttered window fell across manuscript pages spread across the desk. Kerry glanced up from the unpublished memoir of an early associate and wished she could be outside catching some rays. The room felt like a cave, and her current chore was just busywork.

Rose and Noreen had run with the notion that former residents of Wisdom Court might have recorded odd events paralleling Andrea's experiences. "We can't afford to ignore any other strange things happening at Wisdom Court," Noreen said, "and since you're already going through the materials, you can keep an eye out for similarities."

Kerry surveyed the files on her desk glumly. Plenty of interesting women had been associates at Wisdom Court, but so far the documents she'd scanned had been about their authors' professional development. No breathless narratives about encounters with the supernatural had shown up yet.

"Boring," Kerry muttered. Noreen was trying to find the location of the landscape in Andrea's sketches while Dolores checked through Wisdom Court art archives for any similar drawings. She reached for another document and then let it drop back onto the desk. It wouldn't hurt to take a break. She could read a little more of Jessamine's diary first.

Kerry retrieved the key from under the lamp base and opened the desk drawer, ignoring a twinge of guilt. She'd left Jessamine in late July. The entries following her second meeting with Kelvin Haslett had focused on his virtues. Jessamine had been taken with his manners, his humor, and his talents. He'd been something of an artist, carrying with him a sketchpad wherever he went. Kerry wished she could see some of the sketches Jessamine had described, particularly what sounded like a romanticized drawing of Jessamine herself.

> *August 2, 1909*
>
> *I hardly know how to write this. In truth, I shouldn't write about it, but how else can I control my feelings? My heart has never been so full. The world is not the same place it was yesterday.*
>
> *When I saw Mr. Haslett—Kelvin—today (just to write his name makes my heart beat faster) I was upset from a row with Mrs. Selkirk. She said Mr. T. has complained that I am shirking my duties to spend time at the Chautauqua. She claimed he had no clean shirt to wear, but I ironed four of them three days ago. She is the one complaining, because she is jealous of the freedom Mr. T. allows me.*
>
> *I left in a temper. I was already late for the lecture and I walked faster than usual. Mr. Haslett came out of nowhere and I ran into him! He seized my arms to keep me from falling. His hands are very strong and quite warm. Before I could even think, Mr. Haslett*

(Kelvin!) embraced me! I nearly swooned. I'm sure my cheeks were red as peonies. When I pulled away, Mr. Haslett—Kelvin—put his palms to my cheeks and said, "I am not taking liberties with you, Jessamine. My feelings are both sincere and honorable."

Dear Diary, my heart pounded so, I thought it might burst from my bodice. It pounds now when I recall what I did. I lifted my hands to his shoulders and pulled his head down. I kissed him with all the regard I have for him. After his surprise, Kelvin kissed me back. If I felt faint before, it was nothing to what I felt then. If angels had given us wings, we'd have flown away right then. How I wish Mama and Papa could know him. He's such a fine man. He wished to go to Mr. T. at once to declare his intentions. I said not to. Mr. T. is not my father. I will tell him myself when Kelvin is not present.

Kerry set down the diary. She pressed the pad of her thumb against the nagging ache between her brows. Jessamine should have paid more attention to her penmanship, she thought irritably. A lady of her day could be told by her handwriting. Such hen scratching was not acceptable. Shaking her head at the low buzzing in her ears, she turned the page.

The sudden ring of the desk telephone startled her. She knocked the receiver off the base as she answered. "Hello?"

"What're you up to, girlfriend?" Elizabeth's warm voice purred in her ear.

Kerry glanced at the diary. "Just reading through some source material. Why?"

"I'm going for a walk and I'm looking for some

company. You interested?"

Kerry was swept with a desire for fresh air and exercise. A walk in the sunshine would clear her head and help her get back to the stack of memoirs.

"Kerry? It's just a walk. Should be a no-brainer in the decision stakes."

"Sorry. That's the problem. My brain's fuzzy from too much reading. When are you going?"

" 'bout half an hour. You in?"

"I'm in."

"See you in a while, then."

Kerry replaced the receiver. Her gaze drifted over the page where she'd stopped reading. Maybe just a little more.

CHAPTER 17

August 3, 1909

...Kelvin was waiting for me this afternoon near our special place. He spun me in his arms and my heart flew into my throat, just as it did at the circus last week when we rode the big swings. Each time he kisses me, I forget everything.

Kelvin pulled me into the shelter of the big rocks and spread his coat under the ledge. I lay with him there and he knew me. It was wrong in the eyes of God, but I'm not sorry. It was so beautiful. I heard rocks shifting against each other and when I told Kelvin he said we would be remembered in the rocks.

Afterward Kelvin held me, and gave me a small box he took from his coat pocket. His eyes held so much love I couldn't look away. He helped open it and I found a green velvet case.

Inside were two silver disks, one smaller than the other. "They're talismans," he said. "We

*each keep one and therein possess the other."
The bigger disk, an inch and a half across,
hung from a silver chain. Lines extended from
the center of the disk, and a small triangle lay
flat against it. He lifted the triangle and the
jewel was a tiny sundial!*

*Kelvin smiled at my pleasure, and raised the
smaller silver circle from the case. "It's a fob
I'll attach to my watch chain." He showed me
how the gnomon folded out on his disk as
well. On the back of both were engraved the
words, Our Time. "This summer has been
ours alone." He spoke with such sweet gravity
I found it hard to hold back tears.*

*"Will you wear this for me?" I nodded and he
put the chain around my neck and fastened it,
and kissed me with great devotion. "I love
you. I want you to be my wife." My eyes swam
with tears until he complained at my
melancholy. I mopped my eyes with his
handkerchief and showed a sunny face. Yet I
felt such sorrow that my parents will not know
him. Death is cruel, not once but countless
times. When I said that aloud, he held me
close and kissed me again.*

Kerry winced at the sudden pull of her hair, now
wrapped around her index finger. She freed it and
grabbed at a tissue to wipe her eyes. She tugged open
the desk drawer and withdrew the small case hidden
with Jessamine's diary. Gently she opened it. The
pendant was tarnished, but now she could make out
the words *Our Time*. She traced the letters with her
fingertip. Her throat ached.

A thump sounded from the front of the house.
"Crap. The walk!" Kerry leapt to her feet and hurried

from the study. Scrambling for the key, she finally swung the door open where Elizabeth waited. Her curvaceous body filled spandex shorts and a tee shirt dedicated to Buffy the Vampire Slayer. In Nikes and a blue sweatband, she was ready for action.

Elizabeth cast a quick glance over Kerry's rumpled shirt and cut-off jeans, and her bare feet. "I can see you're rarin' to go, girl." She studied Kerry's face. "Have you been crying? What's the matter, honey?"

The kindness in her voice brought Kerry to the edge of tears again. "I got caught up in something, that's all. Can you wait? I'll put on some shoes."

"Take your time."

Kerry opened the door more widely. "Come on in." She hurried toward her bedroom, aware of Elizabeth's curious gaze following her.

In the house across the square, Dolores stared at a lump of clay in frustration. It said nothing to her. In her mind she could almost envision…something, but words kept getting in the way. *Death, grief, end of the story.* She had the words she needed but no image for the last figure in the Wrapture exhibit.

She snatched up the nearly empty pack of cigarettes. A smoke might help her focus, maybe break through the logjam.

Shaking one from the pack, she stuck it in her mouth. It was the rough surface of the lighter wheel against the pad of her thumb that brought her up short. "*Dio.*" She'd overdone it yesterday and now her body was ready to slip right back into the old pack a day routine.

She ground the cigarette into the pottery bowl she'd used as an ashtray and picked up the pack. "Been there, done that, not going back." She threw the wrinkled mass into the wastebasket.

Gotta get out of here. Dolores grabbed a notebook and stuck a couple of pencils into the center pocket of her bib overalls. Fleeing the scene of the crime, she thought, locking the door.

Elizabeth and Kerry were coming down the steps of the other associate house as she came outside. "Where're you off to?"

Dolores skipped down the brick tiers. "My head's either empty or full of shit. I figured getting out for a while might help me decide which."

"Me and Kerry are just heading for a walk. Wanna come?" Elizabeth glanced down at herself with a mocking smile. "This being Boulder I figured I'd better go with formal wear, but Kerry here ruins it with cut-offs."

"Yeah, right." Kerry lifted a brow. "Just because you're a slave to Nike, don't put down my poor but honest outfit."

Elizabeth clicked her tongue. "Dolores, I reckon your overalls will trip up the image police enough so I can stop worrying about being overdressed."

"Bite me."

Elizabeth laughed. She swung open the iron gate, and pulled it shut behind them. The clang of metal scared a crow off its perch in the willow tree.

Clouds drifted in the delftware sky. Their shoes crunched on the gravel road, and redwing blackbirds trilled over the bickering of sparrows. When they reached the sidewalk, Elizabeth lengthened her stride, Kerry and Dolores keeping up. The concrete path was downhill and for a few steps they could see the city outstretched like a crazy quilt. As they went on, trees blocked the panorama.

They'd walked the four blocks east to Ninth Street before Elizabeth broke the silence. "Have you two been able to get any work done today? 'Cause I sure haven't." She didn't look at either one of them, just kept striding, moving her arms in exaggerated swings.

A vague recollection had been teasing at the edge of Dolores's mind. Something she'd seen, maybe something she'd read about was tugging faintly like a minnow nibbling on bait. "Hmmm?"

"This whole thing with Andrea's been bothering me. I haven't been able to think about anything else. I was remembering some of the stuff I've read about herbs and potions, some of the side effects, you know? You'd be surprised how many things can cause hallucinations."

Kerry and Dolores exchanged a puzzled look. "Potions? You're back to the somebody's-drugging-her bit?"

"Not really, but I keep thinking there's something we're not seeing. I even went online looking into salt deprivation. You wouldn't believe what that'll do to you."

"I'll take your word for it." Kerry picked up the pace.

Dolores thought about the artwork she'd sifted through that morning. Nothing had remotely resembled Andrea's sketches. "The only idea that really bothered me was possession. You know, like being possessed by the devil?" Even in the sunshine Dolores shivered at the thought.

Elizabeth nodded. "Yeah, I could see that perturbed you. For a minute there, you looked kinda queasy."

Dolores could feel sweat on her scalp. She gathered her black hair together at the back of her neck and tied it into a loose knot at the base of her skull. "I'm sure you've heard me mention my mother."

"A time or two."

"Church twice a week and confession every Sunday. I don't know if she was always so dedicated, but after my brother died she needed the Church more than before."

A cherry red Ford pickup roared past them, the three bare-chested young men in the back waving enthusiastically at them. The driver saluted them with the horn. Elizabeth waved back. "How old were you when your brother died?"

"Eight." For a moment the daylight faded and Dolores was again the thin little girl outside the drama that was Reuben's funeral. "He was killed in Vietnam."

"Tough break."

"Yeah." As the youngest child, she'd felt the withdrawal of their mother the most. Sometimes it seemed the arched corridors of the church had devoured her like the whale had swallowed Jonah. "My mother believes it all. She was big on the idea of possession. When I was in my teens, she told me I was possessed by the devil."

"God."

At Kerry's exclamation, Dolores shrugged uncomfortably. "Talking about it yesterday brought it back for a minute."

Elizabeth's wide mouth twisted in a smile. "What did your mother think about your grandmother's tale of seeing her father after he was dead?"

Burning eyes and straight, tight lips, thought Dolores. Terrifying rage. "To her it was blasphemy. We weren't allowed to talk about it."

"Honey, that must've been hard on you."

Dolores shrugged. "It's probably what made me an artist."

Elizabeth put one arm around her shoulders in a hug. "Well, then, I guess it was worth it, 'cause you sure are a good one."

When they reached Clifford's, Kerry wanted to get

bottled water. Coming out of the little stone store, Dolores saw the Columbia Cemetery across the street. Behind it the jagged profile of the foothills guarded the sleeping graves. In an instant she recalled seeing Andrea at the edge of the graveyard when she'd stopped to give her a ride. She'd glimpsed something. "That's what I was trying to remember," she said aloud. "It was a headstone."

Kerry lowered the water bottle from her mouth. "And you're excited about this because?"

Dolores waited impatiently for the lines of cars to come to an end. A silver Lexus paused for her to pass, and she headed across the street, Elizabeth and Kerry behind her. "I've been trying to think of a way to end the show, a climax piece. I saw something here that struck a chord. I just can't remember what it was."

They entered the graveyard through the opening in the iron-paling fence. The grassy expanse was set apart from the traffic flow of the street, as well as the surrounding residential area. Here the clamor of life was hushed, leafy trees abating even the bright sunlight.

Elizabeth surveyed the old city of the dead. "You really were talking about an end for your show, weren't you?" When Dolores didn't answer, she began to wander through the rows of gravestones, Kerry following. A magpie complained at their intrusion, flying from one tree to another as they went further into the cemetery.

Dolores rambled toward the southeast corner of the graveyard. What teased her memory must have been seen from that angle since she'd stopped just outside the gate to pick up Andrea. Threading her way through the headstones, she tried to let her mind go blank so she could recognize what she'd seen. In a few moments she found it, an hourglass atop a weathered granite tombstone. An hourglass, she thought in satisfaction, a way of measuring time, the template for the hourglass figure, symbol of body image for women from birth to grave. Perfect.

On closer inspection, the grave was that of one Sylvester Thomas Bedford, 1839-1905, Husband and Father. The hourglass was pockmarked from erosion.

"Did you find what you're looking for?" Elizabeth moved toward her, providing a running commentary. "Listen to this one: *Life holds no pleasures but in waiting for the Divine.* Kinda sad, isn't it?"

"Yeah." Dolores was imagining the hourglass form of a woman dressed in…what? What if she tried to make something replicating sand? How could she get the shininess along with the granular quality?

"Listen to these names," called Kerry. "*Ersie* and here's one called *Edrie.*" She came closer. "And *Frantie!* Surely that's not a nickname. *Frantie.* I've never encountered that one before. *Emergine.* Pretty, huh?"

Dolores, with images of hourglasses filling her imagination, looked around for Elizabeth. She found her in front of a sandstone tablet under a maple tree. "Got a good one?"

Elizabeth glanced up, smile crooked. "I was thinking how when you notice something, you suddenly start seeing it everywhere. Like when I was pregnant every other woman I saw was, too. This time it's sundials. I hadn't seen one in years. First was that sundial Andrea drew that freaked you out, Kerry. Now here's another one." She gestured toward the headstone. "Sundials are in the air, I guess."

Kerry had come over to the grave. At the center of the square granite tombstone was an engraving of a sundial, lines radiating like the rays of the sun with a brass gnomon at its midpoint. Under it was written:

Alice Thornton, 1892-1954. *She lived at the edge of the shadow.*

Elizabeth sighed. "That sounds bitter."

Kerry had moved to the adjacent marker and was peering at the inscription. "This is almost worn away. Here, can you read this name?"

Elizabeth came up beside Dolores. "It's nearly all gone isn't it?" She felt the shallow lettering on the sandstone marker with her fingertips. "Stat-no, that's a 'n.' Stanley. That's it, Stanley. Thorn-no, it's longer-oh, it's Thornton, too, right? Eighteen forty-nine to nineteen twenty-something. Maybe a four, or a nine. The weather's done a job on this."

Kerry muttered something under her breath. The tiny sprinkling of freckles across her nose stood out in relief against her skin.

Dolores looked at her in curiosity. "You're pale as milk, Kerry. What's wrong?"

"Who was Alice?" Kerry walked to the headstone on the other side of Stanley. "God, this one's more impossible to read than the other. Can either of you make it out?"

There was such urgency in her voice that Dolores knelt to examine the stone. Much of its lettering had been worn away. "Betty? Maybe Bettina." She glanced up at Kerry. "Does it really matter?"

Kerry frowned. "I don't know. Stanley Thornton was a widower. This Betty was probably his first wife. But here's Alice and there's a sundial on her stone. A *sundial.* Who the hell was Alice?"

Elizabeth drew closer and put one hand on her shoulder. "Kerry, give us a break, okay? We don't know what you're talking about."

Kerry blinked at her.

Dolores shivered in the shade. She grabbed Kerry's hand and led her to a sunlit wire bench. "Come and sit down. Tell us what's bothering you."

"I didn't mean to go mental on you." Kerry looked over at the headstone. "I've been reading that diary we found in the attic. The girl's name was Jessamine."

She told them about Jessamine's life in Stanley Thornton's house and her growing relationship with Kelvin Haslett. "The part I was reading today, just before you got there, Elizabeth, was when Kelvin gave Jessamine the sundial pendant, the one we found. He called it a talisman and he had one, too, a watch fob in the same design, only smaller. Each one was engraved with the words, *Our Time.* They loved each other so much."

Elizabeth pulled a tissue from one pocket and handed it to Kerry. "Here, honey."

Kerry looked at it in surprise.

"Wipe your tears, *jita,"* Dolores said softly. To her dismay, Kerry buried her face in it. "What is it?"

Kerry blew her nose. "There I was, reading about this incredibly tender moment between two people who were so much in love it makes you hurt. Then we come down here and find that headstone. It just hit me that all those people are dead now. The love, the promise between them…all dead and buried. It makes me sad."

Dolores patted her hand. "What happened to them?"

Kerry released a shaky breath. "I don't know. I haven't finished the diary."

Elizabeth stretched out her legs and leaned against the back of the bench. "So, what about the sundials? And the business about the names?"

Kerry shifted on the bench. "The diary doesn't mention anybody named Alice. Stanley Thornton could've had a lady friend Jessamine never knew about, somebody he later married. But the sundial was Jessamine's and Kelvin's. It doesn't make any sense."

The magpie that had challenged them earlier landed nearby in a flash of blue-black and white feathers. It cocked an interested eye toward them and strutted closer. Elizabeth stood up. "Well, honey, it looks to me like there's only one option."

"What's that?"

Elizabeth held out her hand. When Kerry took it, she pulled her to her feet. "We'd better get home. You've got some more reading to do."

CHAPTER 18

Rose slipped out of Andrea's bedroom and shut the door.

"How's Neal?" Andrea asked.

"Jerri said it's probably the same virus his son has, which accounts for the fever. He's dehydrated, so we need to push liquids. His housekeeper's out of town and no one else is at his place. I told Jerri he could stay here until he's well enough to be on his own. It's either that or the hospital. She'll send a visiting nurse to check on him tonight."

Andrea rubbed a sore spot on her arm, trying to avoid the memory of Neal's hands clutching at her. By tomorrow she'd have bruises. "He'll stay in my room?"

"I hope you don't mind." Rose pushed gray-blonde curls away from her face in a harried gesture. "We can set up a cot somewhere for you, at least for tonight. I don't think moving him is the best thing."

"No, of course not." Andrea thought about getting what she'd need for the night, and decided to deal with it later.

Rose's gray eyes sharpened. "Andrea, you still

haven't said much about what happened. You're okay, right?"

"I guess so." The jump from desire to terror had been hard enough without the ongoing sense of connection she felt with Neal. She saw the deepening concern in Rose's face. "I'm fine."

"Okay. I won't hover. If you want to talk, I'll be here." Rose glanced at her watch. "Except for the next couple of hours. I've got a meeting at the bank. What a day." She headed for the stairs. "I need to check with Aura Lee before I go. Come with me while I let her know what's going on."

After giving Aura Lee a quick update, Rose raced off to change clothes for her appointment.

Aura Lee led Andrea to her own living area. Strudel barked in welcome, tail wagging madly. "Come in, child. You need to get away from the fuss. You've had no time to settle in at all. You can relax here for a while."

Her parlor was crowded with bits and pieces collected over a lifetime. One window held glass shelves where crystal animals bent the sun into glimmering colors.

Aura Lee urged her into a gold damask chair and nudged a fringed footstool under her feet. Strudel put her forepaws on the chair cushion and barked. Andrea lifted the little dog up to sit beside her. Laying her head on Andrea's lap she gazed at her with deep brown eyes, and Andrea petted her.

"Rest for a minute while I check on Neal," said Aura Lee. "I won't be gone long."

Aura Lee returned twenty minutes later with tea. "Neal's asleep."

She made room for the tray on the ebony table at Andrea's feet. "Put these there beside you." She handed across a stack of paper and pens and Andrea set them on the drum table next to her chair.

Aura Lee handed her a cup. "Chamomile with honey and lavender. It's very soothing."

"Thanks." Andrea took a closer look at the bronze sculpture beside her. From a broken Humpty-Dumpty egg arose a slender dinosaur dressed in a flowing gown. In the bend of one scaly arm lay scrolls; the other held a potted plant.

"It's Athena springing from the head of Zeus." Aura Lee settled into the mission armchair, sighing as the red cushions adjusted to her weight. "Jane Bridgewell, an associate here a few years ago, made it. She ruined me for being able to see the Greek pantheon any differently."

Andrea wondered uneasily if she'd start linking the gods with *Jurassic Park.* A brass candelabrum on the pocket organ in the corner caught her eye. "I didn't know you played the organ."

Aura Lee followed her gaze. "I don't. That was my mother's. I tried to learn but hated the practicing. It's a waste, but having it there reminds me of Mama. Drink your tea before it gets cold."

Andrea obeyed. "It's very good." She cradled the blue cup to warm her hands. "You don't need to coddle me, you know. I'm sure you have tons to do."

"Don't be silly." Aura Lee's smile was kind. "You've been in an energy storm since you got here. Wouldn't it be interesting to throw the I Ching for clues?"

Her chair was sinfully comfortable. Andrea nestled deeper into it and Strudel cuddled against her. "I wouldn't know what they meant."

"And you an artist? You don't have to believe in order to gain its benefits. Of course," she added in a thoughtful voice, "it helps."

"I think I believe in afternoon tea." Andrea sipped

from her cup again. "It's so civilized."

"Cottie insisted on it. She said it was the best part of her heritage."

"She was English?"

Aura Lee's eyes crinkled. "Oh, my, yes. She never talked about it but you couldn't mistake her for anything else. She had the most lovely accent."

"What part of England did she come from?"

"I don't know. She was closemouthed about her early life. As we got older, I asked more than once if she had any family members who should be notified…" Aura Lee paused. She shook her head and heaved a sigh. "The only thing Cottie ever said was 'All in bad time, Aurelia. All in bad time.' Then she'd smile one of her vague smiles and that would be that."

The sadness in her voice suggested a change of subject. "All in bad time?"

Aura Lee chuckled. "It was her little joke. The old clock in the foyer has been seventeen minutes fast as long as I've been here. She meant to have it repaired but never got around to it. Every time it chimes it reminds me of her." She sipped her tea. "There's something about clocks in this house anyway. The one in the library will only strike eight bells, no matter what time it is. I used to think it might be a sign of supernatural interference, but that's anybody's guess."

Andrea suppressed a smile at the thought of a haunted clock. Then she realized that Aura Lee had spoken again. "What did you say?"

Aura Lee carefully poured more tea into her cup. "I asked if you'd help me out with something, though I'm a little nervous about involving you."

"What did you have in mind?"

"You were at the séance, of course."

Andrea nodded.

"You recall the invitation to the spirits? We opened

the door to them. Ordinarily you wrap up everything at the end of the séance, but we got so excited because of the wind and Strudel that…well, we didn't close the circle."

"And that's a problem?"

Aura Lee's eyes widened. "Oh, yes! I'm not saying the spirits who attended were bad or anything, but we don't really know. It was a blanket invitation, after all. If some of them are dubious in nature, then we have to encourage them to return to the Other Side." She leaned toward Andrea with an anxious face. "I've been so worried about it. Would you be willing to help me with the ritual?"

Andrea groaned inwardly. "What's involved?"

"First we need to name the directions again and sort of reestablish the circle, if you see what I mean."

Andrea wanted to say no, she didn't want to go through the charade. Another glance at Aura Lee's pleading eyes stopped her. "All right."

"We need to breathe deeply." Aura Lee said apologetically. She struck a match and lit one of the candles. From a low shelf under the window she pulled a bound clump of dried, silvery leaves and held it to the candle's flame. "It's a sage smudge. To cleanse the room."

Soon smoke veiled the air. Andrea thought it smelled like marijuana.

Aura Lee put the smudge in a pottery bowl and moved it to one side of the table. The salver she took from another shelf was piled with dried leaves. "I'm using my own mix of herbs to summon the spirits. Balm of Gilead, mastic, and dittany are what people typically use, but I've added some mullein as well, just to be safe." She placed the mixture at the center of the table. "Now we call the Guardians."

As at the séance, each of the guardians of the four

directions was asked to protect and bind the circle. "Even if our circle is a little sparse," Aura Lee whispered in an aside.

Andrea coughed.

Squeezing her eyes shut, Aura Lee swayed as she intoned, "We ask the shades summoned two nights ago to assemble here. We mean you no harm. The door is open still. We invite you to pass through that doorway to return whence you came. You are needed on the Other Side."

Andrea's eyes were watering at the thickening smoke. She heard Aura Lee begin the chant again. A cough welled up in her throat and she reached hastily for the teacup beside her. Ignoring Aura Lee's reproachful face, Andrea gulped the tea and replaced the cup.

"We welcome all summoned to our circle. We were remiss in not helping you cross back to the Other Side." Aura Lee's voice boomed out now, as if she addressed a congregation. "We welcomed your aid. Now we pray for your safe passage."

Andrea's eyelids lowered, then closed. She felt tendrils of aromatic smoke filling her lungs, seeping further to the inner recesses of her body. Behind her eyes she could see images of her cells floating on smoke into the room as she exhaled, becoming part of the whole.

"We ask that you return now," entreated Aura Lee from a great distance. "We urge you to go home."

The back of the chair moved and Andrea's eyelids lifted. The room was dusky, furnishings distorted in the shadows. Her nose wrinkled at the pungent odors in the air. For a moment she couldn't remember where she was, but when she glimpsed the bronze reptilian Athena, the afternoon's activities flooded back into her mind. At a rustling behind her she swung round. Aura Lee stood over her, the very picture of consternation. "What's the matter?"

Aura Lee blinked. "Uh, nothing, dear. I just wanted to see what you were working on. I'm sorry I disturbed you." She hurried to her chair. "I know today has been exhausting."

Andrea frowned. "I was working on something? I thought we were closing the circle." She glanced down at the stack of papers in her lap. On the top sheet was a sketch, half obscured given that Strudel rested her head and both paws across it.

Pulse jumping, Andrea slid out the page for closer inspection. The young man of the earlier drawings grabbed at the jagged rocks ahead of him, clearly about to fall into the fissure behind him. His fingertips were a scant inch away from any chance of safety. "My God," she breathed. She'd drawn scenes from his life, and now, maybe his impending death.

Andrea looked up from the drawing, catching the dismay on Aura Lee's face. "What?"

"Nothing." Aura Lee's gaze ricocheted off her own. She leaned forward to fuss with the tea tray.

Into Andrea's mind came the image of Aura Lee with the tea tray, handing her the stack of papers to put on the table beside her. Had she hoped for another sketch?

"You set it up, didn't you? The same weird herbs as at the séance, this time with drawing supplies handy."

Aura Lee clasped her hands in distress. "I didn't mean for it to happen. It wasn't—"

A brisk rapping at the door was followed by Rose's entrance. She sniffed the air and glanced at Aura Lee. "It smells like a pot party in here."

"No such luck." Andrea pushed herself out of the chair. "It would've been a lot more fun."

Aura Lee sputtered, but Rose ignored her. "What d'you mean?"

Rose had been the one to hand her off to Aura Lee. "You mean you weren't part of the set up?"

"For heaven's sake, quit talking in riddles and tell me what's going on!"

"It's my fault," Aura Lee blurted before Andrea could answer. "I didn't mean to—it was a last gasp effort."

"At what?" Aura Lee was silent, and Rose let out a deep breath. "Come on, it's been a rough day. Get it over with."

"All right," Aura Lee said in misery. She explained asking for Andrea's help to close the circle opened at the séance. Andrea sat back down as she spoke.

"That's all I meant to do, but then I thought, we never tried automatic writing." Aura Lee twisted her hands together. "I thought maybe Cottie could get a message to me through her while she was here. It's obvious she's already channeling somebody—that's how she's making those sketches. She'd be able to intercept what Cottie sent. That's all I had in mind," she said to Andrea. "I swear it."

"Why didn't you ask her?" The cool disapproval in Rose's voice was softened by the compassion in her eyes. "I don't know the protocol for the situation, but I expect getting her permission was required."

Andrea listened, anger simmering, but Rose's effort to determine the etiquette of using her to contact the dead had her biting back a reluctant smile.

Aura Lee turned a mournful gaze toward Andrea. "If I'd asked, would you have helped?"

Her impulse to smile vanished. "No way. You know why?" Aura Lee shook her head. "Because I'm scared. You don't understand how horrible this is. You're convinced I'm channeling somebody? I'm trying to convince myself I'm not losing my mind. How do you think it makes me feel having you set me up for it again?"

Aura Lee blinked, her face folding into anxiety. "Oh, my. I didn't think. I'm so sorry."

A tapping at the door was followed by Noreen's voice. "Aura Lee, are you there?"

Rose pulled open the door and Noreen lurched in. Her hair was in disarray, her eyelids at half-mast. "Thank the gods you're here. I came to beg some tea but—" She stopped short at the sight of the three of them. "Sorry if I'm interrupting."

Aura Lee whipped a tissue from her sleeve and wiped her eyes. "No problem." She headed to the kitchen.

"Scones? Brownies, maybe?" Noreen called after her. "That's what I really need." She glanced at Rose. "Something wrong?"

Rose slumped into the red chair. "Andrea's drawn another sketch."

"Really. May I see it? I've gone through so many landscape photos my eyes are crossing. Maybe something new will help." She took the paper Andrea held out to her and fumbled for the reading glasses on the chain around her neck. She scrutinized the sketch, and when she looked up from it, her expression bleak. "Our young man's situation has worsened."

Andrea's lips twisted. "It's more hopeless than the earlier ones."

Noreen sat on the footstool. "You've had different feelings about the sketches?"

"I guess so." Andrea thought for a moment. "Yeah."

Aura Lee sailed in with a tray loaded with cups and a steaming teapot. Strudel sat up for a closer look. The door to the kitchen swung shut, sending a lemony scent across the room. Noreen breathed deeply. "Do I detect lemon shortbread?"

Rose cleared space for the tray. "I smelled it this morning when it was baking. Anything I can do to help?"

"Thanks, it's under control." Aura Lee set the tray down. "Start the tea around while I get the shortbread."

Strudel's black nose twitched and her ears bent forward in anticipation. Her wagging tail speeded up as Aura Lee returned with a plate of shortbread and a small dish she set in front of the dog. The contents vanished in the swipe of a pink tongue.

"She'll beg, but don't give her anymore," Aura Lee warned. "She's had plenty."

"But she's so cute." Andrea bit into the square of shortbread and closed her eyes in reaction to the buttery, tangy flavor melting in her mouth. "Never mind," she mumbled. "Nobody's getting any of this away from me."

"A conniver is what she is," Aura Lee said darkly. When she saw the look on Andrea's face she flushed bright pink.

Noreen observed the by-play but just reached for her tea. "I stumbled across something online. If you don't mind," she said to Andrea, "I'd like to ask you a few questions."

"What about?"

Noreen pressed a finger against the crumbs on her plate and licked them off. "What was your principal feeling about the first sketch?"

Andrea responded without thinking. "I was scared to death."

Retrieving a notebook from one pocket, Noreen pulled a pen from another. "Because?"

"It was drawn in my own style but I'd never seen it, never thought about it, and didn't remember making it."

Rose frowned. "Why ask about her emotional responses? I thought you wanted the facts behind the sketches."

Noreen nodded. "Exactly so. Emotions can be factual information. The feelings surrounding an event may be as important as the event itself. *Emotions perfume the span of man like rain on a spring day.* Althea Morgan Shipley. Eighteen thirty-two to eighteen seventy-nine."

Andrea frowned. "I don't see the connection."

Noreen smiled. "No? Would you tell me how you came to draw this latest one?"

Andrea glanced toward Aura Lee. The older woman set her cup onto the table with care, clearly waiting for Andrea to expose her. "I fell asleep. There was some paper nearby and a pencil. When I woke up, the sketch was finished."

"Had you drunk any alcohol?"

"No. We burned some sage and, I've forgotten what else."

"Dittany, Balm of Gilead, mastic, and mullein," said Aura Lee. She watched Noreen's pen move across her notebook page. "The same herbs we used at the séance, except for the mullein."

"Hmmm. Are any of these likely to produce hallucinations?" Noreen asked Aura Lee. "Or create a state of intoxication?"

Aura Lee shook her head. "I don't think so. They're used to allow manifestations of spirits."

"Did you see any spirits?"

"I just drew a picture."

"And you, Aura Lee? Did you see or feel anything different in the room?"

Aura Lee sighed. "No."

"Were either of you aware of any feelings different than your own?" When they both shook their heads, Noreen sat back in her chair, looking at her notes.

"I've been reading about people's perceptions during hauntings. Many accounts report feelings 'left behind.' I'm sure you've heard about cold spots some people encounter in haunted houses. Animals react to such places as well."

"Like Strudel at the séance!" Aura Lee exclaimed.

"Exactly." Noreen took another piece of shortbread. "Accounts tell of dogs sensing the qualities of certain people, as if they can smell evil or fear." Thoughtfully, she added, "I wonder if the scents of our emotions are released into the air."

Rose had folded her legs into the lotus position and now she leaned forward, elbows on her knees. "Like instinctive reactions, pheromones and sexual attraction."

"It might explain things like mobs or hysteria," Andrea said, but she couldn't see any correlation to her sketches.

"If that were true," Aura Lee said, "how could people survive living in the world? Walking down the street would swamp a person with waves of feeling from passersby."

Noreen smiled. "Good question. I think humans had to evolve to the point where they couldn't perceive the clouds of feeling around every person. They had to shut down the receptors to maintain their sanity."

"Hence the development of language, right?" Rose reached for another shortbread bar. "Tamping down intuitive responses, as hearing and sight became more important, required another way of communicating. Are you suggesting so-called intuitive people have retained something of the ability to smell emotions?"

"Or feel, as shown through galvanic skin response,"

Noreen said. "Or taste. Carry it a step further. When people die—especially under traumatic or violent circumstances—what if they sometimes leave behind collections of intense emotional molecules, ones only certain people can sense? To the rest of us, there's nothing there. To the acute or intuitive person, there's a presence, a lingering residue, a—"

Aura Lee's eyes were alight with excitement. "A ghost."

"What's in a name?" Noreen quoted softly.

Rose stared at her. "So you think those lingering clouds of feelings could affect the emotions of the people who perceive them?"

"I don't see why not." Noreen set her cup onto the saucer. "If the emotion molecules were cohesive enough, wouldn't it be like passing through a cloud of perfume? Your skin would take on the scent as you walked through it. You would breathe in the residue. Why couldn't the molecules then progress through your body, affecting your mood?"

Aura Lee was deeply absorbed. "These collections of feelings would be like shadows, wouldn't they? Casting their presence on everyone, but with only a few people noticing them."

"Or," Rose said, "perhaps people would be affected by them, but would only perceive them as moods. As Andrea said, wouldn't it be an interesting explanation for mob violence or mass hallucination? You could say those were caused by an overabundance of perceivers being grouped together."

Andrea shifted in her chair. "But how could you ever measure these things objectively? We're talking about things that are subjective by their very nature."

Noreen shrugged. "There's no such thing as absolute objectivity. My perceptions are always going to be unique to me because I'm the one perceiving them. It's like the Heisenberg Uncertainty Principle in quantum physics. Observation affects outcome. The act of watching something affects the way it turns out. The observer is a part of the equation."

"Which is why you get so many approaches to the lingering emotional residue." Rose smiled. "ESP, the psychic connection, reading the tarot. People have created or found different ways to link with and explain the emotions they perceive."

Noreen poured more tea into her cup. "One of my dearest friends is devoted to astrology. Now, I can see no merit in the idea that the stars or planets or the Milky Way rule our lives. But my friend uses the vocabulary of that belief system to explain the world. She's one of the wisest people I know."

Aura Lee nodded happily.

"But what does that have to do with my sketches? Why me?"

"Why not you?" Noreen's eyes kindled with enthusiasm. "In some ways you're the ideal choice to channel information about this young man you've sketched. You're a stranger here and you've just arrived. You're an artist who has spent her career capturing the images of people described to you. You're probably the perfect person to receive the emotional molecules left behind by this man."

Andrea shook her head. "I don't get it. Heisenberg principle or not, why isn't Dolores sculpting figures representing this guy? Why isn't Kerry writing about him?"

Noreen leaned forward. "Maybe they are! The observer affects the outcome of the observation. When you examine something, you bring your own past to the experience, as well as your own method. Who's to say Dolores hasn't sculpted something inspired by our nameless young man? Or that Kerry hasn't written something about him? But you, because you've been a forensic artist, you're the one who sketches the events that produced the feelings he left behind."

Andrea thought of the sense of deep connection she'd felt while making sketches from people's descriptions. Was Noreen's theory credible? Was it really so difficult to believe remnants were left behind after death, that she'd somehow tapped into lingering fragments of a troubled spirit?

"There is one thing, though," Rose said thoughtfully. "Why is Andrea receiving these messages? More accurately, why are the emotional remains still here to be received?"

"In other words," said Noreen, "is there a purpose behind their being received by Andrea? That is indeed the question." She turned to Andrea with eagerness. "Have you had any answer to it? Have any of the feelings given you some direction?"

Andrea was hit with a wave of fatigue. Feelings, sketches, the by-play among the Wisdom Court women, all were wearing her down, using her up. "The emotions I've felt most are fear and distrust of myself. I've been in a trance or asleep, just an unwilling utensil."

The expressions of concern on the other women's faces deepened Andrea's despair. "The idea of an entity waiting to communicate through me is dreadful. I want it to stop."

Aura Lee was on the edge of tears. "I'm so sorry for what I did. I didn't think."

"I hope you actually closed that door," Andrea said numbly. She threaded her way past the table and headed for the door. "I can't think anymore today."

Aura Lee reached for her. "But, Andrea—"

"Let her go," Rose said quietly.

CHAPTER 19

Sunshine through the windowpanes cast squares onto the oak floor. Like stepping-stones, Kerry thought uncomfortably and frowned at the idea. Elizabeth hadn't been led to Stanley Thornton's grave. The man lived and died in Boulder. Of course he was buried in a local cemetery. That she'd been reading about him in Jessamine's diary had no bearing on their finding his headstone. Neither did the sundial on the marker for the unknown Alice Thornton. But there'd been that odd moment of drift between then and now.

Kerry tugged the study door open and marched to her desk. Getting bent out of shape over a coincidence was a waste of time. She simply needed to read more in order to answer her questions.

She opened Jessamine's diary and riffled through the pages of the sections she'd previously read. She looked at the next entry with surprise. The writing was different from Jessamine's usual tight scribble. Her pen had *scratched* over the page, in several places nearly tearing the paper. Several ink splotches marked places where the pen had bled into the passage.

August 5, 1909

I am so mortified I can hardly write about it.

I went to our place to meet Kelvin—Mr. T. took Mrs. Selkirk to town for supplies today, so I skimped my chores, anxious to see K. I was there before him, and waited, so excited. I heard him coming, but it was Jack Wheaton walking toward me. He is a particular friend of Edward Selkirk and just as nasty. He was smiling and coming near. I started back toward the trail, but Jack took my arm. When I pulled away, he laughed. He said if I needed somebody to pass the time with, he was happy to oblige. "I can't let you go home unhappy, now can I?"

Then it struck me. He saw us that day when we lay together. I knew I heard someone. Jack was treating me like a fallen woman! I was shamed. I saw what Kelvin and I did through his mean, piggy eyes. It was the best thing in my life and he soiled it. I wanted to hit him, to kill him. When I walked away Jack came after me. I told him to let me be. He wrenched my arm and I screamed. Then Kelvin was there and he dragged Jack away from me. They fought—it was frightful. Kelvin's nose bled down his shirt and Jack spat out teeth. Kelvin knocked Jack to the ground and came to pull me away. We stumbled down the trail toward home leaning on each other. A storm came out of nowhere and we were drenched in minutes.

We got to the farm and thank God the buckboard wasn't back yet. We cleaned up in the kitchen. Kelvin's nose isn't broken, but his knuckles are so bruised. He sat with his head hanging for the longest time. When I told him what Jack said, Kelvin cursed him. He said it makes no difference; soon we'll be gone.

I asked why and he said Dr. Tweedham was called back to Boston and he has to go with him. I began to cry, but Kelvin held me and said I'd come with him. He cupped my cheeks in his poor hands. "We'll marry now." His voice made my heart beat faster. "I can't leave you here." He wanted me to go with him then but I have to tell Mr. T. about Kelvin. He's been real good to me and I can't walk away without him knowing why.

Kelvin said we leave day after tomorrow and I have to get ready. I don't have much, some clothes and mementos. Tomorrow I'll clean and help Mrs. Selkirk fix meals for Mr. T. I can't stay in K.'s rooms anyway. I don't want Dr. Tweedham to look at me like Jack Wheaton did. Kelvin agreed. He said goodbye and held me close. Mr. T. and Mrs. Selkirk came in right then and I felt like sinking into the floor. Mr. T. gaped at us but was civil to Kelvin when I introduced them. Mrs. Selkirk was scandalized and brushed past me like I was dirt. We told Mr. T. our plans, and I described our courtship over the summer. Mr. T. saw Dr. Tweedham's leaving means we should get married fast.

Mr. T. invited Kelvin to stay for supper. "I got the mail," he said. "My sister comes tomorrow so she can help with the wedding." He dug out a bottle of spirits to toast us with. Soon he and K. were very jolly. Mr. T. is a kind man.

*I am to be married! I write the words and my
fingers shake. The pendant Kelvin gave me is
in front of me. Our Time. Soon it will always
be our time.*

Kerry rubbed at her eyes, sore from straining to
decipher Jessamine's handwriting. I should take a
break, she thought, but curiosity was driving her. She
pressed a warm washcloth to her eyes and rested for a
while, irritated by the faint hum in her ears. It wasn't
long before she was struggling further with
Jessamine's penmanship.

August 6, 1909

Dear Diary,

*It is my last day in Boulder. It's rained all
night and day.*

*I've worked hard to set things up for Mr. T. I
can't wash but a few shirts at a time since I
have to dry them at the stove. I stewed a
chicken with some root vegetables and baked
gingerbread and two loaves of bread. Mrs.
Selkirk sniffed at my work but stayed out of my
way.*

*Mr. T. met his sister Mrs. Wolcott at the
station. By the time they got here, they were
wet and cold to the bone. Mrs. Selkirk dished
up the chicken and they ate it all. When Mrs.
W. said it was good, Mrs. S. said thanks and
didn't mention I'd cooked it. I took dishes into
the kitchen and Edward was by the fire. He
winked at me and I wanted to kick him. He
keeps his hands to himself when Mr. T isn't
around, but he's disrespectful all the same. I
won't be sorry to leave him behind.*

Kelvin telephoned from the Hotel Boulderado

when I was in the barn getting coal oil and Mr. T didn't come get me. I telephoned the hotel when he told me K. called. I couldn't reach him and I didn't want to speak with Dr. Tweedham because we haven't met, and the connection was very poor.

Later Thursday night:

I visited with Mr. T. and Mrs. Wolcott after supper while I mended socks. We talked about my time here and Mr. T. said he would miss me. Mrs. W. changed the subject. I'm happy to be getting married but this old farmhouse and Mr. T. will be fond memories. I said as much to him and he looked sad. Mrs. W. looked like she wanted to spit nails. I left for my room and Edward came out to the hall after me. He blocked my way and grabbed me. Before I could stop him, he kissed me! His tooth cut my lip and I tasted blood. "Wheaton said you was a quail, and he seen you at it." I slapped his face and he looked real ugly at me. If Mrs. W. hadn't come into the hall, I don't know what he would've done. Jack Wheaton told him! I wish God would strike them both dead!

I ran to my room, real upset, and wasted time pacing and wishing I'd knocked his head off. If he tells anybody else what Jack Wheaton saw—it gives me the shivers to think on it. But the only one that matters is Kelvin, and he already knows.

I calmed down and sat at the dressing table to take down my hair. After I started my 100 strokes the strangest thing happened. In the mirror my hair was darkening. My face changed. My blue eyes turned almost black

*and my nose got longer and straighter. I was
so scared but I couldn't look away. It wasn't
my face anymore. I was looking at Kelvin, into
his eyes. After a bit my own face came back
and I was in the looking glass. I thought I
would swoon.*

*I belong to Kelvin and he belongs to me. But
tonight I saw us become one person. We will
be together forever.*

Kerry turned the page and found it empty.

"No. It *can't* end here." She hunted through the
following pages but they were blank. When she
caught sight of the familiar script toward the end of
the diary, she exhaled in relief and pulled the book
near.

The writing was tiny and the words uneven and
difficult to make out. Faded ink smudges further
obscured them. Kerry fumbled for the magnifying
glass in her desk drawer.

*This is my last entry. A diary is a stupid thing
for a grown woman. I am no lovesick girl
now.*

*I waited for Kelvin all that Friday. He never
came. Mr. T. fussed over me and Mrs. Wolcott
kept wondering until I went out into the rain
to wait by myself. Edward came out for more
wood and sneered at me. "What d'you
expect?" I went back to the house before I
tried to hurt him.*

*I telephoned the hotel. The clerk told me Dr.
Tweedham and his assistant left on the early
train. The tone in his voice made me think
there might have been other calls like mine.
Maybe I'm not the only woman in Boulder
cheated by Mr. Haslett.*

I took sick after that day and didn't leave my bed until mid-September. I prayed to die, but God doesn't listen to me.

Mr. Thornton—he asked me to call him by his given name, Stanley—was kind. He made Mrs. Selkirk care for me and didn't fuss at me. He didn't mention Mr. Haslett. I'm grateful for that. Yesterday he asked me to be his wife. He said he knows I don't love him, but his feelings for me are strong enough to support marriage between us. I accepted his offer. I don't care about Mrs. Selkirk and Edward. I'll fire her and he can rot however he wants.

This is the last time I will ever read these pages. I was foolish to believe Mr. Haslett cared for me. I want to throw this diary away but I can't, though it would be for the best. I'll hide it with the pendant. I've studied the sundial on it till I can't stand the sight of it.

Goodbye to Jessamine. She believed in love and in a man's honor. My middle name is the same as my mother's. Alice. A plain name without airs. It suits me better now.

My last word on this is a poem, the only one I ever wrote:

The line midst love and hate—

Like light and dark—

Lies at the edge of the shadow.

Alice Cunningham
October 20, 1909

Kerry rubbed her eyes, surprised when her hands came away wet. Alice. That explained the headstone at Columbia Cemetery. Jessamine Cunningham became Alice, second wife to Stanley Thornton. The young girl, so deeply in love, became the woman whose headstone quoted the bitter verse in her diary.

How could Kelvin have betrayed her? Had Jessamine been too inexperienced to see him for what he was? Was the tender lover an opportunist preying on the lonely girl?

It didn't feel right. Kerry groped for a tissue. The unfairness of it bothered her the most. Jessamine lost her whole family and then was abandoned by the man she loved—no, not Jessamine. Alice.

The phone rang as Kerry was blowing her nose. "Hello?" After a pause, Elizabeth's said, "Are you crying again? What's wrong now?"

"Nothing. I just finished the diary." Kerry forced a cheerful note into her voice. "No happy ending this time, I'm afraid."

"Don't move, honey," Elizabeth ordered. "I'll be right over."

Within minutes the doorbell sounded. When Kerry opened the door Elizabeth walked through it, Dolores at her heels. Both of them regarded her closely as she swung the door shut.

Kerry tried for a smile. "You didn't have to interrupt what you were doing. I just had a bad reaction to the diary. I told you how real it seemed."

Elizabeth enfolded her in a hug. "Honey, you don't have to explain it to me. I've been known to cry over dog food commercials. I told Dolores you sounded like you needed some moral support." Hands on Kerry's shoulders, she pushed her away far enough to look into her face. Her chocolate brown eyes were anxious. "What happened?"

"What I should have expected, I guess. Come in and I'll show you."

They followed her into the study and she handed over the journal. "I told you most of it at the cemetery.

The last part is the buzz kill."

They sat down and Elizabeth held the book between them. After a moment Dolores glanced up. "The handwriting's terrible."

"I know." Kerry held out the magnifying glass. "It's better with this."

The two read in silence. Kerry watched them, aware of a new appreciation for both of them. Neither had hesitated. They showed up because they thought she needed help. Elizabeth inhaled sharply. "What?"

"His—Kelvin's—face in the mirror." Kerry raised her eyebrows and Elizabeth made an irritated sound. "Jessamine looks in the mirror and Kelvin's face kinda slips over it? What does that remind you of?"

Kerry shrugged. The girl was longing for her lover. She'd seen his face instead of her own. "I don't know what you mean."

Elizabeth pursed her lips. "Sounds like what Andrea was talkin' about, don't you think?"

Dolores's eyes rounded in surprise. "You're right! That's how Andrea described it with Neal in the rain, as though the guy in the sketches just slid right over him. *That* is spooky." She returned to the diary, continuing to read along with Elizabeth. When she came to the end her eyes swam with tears. *"Jita,* this is awful."

Elizabeth finished. "Damn the bastard." She scooped the diary off her lap and slammed it onto the desk. "He went after that poor girl for a summer fling. When it looked like he'd have to come through for her, he booked right out of town."

Kerry shook her head. "I don't know. He could've left with his boss and not said anything to Jessamine. Instead, he talked about marriage and kicked that Wheaton dude's ass."

"But then he leaves?" Dolores picked up the diary to

read some earlier pages. "Listen to this, Elizabeth." She read the passage when Kelvin gave Jessamine the pendant. "It's so lovely. How could he do that and then leave her high and dry? Maybe something happened to him."

Elizabeth snorted. "What could've happened to him? Frostbite from cold feet, maybe. Besides, if he *had* run into trouble, somebody would've found out about it, wouldn't they? Jessamine would've heard about it."

"Yeah, but she got sick," Kerry said. "Remember, she talks about Stanley's kindness, how he made that Selkirk woman take care of her. What did she say? That she'd been in bed until September or so? Let me see that, Dolores."

Kerry searched for the lines and reached for the magnifying glass. "Okay, here...*I didn't leave my bed until mid-September.* And the previous entry was in early August. Wow, she spent over a month in bed. What was it, do you think, some kind of fever?"

Elizabeth frowned. "What do you bet it was a miscarriage?"

"Oh, no," Kerry said. It hadn't even occurred to her. "You're probably right."

Dolores held out her hand. "Hey, gimme." Kerry handed it over and she reread a section. When she finished, she glanced up. "She worked as a servant and doesn't mention friends except for Mr. T. and Kelvin. She wouldn't necessarily have known if something prevented Kelvin from showing up."

Kerry considered it. "But somebody would've said something eventually. Boulder wasn't that big a town."

Dolores shrugged. "So I guess Kelvin was just a good-looking rat."

"I guess so." Kerry hated the sense of loss she felt.

"She'd already gone through so much. I was hoping she went off with Kelvin and had a bunch of kids. I wanted Kelvin to be her reward." She looked away from the sympathy in Elizabeth's eyes. "Instead she died a bitter woman, judging by that headstone. By then Stanley was gone. She was alone again."

"Some folks get dumped on." Elizabeth's voice was sad. "Jessamine was one of them. It doesn't make sense or show any justice. I've known people like that, good people who couldn't buy a break. I reckon you have, too."

Kerry nodded. "I wanted it to be different for Jessamine."

Dolores finished leafing through the diary and closed the cover. She set it on the desk but misjudged the distance and the volume fell to the floor. "Sorry." When she picked it up, she saw an edge of paper showing under the back cover. "What's this?"

Kerry took the diary, opening it to the back. The lining had come loose, revealing the corner of a paper. She pinched the border and tugged. A photograph slipped out onto the blotter. Kerry inhaled sharply.

"What is it?" Elizabeth came round the corner of the desk and Dolores leaned over the front. Silently they stared at the picture.

"Oh, my God," Dolores whispered. "I don't believe it."

CHAPTER 20

Avoiding everyone after she left Aura Lee's suite was as simple as walking out the front door. Andrea retrieved her spare car key inside the rear bumper and drove away.

She took Broadway past the university, dodging students swarming toward shops across from the campus. Down the hill was central Boulder, where cobblestone walks united brick storefronts on the Pearl Street Mall. Neo-hippies in tie-dye and businessmen in suits and ties waited for the traffic lights. Maybe schizophrenia is the norm in this place, she thought bitterly.

Should she leave Boulder? She could send for her stuff when she got back to Tacoma, but then what? The Department had hired a replacement for her, and she'd rented out her house for the coming year. But she had a choice: go back to her old life with her sanity almost intact or stay for further adventures among the ghosties and ghoulies of Wisdom Court.

Andrea drove north past the hospital and looked unseeing as condominiums and bungalows gave way to suburban houses behind old-growth shrubbery and trees. Broadway climbed a hill lined with shoppettes and fenced pastures where horses grazed on silver-green prairie grass. A sign said Lyons was ten miles north and she kept going.

The highway curved around foothills that might have been sketched onto the landscape with charcoal. Stark granite boulders cast shadows over the road. She saw a place along the shoulder of the highway and veered into it without warning. The driver behind her leaned on the horn and roared past her.

What the hell am I doing? Andrea rested her head against the steering wheel and waited for her heart to stop pounding. In a few minutes she carefully turned back toward Boulder. She drove mechanically, taking care with every shift of the gears, every tap on the brakes.

She didn't dare leave Wisdom Court without knowing why such strange things were happening to her. If she did, she'd never be able to trust herself again, wherever she went. Reluctantly she drove back up the hill, tired and no surer of what to do than when she'd left. A headache pounded at her temples.

The grandfather clock chimed as Andrea entered the house. The heavy oak door thudded behind her while she waited through the bells. It was ten o'clock—minus seventeen minutes, according to Aura Lee. All in bad time. In the vibrating air she heard nothing, not even an inquiring bark from Strudel. She started up the stairs, hoping she'd be able to get what she needed from her room and find a place to spend the night. As sick as he was, Neal was bound to be asleep.

The door hinges squeaked. Remaining still she listened for movement from Neal, and when it didn't come, eased open the door far enough to slip inside. She was halfway across the floor to the chest of drawers when the light beside the bed winked on.

"You don't have to sneak around," Neal said in a gravelly voice. "It's your room."

Damn, Andrea thought, and took a deep breath. "Sorry. I was trying to be quiet."

The bedclothes rustled as he shifted position. "I've been thinking."

She pulled out a drawer and searched hastily for the lavender T-shirt and leggings she'd been using as sleepwear.

Neal coughed, and the loose, rough sound made Andrea wince in sympathy. "Aren't you going to ask me what I've been thinking about?"

Andrea frowned into the drawer. "You need to sleep." She retrieved the nightclothes and pushed the drawer too hard, shaking the chest. One of the framed pictures on top of it fell to the floor. "Dammit."

"Andrea, what's the matter now?"

She bent to pick up the picture and checked the glass across Grace's smiling face. "What are you talking about? There's nothing wrong." She hurried toward the bathroom.

"Then why're you acting like I've got leprosy and typhoid both?"

"I'm just tired. We can talk tomorrow." She grabbed the toiletry bag on the counter and switched off the bathroom light.

He whispered, "Andrea, give me a break here." The day's growth of beard added shadows to the planes of his face. His eyes were bloodshot and weary, and he slumped against his pillows.

"I'm sorry." She drew near the bed and tried to smile. "What have you been thinking about?"

The corners of his mouth lifted. "That's better." He extended his hand and without thinking she put hers into it. "I'm pretty foggy about what happened today, in and out of a fever. But I have the sinking feeling I came on too strong." He brushed his thumb over her knuckles. "Am I right?"

He was touching only the tops of her fingers, yet her eyes drifted shut as she savored the caress.

"Andrea?"

She opened her eyes. "What?"

"I said I thought I'd frightened you today." He considered her with the smile back in his eyes. "Maybe not so much?"

Her color rose.

His eyes were somber. "If I did anything to scare you, I'm sorry."

"Neal, I—" Andrea stopped. How could she begin to explain to him what she was trying to figure out for herself? "Everything's so mixed up." What she saw in his eyes made her reckless. Moving closer, she set aside the items she'd come for. "Would you hold me?"

Neal moved over to make room and she lay down beside him. He wrapped his arms around her. "What's the matter?" he asked, voice rumbling in her ear. She shook her head against his shoulder. "Then we'll just hold on for now."

Andrea waited until Neal was asleep and eased off the bed, gathering her night things. She pulled the door shut, letting the spring bolt slide home before she released the knob.

As she slipped through the kitchen, a door opened. Rose wore a flowing gray robe belted tightly around her waist. Her loose curls were silvery in the light from the wall sconce. "Andrea, there you are. There's a cot for you in the studio. I left some extra pillows and blankets, but I'll show you where to get more just in case." She led her to the linen closet where the shelves were stacked with bedding. "Help yourself to whatever you need."

"Thanks." Andrea turned back toward the studio.

Rose followed her and as they entered, she took a quick look around, pausing at the uncovered casements. Outside the trees shifted in the rising breeze, leaves fluttering in the light from the windows. "You sure you want to sleep here? We could put the cot in the living room."

"This'll be fine." Andrea set her toiletry bag onto the counter by the sink. Her shoulder brushed against one of the photographs salvaged from the attic. They'd been hung like drying laundry, away from the light.

Rose fussed with the extra pillow. "It looks as though it might rain. I hope you won't get cold."

Andrea sighed. "Rose, did you want to talk about something in particular?"

The older woman turned toward her. "It's what you said this afternoon about feeling like a utensil, feeling used up." She fiddled with the robe sash. "You've had a hard time since you got here. Aura Lee's horrified at what she did, and she's afraid it might drive you away. Please give her—give us—another chance."

Andrea started to respond, but stopped. Finally she said, "I'm too tired to think about it now. Let's get some sleep. Tomorrow we can take another look."

"Okay." Rose started to say something else, then merely smiled. "I'll see you in the morning then. Good night." The studio door clicked quietly shut.

Andrea brushed her teeth and crawled under the covers, tucking them around her against the chilly night air. It'd been warm in Neal's arms, secure, she thought drowsily. Sometimes that was better than sex.

At the whisper of sound, her eyes popped open. The dark was made of shadows and she searched for movement. She sensed a shivering in the air, followed by rustling.

"Who's there?" No answer. She strained to hear over her heartbeat. Finally throwing the covers she ran for the light switch.

In the sudden glare she saw on the floor the piece of twine, photographs still attached to it. Her breath whooshed out in relief and, grabbing the line, she began to coil the end onto the hook screwed into the wall. The photos trembled on the cord, the strangers in them looking out at her as they moved.

A photograph lay on the floor near the cot and she crept back to pick it up. In the picture a young woman posed at the side of an older man. He stood ramrod straight, holding her to him possessively. His ring, a carved lion's head, appeared to snarl in warning from her shoulder. The woman's light hair was pulled back from her heart-shaped face, and the ruffled collar of her bodice accented her pointed chin and tiny earlobes. Her eyes were empty.

Andrea studied the man. Lined forehead under slicked back gray hair, thick brows over amused eyes, blunt nose and thin straight lips. If they were married, as the pose implied, they had different feelings about it. Putting the photograph on the top of the nearest surface she hurried back to the cot.

Wrapped in the blankets, she sought a comfortable position and tried to recreate the relaxation she'd felt in Neal's arms. But as she grew sleepy, it was the image of the young woman with vacant eyes filling her mind.

CHAPTER 21

She wandered on the mountainside through the misty pine forest. The path curved among fallen rocks and trees twisted by the wind. Sure at last of her destination she ran calling, I'm coming, and sensed a joyous response. I'm coming.

A firm hand jostled her shoulder. "Wake up."

Andrea growled and tried to hold onto the tatters of her dream.

"Come on, Andrea. Wake up."

She peered at reddish hair through slitted eyes. Kerry bent over the cot, ready to shake her again. Dolores was beside her.

Andrea's vision cleared enough to make out Elizabeth as well. "What's going on?" Aware of the crick in her neck, she turned her head with care. "What time is it? And why the committee wake-up call?"

Dolores's hands were clasped together and she was vibrating with excitement. "We have the most amazing thing to show you."

Andrea pushed herself up from the cot and shook her hair back from her face. "What?"

"This." Kerry laid a black and white photo on the cot.

When Andrea saw the young man in the picture, her mind went blank. His dark hair was brushed back from a widow's peak and bold brows soared over almond-shaped eyes in the narrow face. On the bottom margin of the photograph was printed in white ink: *Chautauqua 1909, J.B. Sturtevant.*

"It's the guy in your sketches," Dolores whispered. "Don't you recognize him?"

"Of course I do!" Andrea touched the edge of the photograph. When she turned it over, she saw writing in a lower corner. *Kelvin Haslett, July 23, 1909.* "Where was it?"

"Pasted under the cover of this." The small book Kerry handed her was faded and the word *Diary* was written across it in flowing lines. "It was with the stuff we found in the attic. You know, along with the sundial pendant. The one you sketched at Dolores's show?"

A chill crawled down Andrea's spine. "This is giving me the creeps."

Elizabeth's laugh was short. "Ya think?"

Kerry picked up the photo and slid it back into the diary. "Get dressed and we'll tell you what we've found out. A lot of it has to do with your boy here. Oh, and Aura Lee said to tell you she's making waffles."

"I'm all mixed up."

"We're going to work on that." Kerry squeezed her shoulder. "Come on, things will look better with some coffee. If you hurry, we'll let you have the first batch of waffles."

Dolores and Elizabeth walked out the studio door, Kerry trailing behind them. Andrea tugged on jeans, fumbling with the snap. Her mind was whirling. The man of the sketches was real, and he had a name. She hadn't invented him.

As she pulled a green shirt over her head she heard a sound. Kerry had picked up a photo and stared at it intently. "Where did this come from?"

Andrea craned to look over her shoulder. "It was with the batch from the attic. Scared the hell out of me last night."

Kerry's frown deepened. "The man looks familiar."

Andrea slipped into her shoes and looked around for her toiletry bag. She saw it next to the sink and reached past Kerry to get it.

"I don't know who she is, but I've seen him," muttered Kerry, intent on the picture. "But where?"

Andrea headed to the door. "I'll be in for breakfast in a bit."

Kerry nodded absently. "Me, too, in a minute." She picked up the photo. "I'm going to check something first."

They gathered around the kitchen table some twenty minutes later. Neal had come downstairs with Aura Lee monitoring his every step. His unshaven cheeks were pale and he moved slowly, but the glaze of fever had faded from his eyes.

Rose added place settings as Elizabeth and Dolores arrived. When Andrea came in she reached for another plate. "Are we having a meeting?"

"You could say that." Dolores crossed to the wall phone. "I'll give Noreen a call. She needs to be here. Better make some more waffles, Aura Lee."

Andrea slipped into the chair beside Neal. "How do you feel?"

He reached for her hand. "I'll live but I'm still not sure that's a good thing."

His skin was warm against hers, and she savored the grip of his fingers.

As Noreen came in through the back door, Kerry hurried into the room carrying a manila envelope. Aura Lee brought a platter of waffles to the table.

Andrea glimpsed the excitement in Kerry's eyes. "You found something?"

"Wait till you see." Kerry dropped onto her chair and plunged a hand into the envelope. Pulling out a stack of papers, she set them on the table. "This is the file about the house, *this* house. Caldicott researched the place before she bought it and stuck the information here." Her fingers gently slid a yellowed newspaper clipping from the pile. "I looked through it at one point, but not very closely." She took sip of coffee from the cup handed to her. "Mmm. Thanks, Aura Lee."

Andrea craned to see the headline: *Stanley 0. Thornton dies at home.* Her gaze moved to the accompanying photo of a white-haired, wrinkled man glaring at the camera. "It's him!"

"Who?" Dolores had risen to peer over Kerry's shoulder. "Jeez, a smile would've cracked his face. Wait! *That's* Stanley Thornton?"

Kerry placed the photo Andrea had retrieved the night before beside the obituary. Next to Thornton was the young blonde woman with unreadable eyes. "It's Jessamine," Kerry said softly. "It's their wedding picture."

Elizabeth came round the table to see. "Oh, God, she looks like she isn't even there."

Kerry removed the portrait of Kelvin Haslett from the back cover of the diary and set it beside the wedding picture. "And he's the reason why."

Rose gasped as she caught sight of the photograph. "Isn't he—?"

"It's the man Andrea's been drawing!" Aura Lee looked back and forth between Kerry and Andrea.

"How did you find it?"

Elizabeth and Dolores told of the photo's discovery in the diary and Kerry described seeing the wedding portrait that morning. "It was with the photos from the attic."

"It's incredible." Dolores resumed her seat, reaching for her cup. "The spooky part is finding these pictures all at once. What are the odds of that?"

"Forget the odds." Rose looked at them commandingly. "Tell us what you've found out."

"Especially me," Neal added. "What's all this about Andrea's drawings?"

"Gracious. We need to bring you up to date." Noreen told him about Andreas's three sketches of Kelvin Haslett. "The first was the night of Andrea's arrival. You were with her for the second one, the day you hiked in Chautauqua. The third was produced yesterday."

"So *that's* what happened that afternoon." Neal studied Andrea's face. "I couldn't figure out what I'd done to make you freeze up the way you did. I thought I offended you or something."

"I was freaked out." Andrea released his hand, not knowing how he would react to the rest of it. "Every one of those has been done while I was asleep or in a trance. Yesterday Rose and Aura Lee found me painting in my sleep."

"What, the same thing, this Kelvin guy?" At her nod, Neal recaptured her hand in his. "Why aren't you swinging from the chandeliers?"

"I have been," Andrea said. Neal's fingers tightened around her own.

They passed the two pictures around while Kerry told them of Jessamine's summer romance with Kelvin Haslett. She read aloud several excerpts from the diary, including the passage in which Kelvin gave

Jessamine the sundial pendant.

"The day he and Jessamine were to get married and leave for Chicago, Kelvin didn't show up. Jessamine never saw him again. She ended up marrying Stanley Thornton."

"These are fascinating." Noreen's eyes were alight with enthusiasm as she examined the photos.

"So now we know who Kelvin is. And we know that Jessamine lived here," Dolores said. "But what does it mean?"

Noreen nodded thanks to Aura Lee for refilling her teacup. *"Answers are like flowers grown, questions but seeds determining their blossoms.* Elizabeth Bland Cox, nineteen-oh-two. We have the young man's identity and now we have to establish why he keeps appearing in Andrea's sketches."

Elizabeth glowered. "'Specially since he made a point of leaving town without notice back in nineteen-oh-nine."

From the photo propped against the china creamer, Jessamine looked endlessly at nothing. "She was deeply in love with Kelvin," offered Kerry. "They found each other that summer. Both orphans looking for a sense of home, discovering in each other the missing pieces to their lives."

At the sympathetic silence Kerry glanced up. "I know I'm too involved in this thing. But Jessamine was here." She gestured toward the built-in sideboard visible in the dining room. "She polished that mirror, and dusted the furniture and scrubbed these floors. She hid her diary in the attic. It hurts that Kelvin betrayed her. Jessamine believed he was a good man. It really bothers me that she was wrong."

"Do you think it's just a coincidence," Dolores asked, "finding the pictures like we did?"

Noreen shook her head. "I don't believe in

coincidences."

Neal raised a brow. "What do you mean?"

"You've heard of synchronicity, haven't you?" Noreen slowly whirled her reading glasses by one earpiece. "Jung's concept of significance in apparently unrelated events. We have a diary, hidden in it a photograph of a key person written about in it. The same day, a photograph of the diary's author 'falls from the sky.'" She smiled. "Impressive, don't you think?"

"I don't see it." Neal shifted his weight uncomfortably. "The diary was found in the house where the woman lived. Where else would it be? She hid the photograph of her lover in it. Sounds straightforward to me."

Elizabeth stirred cream into her coffee. "One connection, two connections—okay, call it coincidence. But we've got a string of 'em, all having to do with the same people."

An uneasy expression crossed Kerry's face. "That's no reason to jump to a paranormal conclusion."

Elizabeth made an impatient sound. "We've got the diary, the pictures, the sundial. We just happened to find Jessamine' headstone yesterday. Oh, and by the way, we've already gotten to know this guy in the picture 'cause Andrea's been churning out sketches of him. What's paranormal about all that?"

Andrea frowned in bewilderment. "*Why* are we suddenly finding out these details about this small group of people?"

Aura Lee had been folding and refolding her napkin as the others talked. Under lavender eye shadow, her eyes were shrewd. "You're the catalyst, Andrea. Something about you has sparked odd events ever since you arrived."

Kerry snorted. "You're imagining a causal

relationship purely on the basis of those sketches. What about Neal? Andrea said he changed into Kelvin." Across the table Neal choked on his coffee. "Is synchronicity behind that, too?"

Neal was scrubbing at the coffee on his shirt with a napkin. "What in the hell are you talking about?"

Noreen patted his arm in comfort. "That evening you followed Andrea up to the Amphitheater, apparently she saw you change…" She stopped.

Neal's gaze veered to Andrea. "What?" When she remained silent, he looked back at Noreen. "Changed how?"

Noreen looked at Rose in appeal.

Rose let out a breath. "Andrea said your appearance, uh, altered."

"Oh, for God's sake! She said you turned into this guy Kelvin," Elizabeth said bluntly.

"You think I *mutated* into this guy you sketched?" For the first time that day Neal had some color in his face. His stunned gaze fixed on Andrea. "Was *that* why you ran away?"

Her face flamed. "What could I say?"

"Honey, you aren't the man I thought you were?" Elizabeth cracked, surprising a giggle from Dolores.

Rose relaxed into a grin. "Neal, who's that guy I saw you turn into last night?"

Even Kerry got into the spirit. "That was no guy, I was possessed."

Neal stared at them, disillusioned. "So glad I can provide some comic relief." He focused again on Andrea. "The strange thing is, I felt something weird that night. Yesterday when we were…" His cheeks reddened. "I told you later I thought I came on too strong. I felt that same way…did it happen again?" When Andrea didn't answer right away, he persisted. "I've been tied up in knots since you got here. Now

I've been taken over, or some damn thing. When were you going to tell me?"

Andrea studied the weave of the place mat in front of her. "We've known each other for what? Four days? I hoped to figure it out before we talked." The wariness in his face dissolved her embarrassment. "It's more likely that *you* didn't change at all. I perceived a change. I'm probably certifiable."

Noreen nodded, her elfin face solemn. "She was very concerned about your reaction, Neal. I think that's been bothering her almost as much as the fear of having a breakdown."

Andrea closed her eyes in mortification.

"Hey, don't worry about it." Neal leaned in for a kiss, holding it for a long moment. He pulled away, a smile in his eyes. "What's a breakdown to a guy who isn't himself lately?"

Andrea felt her heart thundering. Before she could say anything, Elizabeth patted Neal's shoulder. "You romantic devil, you. How can she resist that?"

To her own surprise, Andrea laughed.

Noreen smiled. "This is all very nice, but something's going on here. I reiterate my theory: we have a ghost."

Aura Lee clapped her hands. "For once I'm not the only person to think it. I swear this is the perfect place for such a thing to happen."

Kerry forked her hands through her hair in frustration. *"Why* is it so perfect?"

"You know how on the map Colorado is shaped like a rectangle?" Aura Lee asked. "To me it looks like a car battery with two points serving as terminals. Colorado Springs is the negative, Boulder the positive. Think about it," she insisted in response to their groans. "In the Springs are headquarters for a bunch of conservative organizations, religious and political. In Boulder you have a lot of liberal groups and alternative religions, too. Colorado Springs the negative, Boulder the positive."

Neal's laughter lasted until he started coughing. "My God," he rasped finally, "if I weren't a wreck, Aura Lee, I'd waltz you around the room."

Aura Lee sent him a fond glance. "Boulder is a place of power. Strange things happen here all the time."

"So we have a string of coincidences in a very short period of time," Noreen said. "We have the sketches and the painting and the two times when Neal looked like this Kelvin fellow. What else?"

Neal cleared his throat. "It's probably nothing, but I keep smelling bay rum."

Dolores's dark brows wrinkled in a frown. "You saying somebody has a drinking problem?"

Elizabeth snorted. "It's a kind of aftershave, girl. Barbers used to put it on men after they shaved them, back in the good old days."

"My grandfather used it," Neal said. "I keep getting whiffs of it."

Noreen frowned thoughtfully. "I have no idea about that one."

"Something odd showed in my workroom," Rose offered reluctantly. "I found my latest fountain taken apart, and its pieces were…rearranged. " In answer to Neal's quizzical look, she added, "All of the stones and crystals were in a circle around the bowl. I hate to ask, but none of you went into the office, did you?"

"Of course not."

"No way."

Rose nodded.

"Rose, remember what I told you about closing the circle?" Aura Lee asked, troubled. "We didn't do that at the séance," she reminded the others.

"We took care of that yesterday during our little get-together," Andrea pointed out. "Right?"

"I'm not sure it worked." Aura Lee was abashed. "So many things are happening. And I still feel Cottie, like she's knocking at a door, trying to get through with a message from the Other Side."

Elizabeth nodded. "Maybe she's tryin' to tell us about these folks."

Kerry stared at the two photographs in front of her. "So we're left with a blithe spirit?"

"Not so blithe." Noreen frowned at the pictures. "What I don't know is how these spirits manifest themselves. Half the fun of traditional ghost stories lies in hoary old vapors and clanking chains. The things we have here are different. I grant you, Andrea's sketches can be compared to automatic writing. But I don't understand Andrea's seeing Neal alter to become Kelvin Haslett. And why at the Amphitheater?"

"A haunting is a haunting," said Aura Lee firmly. "If a house can be haunted, so can a rock formation."

Dolores nodded in agreement. "Believe me, the earth is alive, as alive as we are."

Kerry's green eyes narrowed. "Clay is dirt that sticks together. Just because you have the vision to shape something from it doesn't mean it's a living substance."

Dolores shook her head. "The things I make from clay don't exist until I shape them, yes? And the world the writer invents isn't there until it's written down. They're *ideas.* Scientists say an idea is a vapor caused by electricity and chemicals in the brain, a physical process resulting in a concept leading to a piece of art—a sculpture, a story. Every step of the way, the stuff used in those creations, the ideas, the words, the clay, all are alive."

"Words don't stand alone, don't have a life of their own. Nor does clay, or ideas—"

"Wanna bet?" Dolores inserted softly.

"It takes the human element," Kerry argued. "Characters lie on the page until someone reads the work. Your sculpture stands there until somebody sees it. Messages are sent from creator to recipient, Dolores. You need a person for the object to have meaning."

Dolores glanced down at her hands. "I've held damp clay and felt the pulse of life in it. Ask farmers— they'll tell you the same thing. Why couldn't rocks have been touched by what passed between Kelvin and Jessamine? Why shouldn't a remnant of the love they felt linger where they were together? If a receiver is needed to complete the circuit, you've got both Andrea and Neal in that role, both picking up those signals."

The room fell silent. When the library clock clanged distantly, Noreen chuckled. "I hate to add Einstein to this theoretical stew, but either we have time folding back on itself, our time bordering on past events, or each of us is living one of an infinite number of lives in an infinite number of dimensions. And for some reason, at least two dimensions are intersecting."

"What difference does it make?" Rose demanded. "I want to know what we can do about it. Andrea, you can't live in fear that every time you draw or paint, you'll pick up ghostly communication." Her gray eyes softened. "You can't have a normal relationship with Neal if you're waiting for him transform into Kelvin Haslett."

"This Kelvin Haslett…why hasn't he passed over to the other side?" Noreen asked. "What does he want?"

Elizabeth rested her chin on her folded hands. "My Auntie Olivia said ghosts try to complete their lives because they have no peace. Maybe we have to help him find peace."

"Oh, is that all?" Kerry clasped her hands around her cup.

"I've been thinking," Dolores ventured. "Someone could've done something to Kelvin. Like that Wheaton guy in the diary. He was after Jessamine, wasn't he?"

"Yeah, the big jerk." Kerry opened the diary. "Don't forget, Kelvin kicked his ass. Maybe he decided to get even."

"Could he have *killed* him?" Elizabeth's eyes narrowed. "What if Wheaton and his buddy Edward got together? Maybe they were both rotten enough to have murder in them."

Noreen rubbed her glasses with a tissue, her expression thoughtful. "How could we find out?"

Kerry turned the journal pages. "I could go back over old newspapers, see if Kelvin turned up later. I can try to find other source materials."

"We already have source materials," Rose pointed out. "Andrea's sketches and painting." She looked around the table. "Maybe we've been missing the obvious. In every one of those drawings, Kelvin's in worse trouble. What if the whole *point* of the sketches is to tell us what happened to him?"

CHAPTER 22

After breakfast they separated to each work on her angle of what Aura Lee was now calling the Wisdom Court Haunting. Kerry muttered to herself about nonsense as she went to her quarters.

Andrea had covered the uncompleted painting of Kelvin Haslett so she didn't have to look at it and set up sketching supplies on her drafting table. For two hours she'd tried to reproduce the landscape of the early drawings but had nothing but doodles to show for it.

A tapping came from the studio door. Andrea glanced as Rose came in. "How's it going?"

"I've got nothing." Andrea stood up and raised her arms overhead in a stretch. "It's hard to slip into a trance when you're not even sleepy. If Kelvin has any information to share, he's taking his own sweet time about it."

"Noreen and I were talking about taking a walk. We've both been surfing the web, but we're too wired to be effective."

"Tell me about it." Andrea pushed her hair back. "A walk might be nice. At least I'd get some blood flowing to my brain. Where are you going?"

"It's a choice between the Mall and Chautauqua. Since dogs aren't allowed on the Mall, I'd guess Chautauqua. Lots of smells."

"What the hell. Let me grab a backpack." She unearthed one in the cabinet and stuffed in her sketchpad and several pencils. "Maybe I'll find inspiration up there. None to be had here." She slipped her arms through the loops and settled the pack on her back. "Let's go."

Rose went ahead to get bottled water from the refrigerator. "Noreen and Strudel are in the yard." She followed Andrea out the door and pulled it shut. A sharp breeze had her buttoning her sweater. "Everybody's edgy, waiting for something to happen."

"That about sums it up." Andrea took a deep breath of the sharp air and looked around at the swaying trees. Everything was in motion, leaves fluttering, clouds streaming overhead.

Strudel bounded across the grass toward them, leash trailing behind her. Andrea bent to rub the dachshund's head. "Hi," she said to Noreen.

"Hello, dear." Noreen was in jeans and a hooded sweatshirt. Her shrewd eyes surveyed Andrea, then glanced in question at Rose. "Are we ready?"

"I guess so." Rose retrieved Strudel's leash and the dog pulled her toward the break in the hedge.

Andrea pressed through it, Noreen at her heels. Strudel pulled on the leash and, nose to the ground, eagerly searched for scents, dragging Rose behind her.

Noreen caught up to Andrea, her breath coming faster.

Andrea slowed her pace. "Did you find anything online about Jack Wheaton?"

Noreen shook her head. "Kerry's working on him. I

started hunting for Kelvin's boss, Dr. Tweedham."

"I hadn't even thought about him." Andrea brushed against a bush covered with tight pink buds, and a faint, sweet scent teased at her nostrils. Beside her Noreen's walking shoes crunched on the gravel road. "Find anything?"

"Yes." When Andrea turned to her in surprise, Noreen shook her head. "Nothing helpful so far, but what I'm looking for is memoirs, or journals. The man toured the Chautauqua circuit several times, and anybody worth his salt in those days kept a record of his travels. If we can find them, maybe we could uncover an entry about his dear assistant Kelvin Haslett leaving his position to become a lecturer at Podunk University."

"But then we wouldn't have any idea of what the sketches are about." A flicker squawked from the wind-ravaged blue spruce down the creek bank and flew behind a wild plum bush.

Strudel chased a chipmunk into a thicket, only her wagging tail visible. Rose smiled at them over her shoulder as they approached. "I'm glad we came out. I feel better already. How about you?"

Andrea shrugged. "Anything's better than sitting around waiting."

Rose nodded. "I don't know how you've been able to stay so calm with all that's happened."

"Don't get me wrong. I'm scared." Andrea's eyes narrowed against the sun cutting through thickening clouds. "I haven't been here even a week. If this stuff goes on much longer, I don't know what I'll do."

Strudel backed out of the thicket and shook herself, tags jingling. Tugging on the leash, she scrambled to the bridge over the creek. "I don't know what any of us will do," Rose said, striding behind. "We have to get some resolution or we'll all go crazy from the strain."

Andrea followed over the bridge, pausing as they reached the trail to the Amphitheater. It stair-stepped up the hillside where the trees were stirring in the rising breeze. It felt as if years had passed since she and Neal had come this way. "I think I'll go ahead, if you don't mind. I need some time to myself."

Strudel had followed her nose into the underbrush, and Rose tugged on the leash to keep her from going too far and getting stuck. "That's fine. We'll see you in a bit."

Andrea turned onto the trail. Her chestnut hair rose from her shoulders as another breeze slid down the slope and she dug in one pocket. As she went up the first series of steps, they saw her securing her hair with an elastic band.

"This situation has been quite illuminating," Noreen said quietly. Her own hair had been swept into hedgehog disorder by the fitful air. "Coming from the greenhouse atmosphere of a girls' school to what looks like an actual haunting has taught me more than I ever expected to know."

Rose watched as Andrea rounded a bend in the trail. "It's a leap, all right," she said, trying to decide whether the last few days had been more a learning experience or a nightmare. Strudel strained on the leash, and she started walking again.

Noreen fell into step beside her. "I suspect what's been set into motion has lingered here for a long time."

"And we've been unaware of it." Rose's voice was tight with frustration. "That's what throws me. Have we ignored earlier signs, or *is* it all because Andrea's here?" A dried leaf blew past her, carried on pine-scented air. She rubbed lightly at the cheek grazed by the leaf, trying to fight off a feeling of dread. "Let's go after her."

Noreen glanced at her curiously. "She said she wants to be by herself."

"So we'll go slowly." Rose shot a worried look up the path. "I don't think we ought to let her get too far away." Strudel took that moment to lunge toward a ground squirrel, barking wildly. "Besides, we're letting the dog choose the way, right?"

"When one's course is set by one's desire, blame becomes the instrument of mendacity. Charlotte Evans Clarkson, eighteen seventy-seven to nineteen thirty-one." Noreen followed as Rose pulled Strudel to the Amphitheater route.

"It's just this feeling I have." Rose stumbled on a rock and caught herself, kicking it to the side of the trail. Strudel trotted over to sniff at it. "I keep waiting for that damned other shoe to drop. It's driving me wild."

"It's because we're all wound so tight," Noreen said sympathetically.

Strudel had taken exception to the stone. She scratched madly with her front paws, trying to bury it. Noreen watched in amusement.

At a glimpse of color exposed by the dog's efforts, Rose bent to investigate. The faint green tint she'd seen was likely from a mineral, perhaps copper. Strudel barked fiercely as she scooped up the rock and dropped it into her pocket.

"For your fountains?" Noreen asked.

"Maybe. I'll decide later." The flash of sunlight on mica captured her attention. She dislodged another stone with the toe of her boot, and picked it up. A memory stirred. The image of Andrea's stowing her sketchpad in her backpack combined with the purposeful way she'd moved up the Amphitheater Trail. "She wouldn't try it alone, would she?"

Noreen glanced at her in confusion. "What did you say?"

"She was frustrated because she hadn't sketched anything, and she tucked her sketchpad into her pack. What if she's going where she drew Kelvin before because she thinks she'll be able to connect with him again?"

Noreen's worried gaze moved up the hillside. "I don't like that idea at all. It's one thing to be back at the house, but out here? She keeps drawing him in danger from falling rocks." Her eyes widened. "Do you think *this* could be the place where those things happened to him?"

Stricken, Rose stared at her. "We have to get to her before she can start sketching." She leaned down to pick up Strudel. "Come on."

The telephone woke Neal from a dream. Opening his eyes did little to take him from a bleak landscape of trees and shadows. Andrea's bedroom was dim, so little light at the windows he wondered if he'd slept away the whole afternoon. He groped on the nightstand for his watch. Three forty-eight. He held it to his ear and heard it ticking.

Getting out of bed took more energy than he wanted to admit. He pushed aside the curtains and saw a storm building over the edge of the mountains, clouds stacking like smoke from a fire. Neal wondered if Denny had secured tarps over the lumber behind the house. If not, they'd just have to deal with wet wood. He wasn't going outside to check on it.

Neal had stretched out again on the bed when someone knocked on the door. "Yeah, come on in."

Aura Lee burst through the door, Elizabeth right behind her. "Neal, Rose just called on her cell phone. She kept breaking up, but what I got was Andrea's in some kind of trouble. I know you're sick, but we need your opinion."

"Rose and Noreen took Strudel for a walk," Elizabeth inserted quickly. "Evidently Andrea went with them."

Neal's stomach rolled. "Where were they headed?"

"She said 'trail', but I couldn't understand the rest." Aura Lee shook her fist at the ceiling. "By the Goddess, I hate cell phones! Just when you need them to—"

"I thought I heard your dulcet tones." Kerry peered around the edge of the door and came into the room. "I've been looking for you," she told Elizabeth. Her glance measured the tension in their faces. "What's up?"

"Rose called but the connection was sketchy. Apparently something's going on with Andrea." Elizabeth crossed the room to peer out the window. "The sky's getting darker."

"Dammit, after the other day, you'd think people would have enough sense to stay here when bad weather's rolling in." Neal pushed himself off the bed.

"Did you try to call Rose back?" Kerry looked on, worried, as Neal pulled on his shoes.

"I got a 'no service' message." Aura Lee wrung her hands. "I don't know whether to call Mountain Rescue, or where to send them if I do. What do you think?"

Neal told himself that they were probably on their way back now. Why didn't he believe it?

"Neal." Aura Lee murmured in concern as he tied the laces and got to his feet. "What do you think you're doing?"

He nodded toward the south window. "Look outside. If they aren't already coming up the sidewalk, they're going to get caught in the middle of something. I don't like the look of it at all."

"But you've been sick, you're barely recovered. What can you do except get wet?"

Neal straightened, ignoring his lightheadedness. "Someone needs to make sure they're okay."

"I could go." Elizabeth frowned at him. "I'll go look for them."

She didn't know the area. Neal remembered his father talking about the gully washers that came over Green Mountain in the 'thirties, of the damage done. Of the people who died. It didn't help to recall the earlier storm Andrea was caught in.

Elizabeth came up beside him. "I got two words for you: Hurricane Katrina. You know we're tough in N'Orleans. I can just hustle myself up that hill and get those women down here lickety-split."

"I can go with her," Kerry offered.

He didn't waver more than a moment. "No. You can come with me if you want, but I have to go. It's these damned hero genes. You can't escape 'em."

Kerry groaned.

"Oh, like you would." Elizabeth punched his arm. "Let's see if our friends have enough sense to get out of the rain."

Outside the air was heavy but chilling fast, humidity thickening. The tops of the trees were still. The sudden absence of even a slight breeze had warnings skittering down Neal's spine. He ignored the wave of fatigue threatening him.

Elizabeth was pulling up the zipper of her jacket. "The air's weighty, isn't it?" Beside her, Kerry fastened the snaps down the front of her sweater.

"Yeah." Neal lengthened his stride across the grass of the backyard. "With any luck we'll find them before it hits."

From behind them came a shout. Aura Lee shot out

the back door, her shiny yellow rain poncho flapping around her like wings. "Wait for me!"

Neal stopped short. As she approached, he growled, "What're you doing, Aura Lee? I told you it's probably going to cut loose up there."

Aura Lee put her hands on her hips. "I'm coming. Live with it."

"All right." Neal pushed through the hedge and started across Baseline Road. When Elizabeth put her hand on his arm, he frowned down at her.

"Dolores is behind us," she said. "Hold up a minute."

"What is this, a freaking field trip?" Neal barely kept impatience under control as they waited for Dolores. She was panting when she caught up with them.

"Thanks." She fought to catch her breath. "What are we doing and where are we going?" she asked Elizabeth.

"We're the cavalry, honey, and we're fixing to save our comrades in arms."

CHAPTER 23

Hikers scurried down the trails, some at breakneck speeds. Cars headed out of the parking area at the base of Gregory Canyon as dark clouds piled overhead.

A gust blew back the hood on Aura Lee's poncho and she groped behind her head for it, finally turning her back to the wind to pull it over her hair. "Where are we going?" she shouted at Neal over the flapping of her cape.

"Don't know." Neal leaned against a boulder. The shrubs at its base shuddered in the turbulent air. His breathing was labored, his face gray. It was a few minutes before he moved toward the bridge across the creek.

Elizabeth had witnessed his struggle up the hill from Wisdom Court with growing dismay. "I know better than to tell him to go back," she said to Dolores between breaths. "He's just like my Lovell, always thinking he's the only one who can get something done right."

Ahead of them Neal crossed the bridge, then stopped yet again. His cough was deep. "*Dios,*" exclaimed Dolores. Her long black hair swirled about her anxious face. With a muttered oath, she tied it in a knot at the back of her neck. "He sounds awful." She trotted up to him. "*Jito*, you're gonna get pneumonia out of this little trip."

"Nah." Head bent, Neal fought for breath. "Just a little under the weather…that's all."

Kerry caught up in time to hear him. "You're going to be little under the ground, the way you're going." She peered at the lowering sky, hunching her shoulders. "This is crazy. Where the hell are we going?"

"We'll find her. We have to." His face was composed but his hands trembled, causing him to fumble with the top buttons of his coat as he tightened the collar for warmth.

With no warning lightning flashed overhead, throwing the dark rocks into sudden brilliant relief. The air around them boomed.

"Oh, shit, shit." Elizabeth hunkered down in her jacket. Her heart was racing and panic nibbled at her control. "I hate lightning. Hate it, hate it." She walked quickly, her eyes fixed on the path, and plowed into Kerry, who had stopped dead.

Kerry stared toward a group of pines at the turnoff to the Amphitheater trail. Their branches churned in the rising wind.

Elizabeth followed her gaze and saw nothing to explain her rigid stance. "What is it?" Ahead of them Neal had reached the fork in the trail from the bridge and was turning east onto the Bluebell-Baird path.

Kerry turned toward Elizabeth, auburn bob blowing around her ashen face. "You don't see it?"

Elizabeth searched for something beyond the trees, rocks and mountainside undergrowth. "See what?"

Suddenly Kerry scrambled after Neal. She grabbed his arm and pulled him to a halt. "The Amphitheater!"

she shouted. "We need to go up to the Amphitheater."

Head lowered against the wind, Neal just looked at her, and then retraced his steps to the Amphitheater trailhead.

He'd trudged halfway up the dogleg when Elizabeth caught up to Kerry. "What's the deal?" she yelled. Her words were nearly swallowed in thunder rumbling down the mountain. "Why go this way?"

Kerry leaned against the wind, plodding over the rocky ground. "The scarf on the tree."

"What?" When Kerry didn't answer, but just kept going up the trail, Elizabeth decided to wait until later to find out what she meant. The whole insane trek up the mountain was an act of faith.

Aura Lee stumbled within hailing distance behind Elizabeth as they struggled over the rugged terrain. "Do you think they're all right? Don't you think they'd find cover?"

"They damn well better." Elizabeth pushed against the gusts and forced herself to lengthen her stride. "Come on," she called back to Aura Lee, "they're getting too far ahead of us."

They were across the bridge over the talus before they caught up with Dolores. She'd stopped at the base of another stairway of boulders and was pointing up the hill. "I think I see Rose. Look up there!"

"Where?" Elizabeth stepped up to Dolores's side. Following the direction of her arm, she saw the figure of a woman. Then she slipped out of sight. "Maybe it's Rose. Did you see anybody else?"

"No." Dolores lifted worried eyes to the trail ahead where Neal was making slow headway. A fine, hard mist had begun to fall. Already her face was damp with it. At their feet, the rocks took on a shine. "Man, this'll kill Neal if he lives long enough to get back to the house." She wiped at the moisture across her forehead.

Elizabeth shivered, pulling her jacket closer. "Let's just find those idiots and get everybody out of here." She cursed the slick soles of her shoes as she slid on the wet rocks.

Aura Lee pushed on past them to Kerry's side, precarious on the pebble-strewn surface. "Maybe they've found something up there."

Kerry's green eyes met Aura Lee's grimly. "What? A death wish?" She put her head down and slogged through the puddles.

The rain was coming down in force now and Elizabeth was finding it increasingly difficult to see anything. Neal had moved out of sight. Lightning cracked, and she shrieked as one foot slipped out from under her.

Dolores caught her by one arm and kept her from falling. "Easy! Let's try to get to Neal. He's fifty yards or so ahead of us." Thunder jolted the air. She surveyed the boulders nearby them. "We've got to get out of this before we're hit by lightning."

Aura Lee had a fierce grip on Kerry's shoulder. "Elizabeth! Let's make a run for the rocks over there while we still can." She motioned toward the huge sandstone formation above them.

Kerry scrubbed at the rain coursing down her face. "Are you crazy? We'll fall and break our necks."

"It's either that or the lightning," Elizabeth shouted. "Let's go."

Bunched together they struggled up the broken trail. As they reached the side path to the Amphitheater itself, the sky flared again with lightning. Terrified by the odor of ozone in her nostrils, Elizabeth scrambled toward the shelter of the big rocks forming the front walls. She tripped and fell headlong, unable to catch herself with her hands. Her palms slid over gravel, stinging at the contact.

"Elizabeth!" Aura Lee fell to her knees beside her. "Are you okay?" She lifted her face toward the sky in fury and yelled, "Goddess protect us! Shield us from the thunderbolt!" Roughly she grabbed Elizabeth by the shoulders. Dolores gripped Elizabeth's hand and they tugged her to her feet. They staggered to the base of the rocks, seeking cover.

Behind them Kerry shouted, "I think I see them." She waved at the slope to the rocks forming the rear embankment of the Amphitheater.

Abruptly Dolores dropped Elizabeth's hand and fell back against the stone at their backs. She gaped at the projecting rock above them. "There they are!"

Neal grabbed hold of Andrea's hand, pulling her toward a fissure in the sandstone rising above them. In the erratic light shadows danced around them, quickened by the near-constant lightning. Gasping for breath, he forced her ahead of him across shingle made treacherous by increasing rain. The sky flashed overhead and before he could shove her into shelter, a silhouette lurched toward them, enveloping Andrea in shadow.

Sick with cold, Neal stumbled back, his hand still clutching Andrea's, and she was forced to move with him, away from the shade engulfing her. Unbelieving, Neal watched the foggy darkness twist toward them, slowly taking on substance in the downpour. Shining rain was creating the outline of a man.

Neal backed away, eyes riveted on the growing figure. Like a funnel-cloud it moved toward them, a head forming above hulking shoulders, and stubs at the sides lengthening into arms. He heard harsh, panting breaths and realized they were his own. Beside him Andrea was making high-pitched sounds that were swallowed in the crashing thunder surrounding them.

The skies opened. Sheets of water ran off boulders and the sloping hillside almost immediately. The shape was silvery now, but for cold dark eyes staring at them with malevolence. Legs had developed from the lower murk, and the first, halting steps brought the apparition yet closer.

Neal jerked Andrea backward, not daring to take his gaze from what was stalking them. Now hands were at the ends of the arms, clenched fists swinging at each side as it followed them.

Beside him Andrea stumbled, falling to her knees, and Neal dragged her to her feet. He swung her around and half-carried her to the path. As they reached the trailhead, he felt a sudden thrust at his back, sending him headlong onto the wet, rough surface, forcing Andrea's hand from his. Before he could push himself to his feet, water gushing from the hillside hit at knee level, rolling him over, carrying him down the trail. He heard a scream.

Elizabeth grabbed Aura Lee and Dolores clutched Kerry by the arm. Together they dragged each other toward higher ground at the edge of the sandstone mass and took shelter under a rocky overhang. From their vantage point Elizabeth stared up at the mountain. In the flashing light she saw three figures in front of the soaring rocks. She drew the sleeve of her jacket across her eyes. "Is that Rose or Noreen with them?"

Dolores shook her head. "They're over there." She pointed to the bank near a thicket of bushes and saplings. They could hear Strudel's muffled barking.

Fissures in the jagged rocks behind Andrea and Neal looked alive in the shadows cast by lightning.

The two of them backed away from a third person—Elizabeth couldn't tell who it was—and then Neal swung Andrea around and pulled her with him. The other figure almost fell toward them and Neal lurched to the ground. "What the hell." Yet another shape swayed unsteadily after the other. "Who is *that*?"

"What's going on?" Aura Lee had sunk to the dirt and was clutching her knees to her chest, shivering with cold. "Why aren't they coming down?"

"Madre de Dios!" Dolores jumped to her feet. The rainwater flowing off the rugged confines of the Amphitheater had filled the nooks and hollows in the walls. Now it spilled from hidden places, streaming across the ground, eddying around boulders. Rivulets ran together toward the natural channel formed by the trail, gaining power as they united. Bits of earth broke away and were carried off in the current.

Through the deluge they saw Andrea catch hold of a rock and pull herself up above the water streaming down the hill.

"Where's Neal?" Elizabeth forced her way through the water flowing over her shoes. "I can't see him," she called back to the others. "We have to get up there. Hurry!"

The four of them battled across the roiling water toward the place they'd last seen Neal. As they neared the mouth of the Amphitheater, Elizabeth heard a volley of barking. Rose and Noreen were struggling toward them through mud and water. Noreen had zipped Strudel into her sweatshirt against her chest. The little dog's drenched head poked out from under her chin.

A flurry of dirt and mud scattered past Elizabeth, and she turned to see Andrea sliding down a bluff. She landed on her knees and scrambled to her feet almost immediately, running to them. Her face was bone white, eyes burning with terror. "We've got to get to Neal," she shouted. "The water forced him down the trail."

Lightning sizzled overhead, thunder roaring instantly, swallowing Aura Lee's shriek.

"Sweet Jesus, protect us." Elizabeth forced herself forward. "Let's go."

Slipping, grasping at rocks and bushes, the women fought to stay on their feet as they slid down the trail.

Aura Lee tugged at Kerry's arm. "Look! There he is." She pointed to the bend in the track. Neal was clutching a boulder but water splashed and pushed against him. His legs were shifting over the edge, his hands slipping along the surface of the rock. In a flash of lightning the large stone looked like a living thing locked in battle with him as he fought to maintain his grip.

Elizabeth peered through the downpour, saw Neal slide further down the face of the rock. For one mad instant, she thought the stone tried to fling him off. "Grab him," she yelled. Dolores lunged for Neal's arm just as Aura Lee fell on her, anchoring her by one leg. Kerry came down beside Dolores and seized her other ankle.

"Help me." Dolores had barely said the words when Andrea fell at her side, immediately grasping Neal's arm. Beside her Rose knelt along the edge of the trail. Heedful of the water spilling along the rim, she leaned forward, reaching for Neal's leg with one hand. Elizabeth scurried toward her.

"Watch out!" Noreen's cry halted Elizabeth in mid-step. "The bank is falling away."

"Okay, okay," muttered Elizabeth. Agonized at her helplessness, she watched the others strain to pull Neal up. Lightning cracked again and shadows darted toward Neal and the women clutching him. Flat on the ground, hands fixed around Dolores's leg, Aura Lee chanted prayers.

The women tightened their grips and braced themselves. "Okay—now!" They heaved Neal back onto the trail, Andrea and Dolores falling backwards, Rose sprawling beside them. Neal lay motionless.

In that instant lightning struck the boulder where Neal had dangled moments before. The boom of thunder was deafening. Pain bit at Elizabeth's cheek and she fell to the ground.

Andrea felt hands moving over her body. She couldn't hear for the ringing in her ears. When she opened her eyes, it was to the sight of Aura Lee kneeling at her side. The older woman's face was covered in mud and her eyes were dazed.

After a while, Andrea could hear her ask, "…you all right?"

Andrea took a deep breath and her chest hurt as it filled with cold air. "I'm alive." Her voice cracked and she fell silent. In a rush, the events of the day spilled back into her mind. A pit opened in her stomach. "Neal?" She pulled her fingers from Aura Lee's patting hand and scrambled to her knees, muscles protesting. She scanned the trail anxiously.

Kerry knelt on the ground, forehead against her knees. Beside her Noreen waited as Rose tried to tie a handkerchief around her right hand. Mud streaked Rose's forehead, and she moved at the edge of exhaustion. Braced against an embankment, Elizabeth, her tiny braids dripping water down her face, stared at the shattered boulder at the edge of the trail, her breathing broken by meager sobs. Dolores huddled beside her, trying to rub warmth into her hands. Neal lay at their feet on the path.

Andrea crawled to him, barely registering the

bruising gravel under her knees. "Did lightning hit him?" She groped for his hand.

"I don't think so." Elizabeth released a shaky breath. "I guess none of us were hit."

"Only cuts and bruises so far." Rose knelt beside Andrea and bent over Neal. "Neal?"

He opened one eye and then closed it against the sporadic rain. The scrape on his forehead was garish against his pallid skin. "Bay rum," he rasped. "Almost choked me."

"What?" Andrea laid her head on his chest, ignoring the rivulets trickling around them. She heard the steady beat of his heart and exhaled in relief. He began to cough.

"We have to get him out of this rain. Neal," Rose said more loudly. "Can you stand up?"

"Yeah." Another cough rumbled from his chest. "Let's go home."

Aura Lee bustled nearer. "Should we put my poncho on him?" She flinched at the lightning flash down the hill.

Kerry stood up slowly. "What difference would it make? We're all soaked." Thunder grumbled along the mountainside.

"Think you can make it down?" Rose asked. One by one they nodded, and she returned her attention to Neal. She touched his shoulder. "Can you walk?"

"Sure. Let's go." He had little strength of his own, but with their help he struggled to his feet. Swaying, he looked up the trail, memory seeping back into his eyes.

Elizabeth shuddered. "Let's get the hell out of here."

Andrea braced her shoulder under Neal's right arm and Rose did the same on his left side. They steadied him as they started down the trail. The storm was dwindling into fitful showers and distant thunder. Rocks shifted against each other as they tramped down the washed out trail.

Aura Lee came to an abrupt stop. "By the Goddess!"

Elizabeth bumped into her, nearly knocking her down. "What's the matter?"

"The other one," exclaimed Aura Lee. "The person up there with them."

Elizabeth stared at her numbly. "You saw somebody else, too?"

Dolores surveyed the hillside behind them. "I saw two more, but there's nobody there now."

Andrea pulled at Neal, urging him forward. They had to get off the mountain and her strength was ebbing fast. "Come on, let's *go.*"

Neal mumbled something and coughed. Andrea tightened her hold around his waist and tugged, propelling Rose forward at his other side.

Kerry frowned at Elizabeth and then stepped in front of Andrea, forcing her to stop. "If there's somebody else up there, we've got to—"

"Kerry let it go." Andrea looked into Kerry's bewildered face. "I swear there's nobody else to worry about. Come on." Kerry bit back a retort and followed them down the hill.

CHAPTER 24

Noreen helped Andrea steady her glass. Her teeth knocked against the rim, and it was all she could do to swallow a bit of the brandy. Liquid heat shot down her throat into her chest, making her cough, but the shivering lessened.

"All of it." Noreen tilted the glass again and Andrea emptied it.

"What happened up there?" Kerry reached for the bottle on the coffee table and refilled her own glass.

"That's what we need to figure out." Rose came into the living room slowly, and despite the thick wrap around her shoulders, she was visibly shivering.

Neal eased around her, heading for the sofa. His face was haggard, the scrape on his forehead as vivid as neon. Strudel trailed behind him, and when he sat down next to Andrea, the dog jumped onto the cushion to lie beside him.

"Whatever it was, I don't want to be there if it happens again." Elizabeth's chair was beside the fireplace where flames licked at thick logs. Cocooning in a plaid throw, she tucked her feet under her. "I don't think I'll ever get warm again."

Noreen poured more of the amber liquid. "Here, get this down. We're all suffering from shock."

"Yeah." Kerry's shoulders were hunched, her face colorless. "Shock is what I felt when I saw—whatever it was."

"God, those moving shadows," Elizabeth murmured. "That's what they looked like to me, anyway."

"Spirits in the stone." Aura Lee bore the tea tray to the table and set it down as gently as she could.

"Don't say that." In spite of a hot shower and dry clothes, Dolores looked small and pale. "With the lightning and the rain, who knows what tricks of vision there were up there?"

"Wait a minute," Noreen said. "We need to write down what each of us saw, and we can compare notes. We'll contaminate our recollections if we—"

"There's no way to be scientific about this." Kerry's voice broke in the middle. "I think I saw a *shadow* attack Neal. I can't just write stuff down when I feel like I'm losing my fucking mind!"

"Hey, it's okay." Rose sat and put her arms around her. "Breathe in and out, hold it…come on and breathe with me." Rose's voice was calm and comforting, and soon Kerry settled into the rhythm, gaining control over tiny bubbling sobs.

Rose checked the others and saw they all were matching the cadence of her breath. She gave Kerry a quick hug, then patted her back and reached for her brandy, taking a healthy swallow. "I'm as scared as everybody else but what'll make me feel better is to focus on facts. Noreen, I think we can avoid overlapping our perceptions and conclusions, don't you?"

Noreen's wise old eyes surveyed the group. "We're all observant and I agree—we've been through too much for pens and notepads. We can do it."

"Who wants to go first?" quavered Aura Lee.

Elizabeth shook her head. "Somebody else."

Neal set his glass on the coffee table. "You have to promise not to commit me, okay?"

Rose smiled wryly. "I think we'll all ask for that deal."

"The rain was coming down like—" Neal looked up. "Well, you know what it was like. Andrea and I were already drenched and we could hardly hear each other for the thunder. We were heading for cover when I saw something on those big sandstone rocks." He leaned forward for his glass. "A little more?"

Kerry slid the bottle toward him and he poured a generous measure. "All hell was breaking loose, but I could see a dark shape moving along beside us...on the rock."

"There were two," Andrea whispered.

Neal looked at her. "Seriously?" At her nod, he took a swallow of brandy. "I thought it was a shadow, but when I looked around for something casting it, there wasn't anything."

"You were wet, there was water in your eyes," Noreen pointed out. "You couldn't be expected to see much even if there was something there."

"Except I saw the shape." Neal took another swallow and shuddered. "It kept pace with us. When we got to the end of those vertical rocks, it—God—it *pulled* itself off the stone. And stood there."

"*Madre de dios.*" Dolores pulled the blanket tightly about her ears.

Noreen cleared her throat. "What did the shape look like then? Was it three-dimensional?"

Neal shook his head. "I guess, like a cloud, or a dust-devil, you know? The rain gave it a silvery outline."

"It took on a shape," Andrea added in a shaky voice. "It went from flat to thicker, like smoke, and then it started—it started growing arms."

"Jesus." Kerry shrank into the chair back, her hands clutching her shoulders.

Rose patted her shoulder with a trembling hand. "Could you recognize the figure?"

Neal shot her a look. "I wasn't making comparisons right about then."

"How about you?" Rose asked Andrea. "Any clues to give us some direction?"

Andrea deliberated. "It made me think of Kelvin," she said finally.

"Why?"

She frowned. "I'm not sure. An impression of dark clothes? It reminded me of his dark suit coat in the sketches."

Aura Lee leaned forward. "I don't understand. You've been helping Kelvin, *translating* him. Why would he want to hurt you or Neal?" She looked at the others for support.

"Help him or not, it looked like that shape *pushed* Neal," Elizabeth pointed out. "Now I know there's all kinds of questions you got to ask. If this thing was a ghost, could it have any control over its—what d'you call it—shape, shade, whatever?"

"Ectoplasm," muttered Noreen. "Equally, could it manage its feelings? Remember, Andrea's sketches are of a young man in danger. We don't know what happened to him, if it is indeed Kelvin. If he was caught up in violence, then one could postulate that he died in extreme agitation."

"And was remembered in the rocks," Kerry murmured. She looked at them. "In Jessamine's diary, what he said after she and Kelvin made love up there. Their happiness was so great they would be remembered in the rocks."

A small, muffled sob came from Dolores's blanketed form. She tugged its folds apart, showing her woebegone face. "What if he's been there ever since, waiting for something? Waiting for Jessamine."

Rose's eyes widened. "What if he confused Andrea with Jessamine, and took Neal for a rival?"

Strudel jumped off the sofa and barked once, sharply. She trotted out the door and into the kitchen.

"Maybe we scared her." Elizabeth's smile was sickly.

"We're scaring me." Rose rubbed her head distractedly. "I don't know how we're ever going to sort this out. We can speculate 'til we're ghosts ourselves, but we don't really *know* anything. And I, for one, am not going back up the mountain to ask anybody questions."

Noreen let out a long breath. "I'm with you there. But I have another question." Her gaze went to Neal and Andrea. "Who was the second shape?"

"If one was Jessamine—I mean—if they somehow reunited after Jessamine died, why would they be messing with Neal and Andrea?" Elizabeth scooted closer to the fire. "Wouldn't they be happy together?"

Strudel dragged a sopping coat into the room.

"Strudel!" Rose hurried to her and knelt to pick up her jacket. She looked down at the little dog in puzzlement. "Why in the world would she want this?"

The dachshund barked again, jumping up to catch the bottom edge of the jacket in her mouth. Growling, she pulled it out of Rose's grasp and, tightening her hold, shook the coat as if it were prey. Several items rattled onto the wood floor near the fireplace.

"What the hell?" Kerry knelt to pick up the bits dislodged from the jacket pockets. "A stone, a stick. Yuck, old tissue. More pebbles." Kerry opened her hand, pouring everything into the lazy Susan at the center of the coffee table.

Strudel barked again and leapt onto the low table. She stuck her snout into the bowl and pulled out something small. Jumping down, she carried it to the sofa and resumed her place beside Neal. There she started licking her prize.

"What's that?" Rose tried to get what looked like a small rock, but the dog growled and pulled it to her. "No, Strudel. Leave it. *Leave* it." She scrabbled for the pebble, finally getting it away.

"What is it?" Kerry asked.

"I don't know." Rose picked at it with one fingernail, and dirt flaked off.

"Is that green?" Noreen bent closer. "Rose, didn't you get this up on the trail?"

"Strudel kept digging." Rose rubbed her finger over the rock. "I grabbed it because she wouldn't leave it alone." She scratched away more dirt with her nail, and a larger piece broke off, leaving a rough circular shape. When she scuffed the surface again, a triangular section unfolded and remained upright as several more fragments fell away.

Kerry breathed in sharply, leaning to look at it more closely. "A gnomon. It's a sundial. Could it be—"

"It's got to be Kelvin's watch fob," Elizabeth whispered. "Where did you find it?"

"On the trail to the Amphitheater." Noreen's eyes snapped with excitement. "At the base of the scree, where that walkway goes across."

Dolores crossed herself, lips moving.

"*Can* you think finding that was a coincidence?" Aura Lee almost vibrated with intensity. "We were led, step by step, up that mountain."

Elizabeth's face lit up. "The scarf! Kerry said she saw it on a branch. Didn't you, girl? Tell them."

Kerry shook her head. "I'm still not sure about that."

"Oh, come on!" Elizabeth turned away from her. "We were scramblin' up that mountain, and Neal had us going one way. All of sudden Kerry, here, stopped dead in her tracks and chased after him, telling him we had to go up to the Amphitheater." She glared at Kerry. "And if we hadn't, I don't want to know what would've happened."

"All right! It was the scarf in Jessamine's box." Kerry closed her eyes. "I saw it, there all of a sudden on a branch, and the tree was at the trailhead. I didn't stop to think about it. What if I'd been wrong?" she demanded of Elizabeth. "Did you ever think of that?"

"Woulda, coulda, shoulda." Neal started to cough. When he was able to stop, he reached for Kerry's hand. "Whatever it was that made you do it, I'm grateful it went down that way, okay?"

"Wait." Dolores leaned toward Kerry. "Did you look in the box? Jessamine's box," she added when Kerry frowned at her. "Is the scarf there now?"

"Holy shit." Kerry bolted out of the room. Returning a few minutes later, she carried the faded candy box. "Let's take a look." She pulled open the lid and let out a sigh as she saw the black net material banded in blue.

Aura Lee frowned as Kerry reached for it. "But what could you have seen—"

"Oh." Kerry's eyes widened with shock. "My God." She let the scarf fall to the coffee table.

"What is it?" Dolores demanded. "You're scaring the hell out of me." Her fingertips touched the scarf and every drop of color drained out of her cheeks. "*Dios!*"

Noreen snatched it up. "It's wet."

Rose brushed a finger along the blue sateen edging

the black net. The moisture against her skin was unmistakable. She looked up from the scarf into Noreen's face. Instead of fear, she saw excitement, and felt a bit of her own. "This is incredible."

Noreen grinned. "To say the least." She turned to Neal. "All right, you said you saw this form take shape, and you, Andrea, saw arms. Was there anything else you noticed? Was it only the dark clothing that made you think of Kelvin?"

Andrea frowned, trying to remember. "It was so wild up there, the wind and rain, the lightning—wait." She made herself think about the slowly moving form that had taken shape before her eyes. Blacks and grays, that impression of a coat, but hadn't there been something lighter, something that glimmered? "A ring! It was right where his hand would have been, at the end of the arm thingies." She looked to Neal. "Did you see it? Silver, it could have been, it reflected the lightning."

Neal was shaking his head. "I don't remember, just the shape, and trying to get you out of its reach." He reached clumsily for his glass. "That's what scared me the most."

Kerry held her head between her hands. Like the rest of them, she was sagging with fatigue. "What kind of a ring? Jeweled? Engraved?" A short, hard laugh broke from her throat. "I'm asking about a ghost's jewelry."

"Wait a minute." Noreen pushed herself off the chair and trotted toward the library. "I need to find that picture." When she returned, it was with the stack of papers and photos they'd compiled in their research. "It was right here." After a few moments of riffling, she held up the picture Andrea had found in her studio.

Jessamine looked at them with haunted eyes as

Stanley Thornton smiled, his hand on her shoulder, the snarling lion-head on his finger.

Andrea leaned forward to take the photo from her. "I don't recall the lion. Maybe." Her gaze lifted to Noreen. "You know how crazy that storm was. And I was so scared…what I saw could've been wearing a jeweled tiara for all I know."

"But why would Stanley be up there?" Rose frowned over Andrea's shoulder at the print. "Jessamine I can understand, and Kelvin, too. Why Stanley?"

"Unless," Elizabeth said, "he had something to do with whatever happened to Kelvin." She slipped the photo from Andrea's hand. "Look at those eyes. He's real happy, and it doesn't take a genius to see why." She glanced up at them. "He got the girl."

With a loud crack, the lights went out.

"Now what?" In the glow from the fireplace, Rose stepped over Elizabeth, still on the floor by the hearth, and went to the switch plate beside the door. She flipped the switch up and down and surveyed the group as the three lamps went on. "We're all still alive. That's something."

"You're getting paranoid, Rose," Kerry said in a shaky voice.

"No kidding. I'm also working my way to a heart attack thanks to all the melodrama around here."

From her place on the sofa, Strudel whined, backing up into the blanket Andrea had tucked around her. "Hey, baby, what's the matter?" The dog's eyes were fixed on a spot hear the drapes over the windows across the room. The frantic moan grew louder and Andrea tried to pick her up, but Strudel growled, showing her teeth.

Aura Lee let out a whimper.

"What?" Dolores said in alarm. "What's going on?"

Aura Lee lifted a shaky hand, pointing to the window. What looked like mist was pulsating, pulling slowly together, thickening.

"Jesus." Neal grabbed Andrea's hand, yanking her closer to him. "Let's get out of here."

"Is that—is that—what is that?" Elizabeth struggled to free herself from the blanket.

Noreen eased off the chair and backed toward the door. "Rose, get away from that wall."

"Wait." Rose's command halted all of them. "Wait a minute. Let's see if we can c-com-communicate—" her voice shook pitifully. The color drained from her face.

Kerry took a step toward her and stopped short, pressing against an invisible force. She strained against it and moved forward enough to grab Rose by the hand, and then Noreen, tugging both out of the room. Behind her Neal dragged Andrea and Elizabeth. Kerry had just turned to go back when Aura Lee and Dolores fell through the doorway into the kitchen. A humming sound was growing louder, straining against their ears.

Neal growled, "Get out of the house."

Together, leaning on one another, they stumbled through the kitchen to the back door and down the steps to the yard.

"Oh, my God, oh my God, that was a ghost, wasn't it?" Dolores babbled, still clutching Noreen's arm. "It was so cold, and *something* was forming in there, I saw it."

"Strudel." Wild-eyed, Andrea forced her way among them. "I didn't bring her out, I forgot her. Where is she?"

Neal was already on the steps. As he took hold of the doorknob, the windows went dark. An unearthly howl split the rising hum, and he jerked the door open. Strudel ran out as if chased by demons, and made a beeline for Rose. When she bent down, the little dog jumped into her arms. The others surrounded them, arms around each other as the house lights flashed on and off.

CHAPTER 25

"We can't stay here forever." Kerry frowned at Rose and Noreen. They'd trooped *en masse* to Dolores's place, and it was from her living room they'd watched the lightshow. Now the house looked normal, warm light shining from every window they could see.

"I'm in no rush to go back there," Elizabeth said firmly. "There's a whole lot to be said for havin' daylight when we do."

"We might find out more about the spirits who are active," Aura Lee began half-heartedly.

"As anxious as I am to learn the source of these amazing events," Noreen said drily, "I think waiting for the sun to rise is a good idea." She consulted Rose with a look, and at her nod went on. "When you consider the manifestation began after Elizabeth's comment about Stanley Thornton's marrying Jessamine, I'd speculate he's our ghost."

Neal nodded, his chin brushing against Andrea's hair. They'd ended up on the leather sofa, and leaned against it in a fog of fatigue. "It's not a bad guess, if you believe the ring Andrea saw belonged to

Thornton."

Kerry ranged around the living room restlessly. "If Stanley had something to do with Kelvin's death, then it makes sense—I guess—that he wouldn't rest in peace. And if Kelvin was a victim of something Stanley did, then he wouldn't either."

Elizabeth yawned. "It would explain those two shadows we saw up on the mountain: one Stanley, the other Kelvin. You got the sundial fob to show Kelvin is probably buried under those rocks, and you got Stanley as maybe the one who put him there. Two ghosts, both mad at each other."

Rose sighed. "What about the scarf? Who put it out as a signal flag?"

"Had to be Jessamine," Andrea murmured, eyes closed. "And then she was trying to help Kelvin."

"Help him what?" Elizabeth asked.

"Keep Stanley from killing Neal." Andrea opened her eyes. "Remember, one of those shadows was trying to push Neal over the edge of the trail."

"Or so it seemed. It makes a rough kind of sense." Rose rubbed her face with both hands. "What's worrying me is what do we do now? A spirit was materializing in the living room and God knows what other supernatural things are happening. You, Andrea, have been channeling—for lack of a better word— Kelvin for the five or six days you've been here." Her gaze went to Neal. "We saw something—maybe a ghost—attack you, and there's no guarantee it won't happen again. I'm wondering how long this sideshow will keep playing."

"I guess daylight would be better," Kerry conceded. She glanced at Dolores. "Is it okay if we all spend the night here? I'd offer my place, too, but I've gotta say, I'm not anxious to split us up, you know?"

"I'll drink to that." Elizabeth pushed herself off her

chair. "I vote we call this shindig a slumber party and stay together until the sun comes up. My girls have made me watch too many scary movies to even think about doing anything else."

"Thanks, *jita,"* Dolores said, "now I feel really safe. At least one of you has to sleep in my room, hear?"

"I will." Aura Lee stood up and maneuvered her way between the chair and the coffee table. "The sooner the better."

"Works for me," Rose said. She was no more eager to leave the warm room than anyone else. Beside her Strudel began to scratch at a cushion to make a nest. "Let's get as comfortable as we can."

They hunted up blankets and pillows, and by the time they were settled, Andrea was beyond sleepy. She and Neal stretched out next to each other on the couch. She snuggled into his warmth, grateful for the strength of his arms. "I'm so glad you're here," she murmured, mindful of the women nearby.

"Me, too." Neal's voice rumbled in his chest where her ear rested. "You can protect me if the boogeyman shows up."

Andrea jabbed him with her elbow and his arms tightened around her. She listened to the quiet sounds in the room and her breathing slowed. Soon she drifted into sleep.

No one was awake to notice the cold air snaking into the room from under the front door.

Neal opened his eyes. He yawned, shifting his weight on the sofa. He was alone. "Andrea?" When she didn't answer, he pushed himself up, throwing off the blanket.

"Neal?" Noreen was in the big chair beside the fireplace. "What's wrong?"

"Andrea's not here. Did you see her get up?"

Noreen switched on the lamp, setting off a groan from the floor near the window, where Kerry had camped. "No. Maybe she's in the bathroom."

"Yeah." Neal glanced around the room. Elizabeth was on the floor near Kerry, and Rose was just sitting up on the rug across from the couch. Aura Lee came through the door to the hallway and he asked her if she'd seen Andrea.

She shook her head. "No. I just got up to use the bathroom. The kitchen, maybe?"

He was already on his way, noticing the light was off. No one was there, or, he discovered, in any of the other rooms. By the time he knocked on Dolores's bedroom door, his instincts were on high alert.

Dolores opened the door and looked at him in sleepy confusion.

"Is Andrea in there?"

She shook her head.

Neal headed back into the living room and bent to pick up his shoes. "She's gone."

Rose was already buttoning her sweater, and the others scrambled to their feet. "I wonder why Strudel didn't bark to warn us?" She glanced down at the dog. "Hell, she's still asleep."

"Where could Andrea *be?*" Aura Lee wondered in a shaky voice.

Kerry gestured from the window. "Look." Across the courtyard the lights of the main house were flicking off, one by one.

Neal was at the door and through it before anyone else could move. They caught up with him on the porch as he reached for the doorknob.

"Neal, wait a minute," Rose hissed behind him.

"No."

"Here." She handed him a flashlight. "So you don't break your neck."

The door squeaked as he pulled it open and Kerry groaned from the steps.

"Hush," whispered Elizabeth. Aura Lee and Noreen crowded against her, forcing her through the door and into the foyer. Kerry and Dolores crept in after Rose, Strudel following. Ahead of them Neal walked steadily toward the picture gallery hallway.

Rose fumbled for the light switch but when she pushed it, nothing happened. "Do you smell that?" she asked Noreen. "Ozone?"

"Possibly." Noreen stepped cautiously across the floor and bumped into Elizabeth.

"Neal's headed to the living room," Elizabeth whispered. She moved forward, the others trailing after her. They stopped at the doorway. The fire had died down to embers, adding deeper shadows to the cold gloom.

Rose forced herself to look to the windows and was relieved she couldn't make out the vapor they'd seen before.

Neal turned on the flashlight and moved the beam over the carpet and furniture, but nothing else was there.

In the glow Rose caught sight of material trailing down over the mantel. "Neal, look at the portrait."

He aimed the cone of light at it, where the burgundy drapery sagged halfway over Caldicott Wyntham's face. On the deepest fold they saw white letters: *LEAVE HERE.*

"My God, where *is* she?" Neal looked around the room in frustration. "Fan out and search the place. We don't know what this thing can do to her. I'll start with her bedroom." He strode out, the flashlight beam bouncing in front of him.

"Got any more of those?" Kerry asked Rose. "I tried the switches in the hall and the spare bathroom.

Nothing."

Aura Lee was already making haste toward the kitchen. "We have candles and at least one more flashlight."

"Now you're talkin'." Elizabeth scurried after her, Kerry right behind. When they came back into the living room, they held candles and Aura Lee was wielding a steel flashlight half the size of a baseball bat.

Rose had one ear cocked toward the hallway. "Do you hear that?"

"That humming sound?" Kerry took a step toward the door, and a sharp *crack* stopped her in her tracks. "What was that?"

"Don't know." Elizabeth's hand was shaking, and the flame of her candle set the shadows to dancing.

"Dios, let's go back to the kitchen. We have to find Andrea." Dolores grabbed Kerry's arm and pulled her round. "Come on, we'll look in there."

"We were just in the kitchen. I didn't see anything," Kerry protested.

"What about Andrea's studio?" Rose asked.

"We didn't check it. Let's go."

The air was bitterly cold and they had to force themselves to keep walking. As they approached the kitchen door it began to swing back and forth. "Neal?" Rose called, voice trembling. "Is that you?"

No answer.

Squaring her shoulders, Rose growled, "Grab my hand, somebody, and the next one grab hers. We're going in all together—" She watched the door swing open again. "Now!" They forced the door to stay open and pushed their way into the kitchen. Behind them the door swung faster and harder until it broke loose from the hinge pins and fell against the lintel.

"Keep going," Rose yelled. "Get to the studio. Let's

go."

The French doors of the studio were closed and dark. And locked. Rose rattled the knob fruitlessly. "What the hell? There's no key to this door." The humming was building in volume.

Kerry shook Rose by the shoulder. "Our friend Stanley doesn't want us to go in there." She had to raise her voice to be heard.

"We must go in immediately," Aura Lee declared. "Goddess, protect us now." She swung the oversized flashlight against the glass pane above the knob and shattered it. Smashing the shards along the edges, she cleared enough room to reach through the gap. When she turned the lock the door popped open, and they staggered back at the rush of cold air from the room. The humming was ferocious. Rose forced herself to step inside.

Shadowy motion in front of a large pale square stopped her in her tracks. "Hand me that flashlight." She flicked it on, and in the glow Andrea moved in front of a canvas on an easel.

"What's she doing?" Dolores shouted.

Brush in one hand and palette in the other, Andrea applied paint to the picture. Her eyes were shut, her face vacant of emotion.

"Did you find her?" Neal demanded from the door.

"Lord!" Kerry yelped. Her hand went to her chest. "You scared me."

Neal ignored her and plunged across the room to Andrea. He called her name but she didn't pause, just slapped more color onto the canvas with the jerky animation of a puppet.

Kerry paled with rage. "Stanley Thornton has to be doing this. We found out what he did, what he's kept hidden all these years."

"But what can we do?" demanded Rose. The air was

thickening with menace. "How can we stop him?"

Kerry pushed against the coldness to stand in the center of the studio. "Stanley Thornton!" she shouted. "We know you killed Kelvin Haslett!"

Dolores stared at her open-mouthed, and then nodded stiffly, setting her dark hair into motion. "All of us do," she said loudly. "We've figured out everything." The air began to swirl and the humming increased, more painful to the ears.

Dolores caught hold of Kerry's hand.

"You let Jessamine believe Kelvin abandoned her," Elizabeth yelled. She fumbled for Dolores's other hand and grasped it.

"You caused great harm," Noreen accused, "then and now. Your lies have been found out." She reached for Aura Lee, bracing herself against the air beginning to twist around the room.

"You must leave this place," Rose commanded as she groped to connect with Aura Lee's hand. Papers and jars of paint were rising into a slowly swirling mass.

"We cast you out of this place." Aura Lee took a deep breath and shouted fiercely. "We cast you out!"

Abruptly the humming stopped and everything fell to the floor. Andrea crumpled at Neal's feet and something rattled behind him. He knelt and gathered her into his arms. "She's ice cold," he said over his shoulder. "Let's get her to the fire." He carried her through the kitchen, maneuvering past the broken door and into the living room. The overhead lights blinked on as they trailed after Neal. He set Andrea on the sofa and tucked a throw around her. "Put wood on the coals."

Rose and Kerry fumbled to collect branches from the basket beside the hearth, and soon little tongues of flame were licking at the kindling. Strudel crept into the room and headed toward the warmth.

Neal rubbed Andrea's hands and arms, all the while calling her name. Finally her eyes opened and she looked up at him in confusion. "Neal? What are you doing?"

He held her to him and rested his head against her shoulder. "Thank God. I didn't think you'd come out of it."

"Out of what?" Andrea pulled away enough to sit up. "What are you talking about?"

Rose bent over the back of the sofa. "Do you remember anything?"

"What?" Andrea stopped to sip at the glass Neal held to her lips. Coughing a little, she swallowed more and then pushed it away. "Okay, okay, tell me what's happening."

Together they did. By the time she heard the description of her unconscious painting her face was tight with despair. "I don't remember any of it," she said finally. "The last thing I can think of is when we were at Dolores's house, just getting ready to sleep."

Noreen leaned back in her chair. "No memory of painting?"

"No memory of anything." Andrea laid her head against Neal's shoulder. "What did I paint?"

Rose was half-asleep, but at that she jerked to awareness. "Good question." She looked around the room at the women who sprawled in various stages of exhaustion. "Does anyone want to get the painting, or shall we go take a look at it?"

Aura Lee struggled up from the wingback chair. "I'll get it."

"It's too big for you," Elizabeth protested. "I'll help."

When they jockeyed the large canvas through the door, Rose was surprised at the tears on Aura Lee's cheeks. She got up to help them steer it around a chair and stepped on something sharp. "Ouch." They propped the painting against the wall.

"Oh," Noreen said on a long sigh when she saw it.

It was the work Andrea had begun days before, but no longer was Kelvin Haslett in peril. He paused at a bend in a rocky trail to look at the woman down the path from him. Smiling, he extended his hand to her and she reached for him. Her blonde hair glowed in the sunlight, and her eyes were filled with love. Flowering current bushes and early mist obscured the way they'd come.

"Is that Jessamine?" Kerry asked in a choked voice.

"Of course it is," Aura Lee murmured. "They found each other."

Andrea stared at the work, her eyes shaded with melancholy. "I don't remember."

Neal stretched his arm around her shoulders. "Remember it or not, you painted it. It's brilliant."

Rose bent to search the rug for what she'd stepped on. "You did all this while all hell was breaking loose in the studio. At least…" She stood up holding something in her hand.

Dolores nodded. "I think maybe so much chaos was in there because Stanley was fighting to keep her from finishing the story." She gestured toward the canvas. "It was like a big distraction, you know?"

"Is Stanley gone now?" Andrea asked.

"I hope to God he is." Dolores crossed herself.

"I think he probably is," Rose said in an odd voice. She opened her hand and on her palm was the snarling lion-head ring.

Aura Lee sank toward the floor, and Elizabeth and Kerry grabbed her arms, guiding her to a chair. "Where did you get that?"

"I stepped on it." Rose set the ring on the mantel.

"Do you think it fell off him in there?"

Kerry stared at the ring. "We let him know he lost. After all those years of hiding, we found out what he did. Any power he got from the secret is gone."

"'And the Truth shall set you free,'" Noreen said softly.

Rose smiled sadly. "That's no woman's quote."

Noreen shrugged. "Even a man will get off a good line every once in a while."

Kerry sat down heavily. "I'm too tired to have the nervous breakdown I have coming to me." She yawned, laughing weakly in the middle of it. "One thing for sure, you'll never be able to come up with a quote for all the stuff that's happened here." She grinned at Noreen. "Nobody could."

"On the contrary, I have just the thing," Noreen said gravely. "I'll quote Jessamine herself as to what was between her and Stanley Thornton, between her and Kelvin:

"The line midst love and hate—

like light and dark—

lies at the edge of the shadow."

THE
WISDOM COURT
SERIES

Edge of the Shadow
A Signal Shown
All in Bad Time

Turn the page for an

excerpt from

A

SIGNAL

SHOWN

The Wisdom Court Series

Book Two

Yvonne Montgomery

Brenna was nearly running when she rounded the side of the house. The electric lanterns above the doors of the two associate houses, as well as the yard lights along the fountain at the center of the circular driveway, illuminated the cobblestone expanse. The murmur of the water and the thud of her shoes against the bricks were the only sounds.

Swiftly Brenna leapt up the steps to her building, key in hand. Moments later she was jerking open the door to her flat, slipping inside, turning the latch. The reach for the light switch was instinctive. In the silent living room she heard her rapid breathing and felt the pounding of her heart. What had just happened? She was frightened, but of what? She'd seen no one, had heard nothing threatening.

Brenna went to the sofa and settled onto it. As she put her camera onto the coffee table, it rattled against the glass top, and she saw her hands were trembling. Had it been a panic attack or had she'd picked up on something wrong?

Slowly her breathing evened and she stopped shaking. Pushing herself off the sofa, she went to the kitchen. When she faced the bank of uncovered windows, she stopped in the doorway. *Dammit, stop acting like a scared kid!* She hurried to the cabinet over the counter and yanked a glass off the shelf. Tugging at the cork, she tilted the Bailey's bottle over the glass, knocking it against the rim only twice before the glass was full. Turning her back on the blank panes, she snatched up the bottle. When she reached the living room, her hands were trembling again. She gulped a healthy swig of the liqueur.

Brenna set down the glass and bottle, then sank onto the couch, snagging the green plaid throw from the arm, wrapping it around her shoulders. She didn't have to think about it right now. Probably be better if she didn't. *Too much weird shit going on.* She fumbled for the camera, nearly knocking it off the coffee table before she curled her fingers around it. She'd gotten some shots—enough to warrant going back with the sixteen-millimeter. The lighting would be a bitch to get right, but it'd be worth it to try.

Flicking the switch to run back through the photos she'd taken, she reached again for the glass. Sipping the creamy liqueur, she saw a decent snap of the lichen on the rock, and a stand of pine saplings that wasn't too bad. She'd caught the look of interdependence in the way the spindly young trees leaned against each other, as if too many strong winds had come their way.

When she came to the image of the finger-shadows extending down the hill, Brenna sighed. No way could the small lens capture the impression of claws, but she'd hoped for more than she'd gotten. The dark areas dominated the square screen, with the trees themselves showing up as only lighter vertical shapes. The flash had illuminated the nearest trunks, but that served to focus on the pines rather than the shadows.

How would she manage the contrast?

She moved on to the shots of the house. Her gaze sharpened. A whitish shape was under the roofline, near the attic window. Brenna gently rubbed against the screen with a corner of the throw, but she couldn't tell what it was. No way to tell without more detail. She levered herself off the sofa and headed for the studio and her laptop.

Downloading the snapshots onto the hard drive, Brenna sipped more of the liqueur. She was feeling better. Nothing like a little alcohol to even out the bumps. Bumps in the night, no, things that go bump in the night.

Glancing down at the laptop screen, Brenna saw the download had been completed. She clicked through the shots, stopping at the series she'd taken of Wisdom Court. Another click enlarged them, and she bent over the first shot to check for the anomaly. There it was. She jerked back in shock, and the glass slipped out of her hand onto the rug. "Holy shit."

A chill snaked down her spine. She was looking at a white face in the attic window. From it desperate eyes stared at her.

A SIGNAL SHOWN

available in print and ebook

Yvonne Montgomery became afraid of the dark, after her parents allowed her to see Psycho at the tender age of twelve.

Now Yvonne lives in a shadowy three-story Victorian house in Denver's historic Capitol Hill where her imagination rises to the challenge when the old floor-boards creak for no reason and the window panes rattle without wind.